Outlaw Mamis

Outlaw Mamis

Jasmine Williams,

Niyah Moore, INDIA,

Brandie Davis,

N'TYSE

www.urbanbooks.net

Urban Books, LLC
300 Farmingdale Road, NY-Route 109
Farmingdale, NY 11735

ISBN 13: 978-1-64556-083-8
ISBN 10: 1-64556-083-X

First Mass Market Printing October 2020
First Trade Paperback Printing May 2019
Printed in the United States of America

10 9 8 7 6 5 4 3

Distributed by Kensington Publishing Corp.
Submit Orders to:
Customer Service
400 Hahn Road
Westminster, MD 21157-4627
Phone: 1-800-733-3000
Fax: 1-800-659-2436

Outlaw Mamis

Jasmine Williams,
Niyah Moore, INDIA,
Brandie Davis,
N'TYSE

"Outlaw Mamis is an intense thriller that will have the reader riveted from one drama-filled page to the next. This theatrical ride is one that you will get on and not want to get off. Fall between the pages and fill your library with this gritty urban tale from the desk of some of the hottest pens in the industry."

~ **NeNe Capri,**

national bestselling author
of ***The Pussy Trap***

Dedicated to my childhood friend,
McKinnley "Brian" Hobbs.

May God continue to
protect you. Your ghost ridah for life! :~)

Foreword

There's nothing like a boss chick that knows how to get it by any means necessary. In a world where men reign supreme, *Outlaw Mamis* flips the script and shows that a female can do anything that a male can do . . . if not better. Drama fills the pages, and loyalty tests the limits. But, there's one thing that can't be denied: the crew is vicious, and they came to wreak havoc on the streets.

As a fellow woman in the literary game, I feel a special joy when I see women put it down. N'Tyse has done it again with this gritty, skillfully crafted tale of greed, lust, deception, and the hustle. She takes you through the streets and holds you hostage until the very last sentence.

~ Danielle Marcus,

national bestselling author
of the book turned
to film ***Plug Love***

Blood of my Blood

by

Jasmine Williams

Introduction

"Where the fuck my shit at, Ayana?" A deep, ominous voice jolted me out of my deep sleep.

"I don't know what the fuck you talking 'bout," my mother replied in a snappish tone. "You need to get the fuck outta my h—"

The sound of knuckles crashing into bone echoed throughout the still and quiet apartment.

"You dumb-ass bastard!" I heard my mom screech, followed by sounds of tussling and furniture moving. It was no lie that dope fiends had super strength, because my mother would fight anybody.

I slid out of my bed and tiptoed toward my bedroom door. Afraid that the old door was going to creak when I pulled it open, I peeked through the small sliver.

"Yo, chill the fuck out before I have to murk yo' ass!" the voice boomed again, causing the fine hairs on my arms to stand up. "I know you stole my work, and I'm not leaving here until you give me my shit or give me my money!"

I couldn't see anything, but the more the man talked, familiarity started to set in. I knew that voice.

"Leave my mommy alone," my little brother, Jason, whimpered. "P–please leave her alone."

"Get the fuck off me and go back to bed, lil' nigga!"

"Don't touch my damn baby or I'll kill you in this bitch!" Mama fussed.

Another loud whack, followed by a crashing sound, and my little brother screaming at the top of his lungs caused me to jump back.

"Stop runnin' that mouth and run them legs outta here to get my shit, fuckin' junkie-ass bitch," he spat, his voice laced with hate.

My eyes darted around my room, looking for anything I could use as a weapon. There weren't a lot of options, so I snatched up the small lamp that sat on my nightstand. As I wrapped the cord around the lamp to prevent an accident, I moved out of my room and into the hallway. My heart pounded rapidly as I rounded the corner to find out who the intruder was and what he wanted with my family. Truth was, I was scared as hell, but I would die before anybody did something to them and I didn't at least try to stop it.

Fear was replaced with rage when I peered into the living room and saw a man in a black hoodie standing over my mother and stomping her. Jason was curled up in a ball next to our mom with a mixture of tears and snot running down his innocent face. I tiptoed closer to the scene, careful not to make any noise that would alert the man of my presence.

"You still ain't trying to tell me what you did with my shit? If you don't start talking, your son is gon' be next."

Hearing those words caused me to move more hastily. With light steps, I ran up behind him and raised the lamp above the intruder's head.

"Naima! Help me!" Jason cried out, causing our unwanted guest to abruptly turn around.

POW! POW!

I didn't know which sound was more deafening—the gun clapping, or the wails coming from my family. It all blended together in a chorus of agony. I clutched my stomach, and my hand was met with the warm blood that poured from the fresh bullet hole. It was only because of the initial shock that I was still standing, but as soon as I realized that I'd been shot, I collapsed on the floor. Breathing had never been so difficult before, and I felt my airways filling up with a liquid that was thicker than water. The pain from the gunshot went beyond anything that I'd ever felt or could even imagine. The only thing that hurt worse than that was staring into my cousin's eyes as he stood over me with a smoking gun. In a panic, he tucked the gun and dashed out of our apartment right before total darkness set in.

Chapter One

"Look, I told you to keep yo' damn wheelchair! I know that y'all may think I am, but I ain't handicap. I can walk on my own," I told the jovial nurse.

"I understand, Miss Jenkins, but it's hospital policy. I have to wheel you downstairs and to your car," she informed me as she practically forced me into the wheelchair.

"If it's gon' get me out this place faster, do what you gotta do," I huffed as I sat back and placed my feet in the foot rests.

The nurse handed me the discharge papers and wheeled me into the hallway. "So, do you have someone coming to pick you up?" the nurse asked as she rolled me into the elevator.

"Can we just ride this elevator in silence? I'm really not with all the questions and stuff right now," I snapped.

There was an uncomfortable silence in the elevator, and I instantly felt bad for going off on the nurse the way I had. For the entire four weeks I'd been in the hospital, Nurse Stephanie had been nothing but nice to me. She was the one that told me I was brought to the hospital by ambulance, and that I had lost so much blood that I needed a blood transfusion. She even gave me a pair of sweat pants and a T-shirt to leave the hospital in since my clothes were covered in blood. It wasn't right, but I was only taking my frustrations out on her. It had been thirty days that I was in the hospital, and not one person came to see me. For thirty days, I miserably waited for somebody, anybody, to show me that they cared whether I lived or died. That day never came.

I shouldn't have expected much from my mom since she was nothing but a fuckin' junkie. No matter how many times I got teased about my crackhead mama, went a day or two without a nutritious meal, or had shit stolen from me by her, I still loved my mom. You only get one, and even though I got upset with her quite often, she was still mine. You would think that for once, she would put me before chasing the next high—especially when I was shot behind some bullshit that she was caught up in. I would be lying if I said that shit didn't hurt like a stab to the heart. It was something that I had to charge to the game, though. A drug-addicted mother is never a reliable one, so I was basically on my own.

"I wanna apologize to you for the way I just spoke to you," I told Nurse Stephanie once we were in the lobby. "I got it from here, though, so you can roll this wheelchair right back where it came from." I cracked a semi-smile as I slowly stood up.

Nurse Stephanie helped me out of the chair and gave me a warm smile. "You're fine, Naima. Trust me, I understand. Just be safe out there, because I don't want to see you under these circumstances again."

"Thanks again for everything," I reiterated before I strolled out of the hospital.

I welcomed the bright sun and fresh air. I was overdressed for the late-spring heat in those hot-ass sweats, but that didn't matter. I felt like I had just been released from a jail sentence, so I was taking in everything that

I had taken for granted before I almost lost my life. I never realized how much of a luxury it was to take a deep breath, feel the wind brush against my skin, or to hear birds chirping. None of that meant anything to me until it was about to be snatched away from me.

I didn't know how the hell I was getting home, so I borrowed somebody's phone and called myself a cab. As I sat and waited for the cab, my mind drifted off to my little brother. Jason and I had never been separated for any amount of time. Even though I was only eight years older than him, he was damn near my son. I was the one who bathed him, fed him, and made sure he got on and off the school bus. He was an honor roll student because I helped him with his homework and studying. Lord knows what he'd had to go through in the last thirty days. There was no telling with our mother. I just hoped my baby wasn't going hungry or being neglected. I prayed for her sake that my brother was still in good health when I got to him, because I didn't want to hurt my own mother, but I would—especially if she put sucking dick for drugs before taking care of her own son.

When the taxi finally pulled up, I rose from the bench too quickly, and a sharp pain shot through my stomach.

"Agghh! Fuck!" I growled through gritted teeth as I gripped my stomach where the pain was.

The physical therapy that I'd done in the hospital had helped me tremendously, but apparently, I wasn't as healed as I thought I was. I had been told to continue the physical therapy for six more weeks once I left the hospital, but I had no intention of doing that. The only thing I planned on doing was putting a bullet between the eyes of the person that almost sent me to my maker.

Chapter Two

"Stop at this Walgreen's on the corner coming up. I need to get my prescription filled," I told the cab driver.

Instead of verbally responding, the cabbie nodded his head and pulled into the pharmacy parking lot. Before he could even bring the car to a complete stop, I damn near jumped out of the pungent-smelling vehicle. Had I been in there any longer, I would've been throwing up all over the seats from the foul smell of onions and pigs feet.

As I stood in line at the pharmacy, I looked down at my prescription for the first time. A smile spread across my face when I realized that the doctor had prescribed Percocet for my pain, and there were three refills on the medication. Growing up in the hood, I knew that there were plenty of junkies who would be willing to spend money on the pill. With ninety pills, I could easily make nine hundred dollars off one bottle. Most of the doctors in Hampton Roads knew that these bitches were pill heads, so they had stopped prescribing narcotics to them. That only meant that mine would be in high demand, and junkies wouldn't flinch when I told them that I was letting them go for ten dollars a pill.

After dropping my prescription off with the pharmacy tech and letting her know that I'd be back, I slid back out the front door of the pharmacy. Peeking around the corner to make sure the cabbie wasn't paying attention, I took off running in the opposite direction. The pain in my stomach was enough to make me fold, but I didn't have the money to pay his ass, so I did what I had to do and hauled ass for five minutes straight. I didn't stop running until I made it to my front door. Out of breath, I plopped down on the beat-up lawn chair on my porch.

"Naima!"

My antennas went up when I heard somebody calling my name. The voice was so small that I couldn't tell what direction it came from. After being shot, I was paranoid as fuck, so I kept my head on a swivel. When I saw Charlene, or Cha-Cha, as the hood called her, I rolled my eyes so hard that for a second, I thought they got stuck. She was walking through the cut with a baby on her hip and a toddler trotting beside her.

"What's up, Naima girl?" Cha-Cha greeted as she approached me. "I heard about what happened. I'm so sorry, sis."

"Miss me with that sis bullshit." I waved her off. "Now that I'm back home you miss me so damn much, but where the fuck was you when I was suffering in the hospital for a month? Where the fuck was anybody? I don't fuck with none of y'all! You can't call yourself my friend, but then once it's time to show and prove, you go missing. Fuck outta here!"

Cha-Cha shifted her saggy-diaper-wearing baby to her other hip. "Don't do that, Naima. How the fuck was I supposed to get there with no money, no car, and two damn kids attached to my ass? You're speaking on what friends are supposed to do, but friends are also supposed to understand their friend's situation. You know I would've been there if I could have. Shit, you know more than anybody how hard it is for me to find somebody to watch these damn kids."

"Whatever. I'm not tryna hear no more of your excuses. If it was you in the hospital, I would've hitchhiked to the damn hospital to see about my friend. I guess we're cut from a different cloth, though."

"I can't believe that you're really sitting here questioning over ten years of friendship. It's cool, though. I guess I'll just keep the information that I got on Kenan to myself. See, while you were in the hospital, I was out here being a friend and doing my homework. So, I guess I'm not completely useless." She rolled her eyes.

Hearing her bring up Kenan piqued my interest. I was ready to end the conversation and cut her off for good, but now Cha-Cha had my attention.

"Wait. How do you know that it was Kenan who shot me?" I asked. When the police had come to question me, I told them that I didn't know who shot me. So, I had no clue how that information got leaked. I didn't want anybody to know, because I wanted to handle the shit myself.

"Who doesn't know? You know the news around the hood travels fast. He's been going around bragging about how he shot you and telling people to take that as a lesson not to fuck him over. His words were: 'If I'll shoot family to teach them a lesson, imagine what I'll do to a mothafucka that ain't blood.' According to him, your mama stole some crack out of his room," Cha-Cha rambled on, telling me all the scoop like she worked for the *Enquirer*.

My heart damn near pulsated out of my chest hearing this revelation. I could feel the rage and revenge pumping through my blood. "How does he know it wasn't his crackhead-ass mama that stole the shit? You know what? That doesn't even matter. Do you know where he's at?"

"I'm sure he won't be hard to find. He's been coming through the hood every damn day tryna be flashy and shit. Tyrell, get out of that fuckin' dirt!" she yelled at her three-year-old son.

"Good. Well, I'll be waiting for his ass when he comes back through." I finally stood from the chair and pulled open my screen door. "I'll get up with you later, Cha. I got some shit I need to handle."

I started banging on the door, waiting for somebody to come let me in. I noticed the still quietness on the other side of the door and knocked louder. Usually, Jason would be running up to the door, screaming that someone was knocking, and my mama would be running behind him, telling him that he better not think about touching her door. The silence left an unsettling feeling in the pit of my stomach.

"Mama! Mama!" I yelled as I continuously knocked on the heavy door. I swore I heard my knocks echoing on the other side.

"Jason! It's me! Y'all stop playing and open the door!" I started panicking as I banged until my knuckles were raw. I didn't know what was happening on the other side of the door, but my gut had me expecting the worst.

I felt a hand touch the back of my shoulder, and I turned around, ready to swing.

"Naima, it's just me," Cha-Cha said, throwing up her free hand surrender-style. "You mentioned that no one came to visit you while you were in the hospital. That means you probably don't know about what happened."

When I made eye contact with her, the glimmer of sadness in Cha-Cha's eyes confirmed my gut feeling. "What do you mean? What happened to who?" I asked, my voice cracking with every word.

"Well, your mom got arrested for trying to rob the corner store with a knife. When the cops found out she had a son at home, they came over here and searched the house. They found drugs and paraphernalia in there, so CPS took Jason with them. Once the rental office got wind of the legal trouble your mom was in, and the fact that she had drugs on their property, them bitches put a seventy-two-hour eviction notice on the door. Three days later, they were bringing y'all stuff outside. I got as much of it as I could."

I had to sit down again. It felt like the wind had been knocked out of me. The pain was so unbearable that nothing but silent cries escaped. What happened to my mother was unfortunate, but she brought that on herself for doing that dumb shit. My brother Jason now being part of a system that gave no fucks about a little black boy was what cut me deep. I buried my face into the palms of my hands and bawled so hard that my body shook. Cha-Cha wrapped her arm around my shoulder and tried to comfort me, but my sobs caused her baby girl to break out in tears.

"You know you can come and stay with me for as long as you need to," Cha-Cha said while trying to comfort her fussy baby.

I sniffled, wiped the tears from my face, and shook my head. "Nah, it's cool. I gotta make something shake if I want to get Jason back. If you want to help me, find somebody to keep the kids and be ready by nightfall. It's time to take it back to our wild and reckless days."

Chapter Three

In the still of the night, I was crouched behind a bush in the back of a trap house. Like a predator waiting to catch its prey, I was in perfect position to watch every movement in the house. With a gun tightly gripped in my right hand, I was lurking, waiting for Kenan to emerge. I had already been out there for over an hour, but I was prepared to stay for as long as it took.

Finally, a glimmer of light came through the wooden fence that was slowly opening. I heard his voice before I saw him, so I knew he was coming. I grasped the gun tighter as my adrenaline started pumping. Kenan stepped through the gate with a black duffle bag in his hand. Once he closed it behind him, he walked off without ever checking his surroundings. I quietly hopped from behind the bush and ran up behind him with light feet. Once I was sure that he couldn't hear my footsteps, I stepped in front of him with my gun drawn, stopping him in his tracks.

"Surprise, surprise, muh'fucka!" I whispered harshly, shoving my gun into his stomach, the same place he had shot me.

Kenan started chuckling. "Damn, you still alive? I thought I killed you."

"Well, it looks like you thought fuckin' wrong, huh? That was your mistake, because now I'm here to make sure your mama is standing over your grave. And you know what's even funnier? While she's standing over your body shedding tears, I'll be the one comforting her, and she won't even know that I'm the one that took you away from her."

"You know what else is funny? I already caused you and yo' mama that same pain when I shot you in front of them, put the bug in the cop's ear about her robbing that store, and watched CPS snatch poor li'l Jason up. It's sad 'cause he was innocent in all of this. I didn't have anything against my boy. He was just a liability. See, your mama was the one that got my moms hooked on that shit. If it wasn't for her, I wouldn't have lost the only person that I love in this world. Your junkie-ass mama damn near shoved that shit up her li'l sister's nose. My mama wasn't the same no more after that. Ayana took away somebody that I loved, so it was only right I returned the favor." Kenan smirked.

Kenan had my emotions running high with every word he spoke. I couldn't believe he had been plotting and planning against his own family this entire time. There were so many questions running through my head. I wanted to know why. I wanted to know if he had been secretly hating us our entire lives while he was smiling in my face, pretending that we were cool. What I wanted to know more than anything was why I didn't see this side of Kenan before now. Then, I realized that none of that even mattered now, because Kenan had already signed his death certificate.

"Okay, enough with the small talk. Give me what's in that bag, bitch!" I pushed my gun into the side of Kenan's face, and he grimaced. I didn't want him to know that he had my mind rattled, so I just changed the subject. Talking to him was wasting time. I needed to smoke his ass and get the fuck out of dodge.

"I ain't giving you shit! You gon' have to kill me to get what's in this muh'fuckin' bag!"

A Joker-style grin spread across my face, and I cocked my gun back, making sure that a bullet was in the chamber. "That won't be a problem, 'cause you're gonna die anyway. It's a shame you have to die because your pussy ass is sad that your grown-ass mama became an addict. Last time I checked, nobody can make a grown woman do shit she doesn't wanna do, so apparently your mama wanted to be a junkie. Think about how much worse it's gonna get when she finds out somebody left her son stankin' in the back of a dark alley."

Kenan stood so still that I couldn't tell if he was breathing. Reality must've set in that I wasn't playing with his bitch ass. I was coming to collect his money and his soul. His eyes darted around the dark alley in the back of the trap house. Kenan then looked me up and down like he was sizing me up, probably contemplating whether he could take me down.

Kenan started to chuckle. "You must not know who you're fuckin' with. Even if you kill me, this shit won't end with me. Vince is going to find out who robbed his spot regardless. Don't start a war that you ain't ready for," he said coolly, as if he wasn't fazed by the gun at the side of his head. I knew that he was, because his tone had calmed down drastically from the rowdy one he was just speaking in.

Suddenly, the wooden gate that surrounded the back of the house that Kenan had walked out of swung open. I looked up, and a man with a fitted cap emerged from behind the fence. Kenan started grinning like a fool when he thought he was about to be saved.

"I told you that you wouldn't get away with this shit." He spoke loudly, trying to alert the other man to what was going on.

Fuck! This other nigga wasn't a part of the plan! Now I'm gonna have to kill them both!

"Yo, what the fuck is going on out here?" the man asked. Once he looked over at me and realized what was about to go down, he snatched his gun off his waist.

Pop! Pop!

Pow!

"Grab the bag and let's go!"

I looked down at the smoking gun that was clenched in my palm and smiled. Kenan lay flat on his back with blood seeping underneath his body. He started to cough, and a weird gurgling noise came after, like he was choking on the blood that started to pour from his mouth and down the sides of his face.

I stood over his body and kneeled so that we were face to face. "How does it feel to be the one with bullets in you? Nobody fucks with my family, ever! You're a snake and a rat, and soon they'll both be feasting on your body." I gathered every drop of moisture in my mouth and spit on his face.

When I stood up, I looked around at the crime scene. The other man wasn't moving at all, but what seemed like gallons of his blood started to make puddles around my feet. Seeing all that blood gave me a high that I'm sure no drug could ever give. I admired my handiwork before I shot Kenan one more time in his face, just to make sure he was dead. Brain matter exploded all over the concrete, and I knew for sure he wouldn't be having an open casket funeral.

Cha-Cha grabbed me roughly by the arm and snatched me from the spot that I was standing in. "If you don't bring your ass on, we're going to get caught out here! Get the bag and let's make a run for it!"

The bag had fallen from Kenan's hands before he even hit the ground after I shot him in the chest, so I snatched it up and took off running to the end of the alley. My only fear was getting caught, so I was hauling ass, and Cha-Cha was right beside me.

When Kenan's friend had pulled out his gun, my best friend, Cha-Cha, had jumped out of the bushes she had been hiding in and shot him twice. When it came to doing dirty work, I could always count on her to do it. From the time we were fifteen years old and started out boosting, we had been partners in crime. We learned early that the only way to survive in the hood was to get it in any way possible, so we had been criminals for a while. This was our first time actually committing a double murder, but from the amount of power that I felt, I knew it wouldn't be the last.

Our associate, Deshara, pulled up with the getaway car as soon as we got to the end of the alley. We jumped in the car, and Deshara sped off before we could even get the doors shut. I hurriedly snatched off the red bob wig I'd been wearing. I popped the gray contact lenses out of my eyes and shimmied out of the black Dickies jumpsuit that I had on. Underneath the jumpsuit, I had on an oversized pair of sweatpants and sweatshirt to make me look bigger than I was. It was hot as hell outside, so I was sweaty, but that was my disguise. Cha-Cha took off her outfit, which consisted of the same thing as mine, and we shoved everything into the duffle bag and shoved it under the seat.

We heard police sirens in the distance, and Deshara slowed down once we turned onto the main street. "Oh my gosh, I'm so glad that y'all made it back in one piece! When I heard those gunshots back there, I thought . . . wait a minute! If it wasn't y'all that got shot, but I heard gunshots in the alley . . . y'all were the fucking shooters!" Deshara blurted. "Please tell me that y'all were just shooting warning shots and didn't hit anyone."

The silence that filled the car gave Deshara the answer that she dreaded. She took her eyes off the road and looked back and forth between Cha-Cha and me with her mouth agape. We never confirmed anything because Deshara couldn't tell what she didn't know or see for herself. Deshara didn't know the real reason we were there, because it wasn't her business. We just needed her to be the getaway driver because she was the only one with a car. As far as she knew, we were just on another one of our petty robbing missions.

"Okay, somebody need to tell me what the fuck is going on. Did I just become an accessory to murder? Tell me, dammit!" Deshara screamed. She was very emotional because she knew, just like we did, that if we were to get caught, we would be spending the rest of our days behind bars.

"Girl, calm your ass down! We didn't kill anybody, but we damn sure shot them. I don't know why you're so bent out of shape about it, because if we didn't handle our business, our bodies would be the ones laying in that alley. I'd rather for it to be them than us," Cha-Cha lied. She didn't appear to be fazed by the situation at all.

"Whatever you say. I just can't help but think that this shit is gonna catch up to us one day. When you fuck the streets, they fuck you back harder. These niggas out here don't be playing about their money. We need to quit while we're ahead. That's all I'm saying."

Cha-Cha rolled her eyes and smacked her teeth at the same time. "You always gotta be the Debbie Downer! Don't nobody wanna hear that shit after we just shot two people and stole their money. Don't bring that negativity over here, because you're speaking shit into existence. If we do get caught, it's gonna be your fault because of those nasty vibes you got going on. Just shut the fuck up and think about all this money that we're about to count. You never complain when you're spending that money. Shit, we do the hard part anyway, but you do the most damn complaining."

I didn't say anything, but I agreed with everything that Cha-Cha was saying. I was sick of hearing Deshara complain every single time myself. If Deshara was smart, she would've taken my silence as a warning, but I guess she wasn't as smart as I thought.

"Bitch, we in this shit together. If we go down, I'm getting just as much time as y'all because I helped y'all get away. So, you can kill that shit about y'all doing the hard part. I'm putting myself at risk just like you are. Fuck outta here!" Deshara seethed.

"How are you getting mad when you're the one that started this conversation? We're not holding a gun to your head and making you do this with us. You choose to do it because you need the money just like we do. If you don't like it, don't do it. It's as simple as that," Cha-Cha said.

"Y'all chill out! We just came up on a lot of cash, and y'all in here arguing. Cha-Cha is right, though, De.

You don't have to do this. If you're scared, say you're scared." I smirked.

"Ain't nobody scared! Let's go in here and count this money."

"Okay, but I need to make a quick stop first. Make this left turn right here," I instructed.

Deshara nodded her head and turned onto the dark side street. It looked like a war zone with all the empty and broken beer bottles littered over the street, and most of the streetlights had been shot out. It looked like a place that you would lure somebody to when you wanted to do some dirt and didn't want anyone to find out.

"What's out here? It looks creepy as fuck over h—"

Pow!

A bullet to the dome silenced Deshara forever.

"Damn, Naima! What the fuck did you shoot the bitch for?" Cha-Cha asked as she wiped off the blood that blew back on her face.

"She was a liability. If you get a scary bitch like that in the right situation, she'll start singing like a canary. We can't afford to go to jail because that bitch folded. She knew too much, and she showed too many signs of being a weak link. You know all it takes is one weak link to break the whole chain. Fuck that! I ain't got time. I can't take care of Jason from behind bars, and it would be hard for you to raise two kids from jail. I did us both a favor." I shrugged.

"You would've did me an even bigger favor by letting me pull the trigger. I had the same thing in mind for that bitch. All that talking she was doing tonight, I already knew what time it was. Let's get this bitch out the car."

Cha-Cha climbed out of the back seat and pulled

the driver's door open. As soon as the door flew open, I kicked Deshara's body out of the seat and onto the ground like she was last week's trash. I expeditiously hopped out the car, went in the trunk, and grabbed a T-shirt to wipe up all the blood that was visible on the windshield and dashboard. By the time I was finished, Cha-Cha had jumped in the driver's seat and was ready to pull off.

She sped off the street and gave me a side eye. "I should kick your ass for all that bitch's brains spraying all over my face. You could've at least warned a bitch."

We both busted out laughing, and then discussed what we had to do for the rest of the night: burn the car and all the evidence, and then count the money that we collected.

Chapter Four

"This is enough money for me to pay rent on a nice two-bedroom apartment for a year. I need more, though. Since we have to start from scratch with everything, I need money to furnish the place, buy him new clothes and shoes, keep food in the house, and buy him what he needs for school. Jason has been wanting to take karate and play football for a while now, so I want to make that happen for him. The only way I can make that happen is with more money."

Cha-Cha and I were sitting in her bedroom, counting up the money that we took. There was a total of $26,000 in the bag, and we split it down the middle. Anybody would've been satisfied with that amount of money, especially if they had nothing to begin with. I was on a mission, though, so that just wasn't enough for me. Some people may call it greed, but I called it getting prepared for the worst. I needed a nice-sized stash for a rainy day because in my life, the rain always seemed to pour.

"Well, you know I'm down for whatever. I'm trying to get me and my kids up out these projects by any means necessary. We became products of our environment, but I don't want that for my babies. I'd rather take all the risks now, so they won't have to in the future," Cha-Cha stated. "We meet up with Jacoby tonight to sell him the brick of coke that was in the bag, and he said he'd buy your Percocets off you for a stack. I don't want a cut of that since they're your pills, but after our split for one brick, we'll both have ten thousand more dollars. That's an easy twenty-three thousand that we made with no effort."

"So, why stop there? You said Jacoby wants us to meet up at his after-hours spot, right?" I asked.

"Yeah, he told us to come at two a.m."

"Perfect timing. That's when all the ballers and dope boys are leaving the club and heading over to Jacoby's spot. You can be the one to do business with Jacoby since you're the one with a personal relationship with him. While you're doing that, I'm gonna scope out the scene and find our next prospect. One of these stupid muh'fuckas will want to take me home, and I'll go. You're gonna have to keep a close eye on me, because when I leave, you'll need to follow the car that I get in. I want you to sit outside of the house for forty-five minutes. When I check the layout of the house, I'll send you a text of a way in. Please be in there exactly forty-five minutes after you see me step foot inside."

Before Cha-Cha could respond, my phone started ringing with Aunt Amina's name displayed across the screen. A wicked smile sat upon my face as I snatched up the phone and answered it.

"Hello?"

As soon as I answered, Aunt Amina's wails poured through the receiver. "Naima! They took my baby! Lawd s–somebody done took my baby away from me! Why, Lord? Whyyy?" she sobbed uncontrollably. It almost pained me that I was the one who brought her this tremendous amount of pain, but that feeling quickly went away when I remembered that he wanted me dead first. Fuck him!

"Aunt Amina! What's going on? What are you talking about?" I asked with a hint of anxiety in my voice.

"It's Kenan! They found my baby's body dumped in some damn alley like he wasn't shit! He *was* something! He was my baby! Help me, Jesus! Why didn't they take me with him, too?" she cried.

"What? Nooo!" I screamed out and broke down crying. If I didn't know any better, I would've thought that I was in mourning for real because my acting skills were so superb. "W–what happened? Do the police know anything yet?"

"They don't have anything to go on. The only thing they told me was that it could've possibly been a robbery. They found somebody else dead in the alley too, so they're also saying that it was possible they killed each other. I don't care what happened. I just want whoever did this to my baby to pay. I'll find out who did this shit, and I'll kill them myself. I swear, I'll kill them myself."

I continued to sniffle and sob with my aunt. "Auntie, I promise I'll see what I can find out. Let me try to get a ride to some of the neighborhoods he used to go out, and I'll see what they know."

"Thank you so much, baby. You know what? I have the keys to Kenan's truck. Seeing it sit in front of my house every day is gonna be too painful, so why don't I just let you have it? There's no use for it here, and I'm sure that he would want you to have it."

I almost threw up in my mouth because she really didn't know her son if she thought that he would want me with his truck.

"I really appreciate that, Auntie, but I can't. That's one of the only pieces of your son that you have left."

"Naima, I insist you take this truck. I won't be able to bear looking at it. It's bad enough that I have to live in the house that his scent lingers in. His bedroom is still exactly the way he left it. All of his clothes and shoes are here . . . just everything! Just knowing that he'll never walk through these doors again . . ." Aunt Amina broke out in tears again.

"Okay, Auntie. I'll catch the bus and come get the truck from you. I'm coming to console you, and when you're ready, I'll do what I can to help you with the funeral arrangements."

"I don't even want to think about that right now. I barely have enough money to make rent, let alone have a whole funeral."

"Kenan has plenty of friends that I'm sure won't mind helping with that. Money is no object to most of the dudes he hangs with, so they better come through, or they'll feel my wrath."

For the first time, Aunt Amina let out a small chuckle. "You remind me so much of him. Both Kenan and you get that hothead shit from your mom. I always used to joke with her and tell her that I carried and had her child, because they were definitely two of a kind."

"Yeah, that they were," I mumbled.

"Oh, and Naima, I'm so sorry about what happened to your mom. God, I wish that she was able to come to the funeral. I don't even want to tell her that her nephew is dead while she's in there, because I know it's gonna kill her. Jesus, I need you to help me, Lord! Before Kenan died, he told me that he would make it his mission to get Jason. He was so fucked up about the police snatching him up out of your mama's house while you were in the hospital. He said he tried to get the cops to let Ayana go because she wasn't in her right mind, but they told him that the judge would be the one to make that decision. He felt so helpless in the situation, but he was determined to do something about it. He told me that he was waiting on the right opportunity to get the person that shot you, too. Now he's . . . h–he's gone!"

I rolled my eyes and tried hard not to let the attitude drip through my voice. Amina really had no idea who her son was. It was clear that she didn't know he was behind every unfortunate event that had taken place in my life over the last month. He lied to her about everything and tried to make himself seem like he was a fuckin' saint. Fuck outta here!

I couldn't even stomach talking to her anymore because it was obvious that he had her bamboozled. I wasn't about to keep listening to what a good guy he was when I knew the truth.

"I'll be over there in about an hour, Auntie. I have to get off the phone now so I can charge it up before I get on the bus. Are you gonna be okay until I get there?"

"I'll be fine, baby. I'm just gonna go and look at some of my old photo albums until you come. The rest of the family will probably be here soon, so don't you worry about me doing anything crazy. If we're gonna get Jason back, I have to stay sane."

There's no 'we' in this, bitch. Y'all fuckers should've never let him be placed in the system when he had blood relatives still living.

"Okay, see you soon. Bye now!" I hung up the phone before she could pull me into another conversation.

When I looked up, Cha-Cha had a big cheesy grin on her face. "Bitch, do you deserve an Academy Award or nah? That was some of the best acting I've ever seen in my life!" She chuckled.

"Yeah, and that acting just got us a new getaway car. So, are you down with this plan for tonight?"

"You know I am. Let me just bribe my ho-ass mama with some of this money so she can take a night off the stroll and keep her grandkids. I'll be ready."

"A'ight, cool. I'm about to go sit at my aunt's house for a li'l while and pick up this truck. I have a few other stops to make, but I'll be here to pick you up by ten so we can get ready together and go over the plan one more time."

"I'll be ready."

I grabbed all my belongings and shoved my portion of the money into a purse that I got from Cha-Cha. I felt good knowing that I was taking all the necessary steps to get my brother back.

Chapter Five

Taking a long, hot bubble bath was everything I needed to relax my body and mind. I spent almost every second wondering if Jason was being treated right, if he was eating, and I even found myself wondering what was going through his mind. I needed to calm my thoughts if I was going to pull this mission off without any hiccups, so I sipped on a bottle of champagne as I soaked. After being in the tub so long that my skin pruned up, I let the water out and cut on the shower to wash my body and shave.

"Hurry up in there, girl! I still have to do your hair and makeup and finish getting ready, and time is getting away from us," Cha-Cha fussed just as I was getting out of the shower.

I threw the plush towel that the Aloft hotel provided around my body and started drying off. "Chill out! We won't be late. I'm coming out of the bathroom now."

I emerged from the bathroom wearing a silk robe that I bought from the mall earlier and plopped down in the chair that sat behind a desk. Makeup wasn't my thing, but I was going all out to reel in the bait.

Cha-Cha stood behind me and started parting my hair off in sections to flat-iron it. "Are you nervous about tonight?" she asked me.

"The only thing I'm nervous about is my brother being adopted by a family and it being too late for me to get him back. Why? You having second thoughts?"

"Never that. I was just asking because we've never done anything like this. Actually, going in a person's home and robbing them is a different ball game because we'll be on their turf. That means we have no room for error."

"You ain't gotta tell me some shit I already know. You just worry about yourself and making sure that *you* are on your *P*s and *Q*s. I got everything under control on my end."

I could see Cha-Cha nod her head in the mirror, and she continued to do my hair in a comfortable silence. Once my hair and makeup were complete, I slid into the black freakum dress I had purchased earlier that day. The back of it dipped down to just above my ass crack, showing off the tramp stamp that read *Gemini* on the small of my back. The dress hugged my curves like a second skin, and the sides of my boobs peeked out, making the dress even more sexy. Standing in the bathroom mirror checking myself out, I was impressed with how everything came together. Cha-Cha had placed big doobie curls in my long, thick hair that cascaded down my back. The smoky eye and red lips made my caramel-colored skin pop and set the rest of my look off. She had me looking twenty-five instead of nineteen, so I knew that the men would be drooling over this pretty young thing.

Cha-Cha looked just as good in a much simpler outfit. She was wearing a pair of skin-tight white jeans with an orange off-the-shoulder crop top and gold heels. She was one of those mocha-skinned girls that looked good with blonde hair, and today was no exception. She had straightened the dark blonde weave she had sewn in, and it hung down to her ass.

"Look at you looking like a whole snack. Let's do this shit," Cha-Cha said as she grabbed her oversized purse and headed to the door.

I picked up my own purse and made sure I had my cell phone and my gun before we left. By the time we made it to After Midnight, the parking lot was already packed. All eyes were on us when we stepped out of the black-on-black Suburban. Not giving a fuck about any of the unwanted attention we were receiving, I strutted toward the door. Cha-Cha grabbed my elbow and stopped me midstride.

"We're not going in the regular entrance. Jacoby wants us to come through the back door so nobody will see us," Cha-Cha explained.

"Well, I think it's a little too late for that," I said, nodding my head in the direction of a group of men that were gawking at us.

Cha-Cha looked at them and waved her hand. "Girl, please! They're so drunk that they won't even remember seeing us. Let's go!" she urged as she led the way to the entrance that we were supposed to use. "When we get inside, I'll show you how to get to the club from down here, and then I'll go handle our business. You got the pills, right?"

I dug around in my purse and pulled out the Percs. I had already ripped the label off the bottle, so there was no tracing that shit back to me. I handed them to Cha-Cha before she knocked on the heavy steel door. After a few seconds, a man that was built like a bull opened the door. He was wearing a collared shirt that had *Security* written across the chest with a gun on his hip. The scowl on his face let me know that he wasn't expecting us.

"Who the fuck are y'all, and what the fuck you want?" he asked, completely unfazed by the two pretty faces that stood before him.

Cha-Cha's evil glare matched his as she stared him down. "Who the fuck are *you*, my nigga? The help? You must didn't know that Jacoby was expecting us. Why don't you get your fat ass out the way and let us in?"

Cha-Cha tried to brush past him, but he moved his wide body to the side and blocked her. "The boss ain't told me shit, and until he does, y'all won't be getting in. Not through this door anyway. Walk y'all fine asses around the front and wait in line like everybody else."

"Nigga, fuck you! I'll be sure to let Jacoby know that you're giving us a hard time. I'll have your weak-ass job just like that!" She snapped her fingers for emphasis, and then pulled out her phone and made a phone call. She placed the call on speaker phone while she waited for an answer.

"Yo," a sexy-ass male voice echoed through the speaker.

"What's up, Jacoby? Can you let this fat fuck at the back door know that you're expecting me? He seems to be taking his damn job a little too seriously," Cha-Cha explained.

Jacoby started snickering. "That is what I pay him for, so he's doing right. Chill out on picking with my employees, Cha. You don't never know how to act. Let me holla at him."

"Oh, you're on speaker. He standing here with the dumb face now. You can go ahead and tell him to step aside."

"Aye, Max, go ahead and let her and her friend in. They're the only ones I'm expecting tonight."

Cha-Cha hung up the phone and stuck her tongue out as she moved past Max. When I walked by, he eyed me like he was hungry and I was his favorite meal.

"My bad about that. I was just doing my job. Nothing personal," he said.

"You can keep your apology, boo. I wasn't worried about it," I let him know without breaking my stride.

Cha-Cha and I walked down a hallway that looked like it belonged in a prison. There was nothing special about it at all. The floor was concrete, and the walls were cinderblocks. The muffled music that we heard through the walls had to be coming from the club. I just hoped that shit looked better than the damn dungeon we were in. There were different rooms in this section of the club. I took a quick glimpse in the first one we passed, and I saw a pool table. There were mad niggas in there shooting dice on the floor, whooping and hollering, probably ready to kill each other over that money. The next room we walked by had the door closed.

"That's Jacoby's office right there. He has some stairs in there that lead to a room that overlooks the club. So, I'll be watching you from in there. If you can, try to stay near the bar because that's where I'll have a bird's eye view of you."

"Okay, I'll do that. Don't let that nigga try to downtalk you on the price either!" I told her. Jacoby was a dude that she used to mess with, so I didn't have time for him to be sweet-talking her. She would probably fall for the okey-doke.

Cha-Cha looked at me like I was a fool. "Girl, you don't need to worry about that. Shit, I need this money too. If I was stupid enough to let him talk me down, that would be a smaller cut for both of us. You gotta know that I'm not that damn dumb."

"Just making sure we're on the same page."

"The stairs that'll take you directly to the club is right here." Cha-Cha pointed ahead. "It's another door there, but once you close it, you won't be able to get back in. The door only opens from this side. You want me to come up with you?"

"Nah, I got it." I stepped closer to her and spoke in a hushed tone. "When I get ready to leave, I'm gonna tell him that I have to use the bathroom to give you time to get to the car. Make sure all of our money is there before you leave. And don't forget, forty-five minutes."

Cha-Cha moved her hand around like she was telling me to hurry up and finish. "Yeah, yeah. Forty-five minutes, I know. We've been over this a million times, Naima. Get you a drink or something to relax your nerves."

I giggled at Cha-Cha because she was right; I was being repetitive. I just wanted to be sure that nothing went wrong. We couldn't afford to miss one minor detail. "Let's get this money!"

Cha-Cha grinned and nodded her head. "Let's do it!" She stood there until she could no longer see me walking up the stairs, and I heard her faint footsteps walking away.

The music got louder as I neared the top of the stairs where an entrance to the club was. I took a deep breath and closed my eyes before I opened the door. I needed a moment to gather myself before I did what I had to do. I had never done anything of this magnitude, and I knew that so many different things could go wrong. I was just praying that nothing did. This was all for my brother, and I wouldn't be any good to him if I got locked up or killed in the process.

"I'm coming for you, Jason," I whispered to myself before I finally walked through the door.

I found an empty seat at the bar and sat facing the club so I could scope everything out. The place was packed with thirsty bitches that were already drunk from the club they went to before they came here. They were all on the dance floor twerking, trying to get some attention from the men. I swear that shit was like a human mating call. Some of the men were catching that ass they were throwing, some of them stood around and watched, and some of them weren't paying them any attention at all. I looked around and saw a few potential marks, but since people were still coming in, I decided to wait it out.

I turned around and faced the bartender to order a drink. When I tried to get his attention, he walked past me like he didn't even see me. I went in my purse and pulled out a twenty-dollar bill. Once he finished making the drink he'd skipped me for, I shoved the money in front of his face. This mothafucka had the nerve to walk past me again like I didn't fuckin' exist.

I turned to a girl that was sitting next to me. "Am I invisible?" I asked loud enough for the bartender to hear.

The girl covered her mouth and started laughing. "No, I don't think so. I can see you just fine."

"Okay, I just wanted to make sure before I get to acting a fool in this bitch!"

"Aye, man!" a voice boomed from behind me. "I know you see this lady over here trying to get your attention. Why don't you come see what she wants?"

The bartender hurried to me, looking nervous as fuck. Whoever was behind me had his ass shook. "I apologize, ma'am. I was just trying to help the customers that were here before you. What can I get you?" he asked.

"That's some bullshit and you know it. You walked past me three fuckin' times, heard me calling you, and saw me put my money out. Get me a Sex on the Beach. Make it two because you'll probably ignore me again when I want my next one. And don't put a lot of ice in my shit," I shouted over the music.

I turned around to see the person that had come to my aid. My eyes landed on one of the finest men I had ever seen. He was a shade darker than me, almost cinnamon-like. His locs hung loosely past his shoulders with crinkles that made me think he just took out some braids. The diamonds that he wore in his ear, around his wrist, and on his fingers were simple, but expensive. I knew real diamonds when I saw them, and he had them in abundance. Even the designer sneakers on his feet gave away the fact that he was working with a nice piece of change.

When we made eye contact, I got lost in his gaze as he licked his succulent lips.

You're here for a job, Naima. Imagine that this nigga got a cockeye or something, 'cause he is too fine to focus.

"Thanks for getting that prick's attention for me," I said to the dude right when the bartender came back with my drinks. I handed him the money that was in my hand, but the man pulled my hand back.

"It's not a problem." He handed the bartender a hundred-dollar bill. "You make sure she gets whatever she wants to drink for the rest of the night. If it's any change left, you can keep it," he told the man behind the bar, and then turned his attention back to me. "You gotta be aggressive with that muh'fucka. What's your name, beautiful?"

"Brielle," I told him before I took a sip of my drink. "What's yours?"

"Brielle." My fake name rolled off his tongue. "I like that. My name is Jay. You here with yo' man?"

"Nah, I don't have one of those. I'm here alone. Just wanted to get out of the house and have a drink—or six." I smiled at him, making sure to keep eye contact.

"Ain't nothing wrong with that. You tryna hit the dance floor with me? Might as well enjoy yourself since you came out."

"I don't see any harm in that. Let's go." I stood up from the bar and led the way to the dance floor. I made sure to switch my hips every step of the way, so his eyes could stay glued to my ass. As juicy as this thing was, I knew he was watching.

Once we stepped onto the dance floor, it was like people moved out of the way to make room for us. Jay must've been somebody that had a lot of clout, because the women were looking at me like they wanted me dead. That didn't do nothing but make me give them something to look at.

I started swaying my hips to the beat of G-Eazy's hit song "No Limit." For a minute, Jay stood back and watched me while I occasionally looked back at him and winked my eye. Before long, I had turned the dance floor into a full-blown twerk session. Jay came behind me, and I started throwing my ass all over him. From what I felt, homeboy was working with a monster.

"Damn, girl. You damn sho' know how to move that body," he spoke into my ear as I grinded and worked my ass like I was trying to get pregnant.

"I know how to do a lot more than that," I said seductively.

I didn't think it was possible for his dick to get any harder, but that shit was damn near sticking in my ass. If I kept this up, I would have him exactly where I wanted. I turned around to face him and started grinding my pussy against his dick. A lustful look filled his eyes, and I placed soft kisses on the side of his neck.

"Girl, I'm ready to take yo' ass to the back," he groaned.

"I'm not that type of woman, daddy. If you can't take me to the crib, then you don't want this pussy. I don't fuck in cars, in alleys, or in no public-ass bathroom. I'ma need enough space to give you this work," I sexily whispered in his ear while I grabbed his dick.

"Well, shit! Let's get out of here then. My condo is out in Drift Tide. It's right on South Military Highway. We can be there in five minutes."

"That's cool, but I hope you're ready to pay if you wanna play."

Jay's brows knitted together in confusion. "Damn, it's like that?"

"Damn right it is. I don't know you, and you ain't my man, so pussy ain't free. My mama always taught me not to leave with a wet ass and a dry purse. I normally wouldn't even be considering this, but I've never wanted to fuck nobody as bad as I wanna fuck you right now either."

"I can dig it, ma. Shit, it ain't tricking if you got it. Money ain't shit to me, and I can't lie and say I don't wanna see what that pussy be like. Fuck it. Let's bounce."

"Okay, let me run to the bathroom real quick. I been holding it for too long, and I can't no more. Don't go nowhere, sexy." I kissed him on his soft lips for good measure and ended up liking it more than I should've.

"I'ma be waiting by the door for you." He grinned.

I had to push through the crowd to get to the bathroom. As soon as I locked myself in the stall, I pulled out my phone and texted Cha-Cha to let her know it was time. To kill some time, I made myself use the bathroom, washed my hands, and played around in the mirror. I couldn't believe how easy this was. I was sure that I was going to have to put in some work to get somebody to take me back to their house, but Jay practically fell into my lap. *What a fuckin' fool,* I thought to myself and chuckled out loud.

By the time I finished up in the ladies' room, Cha-Cha had replied to my message, letting me know that she was ready.

Just like he said, Jay was standing at the front of the club waiting for me. He grabbed my hand and walked me to his car. He was pushing a nice-ass dark green Range Rover. That horny fucker didn't even have the decency to open my door and help me in. By the time I climbed into the big-ass truck, he already had the car started and was ready to pull off. Before I could even get my seatbelt on, he sped off so damn fast that my head flew into the seat.

"Damn, mothafucka! I wanna live to see tomorrow!" I snapped.

"I ain't gon' kill you, girl. Just relax and enjoy the ride. You smoke?" he asked, pulling a rolled blunt out of a Backwoods pack in the middle console.

"From time to time, but I'll smoke with you if you got some good shit."

Jay put the blunt to his lips and sparked it up. "That's all I smoke," he said, and then took a deep pull of the weed.

Jay wasn't lying about living right up the street, because we were pulling into a neighborhood before he even passed me the blunt. I checked my surroundings and took in every inch of the scenery. The neighborhood was one long street that branched off into different courts. There was only one way in and out, and Jay lived all the way in the back. The neighborhood was too quiet for me to shoot him and make a quick getaway. This complex looked like it had a neighborhood watch program, a.k.a. nosey neighbors.

Jay passed me the blunt and opened his car door.

"You ready to go in?"

"I didn't come over here for nothing." I took a couple of pulls of the blunt, handed it back to him, and opened my door. I was ready to go in and get it the fuck over with.

Jay led the way to his front door and unlocked it like somebody was chasing us or something. He looked good as fuck, but the way he was acting like he didn't get pussy was a turn-off.

Before we even got in the door good, Jay was all over me. He tried to shove his tongue down my throat and groped my ass. His hand moved under my dress, but I stopped him before he could get to the honey pot.

"Wait a minute! Slow the fuck down!" I pushed him off me. "You need to take your time with me. This ain't no wham, bam, thank you, ma'am. I'm gonna make damn sure that I'm satisfied, too. Damn, can you show me to the bathroom and give me a wash cloth so I can freshen up?"

He nodded his head. "I got you. The bathroom is this way."

I followed him down the hall, and we stopped at a linen closet. He grabbed me a wash cloth, towel, and a fresh bar of soap. We walked a few more steps, and he pushed open the bathroom door and hit the light.

"Go 'head and handle your business. I'll be in my room waiting on you, so don't take forever."

I shut the door on him and rolled my eyes. "Ugh! Thirsty ass!" I mumbled under my breath.

As I looked around the bathroom, I realized that there was a window in there. It was low enough for Cha-Cha to be able to climb through when the time came. Making sure that the water was on full blast to drown out any noise, I slowly lifted the window just enough for Cha-Cha to push it the rest of the way up. After taking a quick ho bath, I walked out of the bathroom and closed the door behind me. There was only light coming from one room, so I figured that one belonged to Jay.

When I walked in the room, this dude was already in the bed, stripped down to his boxers.

"It took you long enough."

"Took me long enough? But you still ain't ready?"

"You're the only one that still got your clothes on. I know you didn't have me bring you all the way here to play games with me," he fussed.

"Nah, I didn't come to play. Which is why I'm not understanding why I don't see my money on the night-stand," I replied with my hand perched on my hip.

Jay sucked his teeth and frowned up his face. "You serious right now? Girl, you're gonna get your money."

"I know I am, and I'm gonna get it now. This is like a slot machine. It don't work until you put the money in it." I grinned.

I pranced toward him while stripping out of my dress. I was completely naked underneath, so when I let the dress slide to the floor around my feet, Jay looked like he was about to drool as he laid eyes on my body. I lifted one of my breasts and flicked my tongue across the nipple. His dick almost busted right through his boxers.

"Trust me," I started as I crawled on the bed and between his legs. "It'll be worth your while, but not until I see my cash."

"A'ight, I'll give you the money first." Jay leaned over the side of the bed and grabbed his jeans off the floor. He pulled some money out of his pocket and threw a few crumpled bills at me.

I counted the money and looked at him like he'd lost his mind. "Two hundred dollars? Nigga, you might as well take me the fuck home. Pick you up one of them cheap hoes from church street. Got me fucked up!" I fussed as I climbed off the bed. I made sure that when I bent over to pick up my dress, Jay got an eyeful of ass and freshly waxed pussy.

"Got damn, girl!" I heard him mumble under his breath.

I abruptly turned around, catching him licking his lips as he stared at me hungrily.

"What the fuck you waiting on? Get dressed so we can bounce. And I'm keeping this li'l punk-ass two hundred dollars for wasting my time."

"Nah, fuck that! I'ma get me some of this pussy tonight," Jay announced as he rolled out of bed. "I got enough money to pay your ass ten times over, so don't try to play me like I'm a broke mothafucka. If you weren't beautiful as fuck with a pretty-ass pussy, yo' ass would've been catching an Uber home right now. I like your personality, though, so I'ma give you yo' li'l money. You pressed about it, so you must need the shit. I don't mind helping out." He went inside of a walk-in closet, and I discreetly moved to the side to see what he was doing.

Watching him like a hawk while his back faced me, I saw him pull up a panel in the floor of the closet. He reached straight down there and pulled some money back up, so it couldn't have been in a safe. I eased back over to the bed and sat down before he came back out of the closet.

This muh'fucka gets stupider by the second!

"I hope this is enough for you, 'cause I ain't giving yo' ass no more than that. Don't even know how tight and wet that pussy is yet, and I'm already cashing out. I hope you like sucking dick," he said as he made the money rain on me.

If I wasn't on a mission, his ass would've been cursed out and beat the fuck up for the disrespect. Since I needed every dime, I collected the money that fell around me on the bed and floor and counted it up. He only gave me three hundred more dollars, but that was cool because I now knew where his stash was.

"Actually, I love sucking dick. But only if you let me do it my way."

I pulled him onto the bed and straddled his lap. Jay's nose rested against my neck, and his light breaths felt good on my skin. When his lips replaced his nose, it felt even better. I got into the groove and moved my hips, letting him feel my wetness through his boxers. I reached behind me and lightly squeezed his balls, rubbing my finger across the gooch. Jay started sucking on my neck with more intensity and caressing my ass.

"I'm ready to feel this dick, daddy," I moaned, gently massaging his balls.

"I'll give it to you after you suck it," he demanded.

"Lay back on the bed," I ordered. He obliged.

I got out of the bed and walked over to my purse, pulling out a pair of handcuffs and a feather. Jay's eyes were wide with shock.

"Yo, what type of shit you on? I just want some head," he explained.

"And that's what you're about to get," I told him as I ran the feather down his chest. "I already told you that I only enjoy doing it when it's done my way. I like to be in full control when it's my time to be the pleaser. It's something about a man experiencing large amounts of pleasure and all he can do is lay still and enjoy it. There's no escaping or trying to gain control of the situation. I'm tellin' you, it'll be the best orgasm you'll ever get. Let's make the best of this night together. After all, this is the first and only time, and you're paying." I mounted the bed, sat on his dick, and placed soft kisses all over his chest. "So, are you trying to have some fun or what?"

"Fuck it. I'm down," Jay responded, telling me exactly what I needed to hear.

I scooted up his body until my pussy was right in his face. When I snatched the handcuffs up off the bed, Jay extended his arms above his head like he was ready for me to cuff him. I took the open opportunity to secure his wrists tightly to the bed post.

"Damn, girl! You got these shits tight like I'm under arrest or something," Jay complained, trying to wriggle his wrists.

"Don't worry about that. Soon you won't be able to feel anything but pleasure." I slid his boxers off and tossed them to the floor before I heaved my ass and pussy right in his face.

Without any more words, I swirled my tongue around the head of his humongous dick. For a few moments, I continued to tease him with my mouth. Jay's groans filled the room, and he started pumping his dick in and out of my mouth.

"Don't be scared now, girl. Stop playing and suck this dick like you said you was."

I crammed my pussy into his mouth, silently letting him know to shut up and eat. He started making circles on my pearl with his tongue, shooting an electric signal from the crown of my head to the tips of my toes. That gave me all the encouragement I needed to slob him down like a ho working for a tip. The only sounds that could be heard were our simultaneous moans and me slurping him up. My legs locked around his neck when I felt the beginning stages of my climax coming on.

"Oooohhh, shit, daddy! Don't stop! I'm about to cum!" I called out as I bucked my hips against his face.

Jay pushed his tongue flat against my clit and made it vibrate. Before I knew it, my essence was raining down on his face. While I was riding the wave of my orgasm, I continued to suck and jerk his dick while playing with his balls.

"Aaahhh, fuck! Hold up! I'm not ready to nut yet. I wanna feel that pussy."

Obliging his request, I slowly removed myself from him and retrieved a condom out of my purse. As soon as I slid it down his girth, I climbed on top right behind it. Trying to fit his entire dick inside of me was a feat, so I eased down slowly as he filled every inch of my walls.

"Ummmm! This dick feels sooo good," I purred in his ear. I wasn't lying either. We hadn't even started good yet, and I was ready to sing from the mountaintops. It's a shame that such a big, pretty dick between the legs of a fine-ass man had to go to waste.

I went into full cowgirl mode and started riding his dick with a purpose. The friction from my clit rubbing against him had me ready to cum all over him for a second time. Jay was handcuffed, but that damn sure didn't stop him from fucking me back. He was moving them hips and hitting spots inside of me that had never been explored. I could feel my juices wetting up the insides of my thigh while his dick pulsated in me.

"Fuck! This pussy was worth every dime of that money. Ride this shit!" he grunted.

His eyes started to roll back, so I knew that the end was near. I threw my legs over his head and spun around on the dick, now riding him with my back facing him. I placed my feet flat on the bed and started bouncing up and down while making my ass cheeks jump, one at a time.

"Shit! I'm 'bout to nut!" Jay let out a deep groan as warm liquid filled up the condom.

I slowly rose from his dick, and the now soft member flopped on his leg. "I'll be back. Let me go get us something to clean off with."

"Hold up. Ain't you gonna untie me?" Jay asked, pulling his arms forward like he was trying to snatch the cuffs from the bed.

I looked back at him and grinned. "Give me a second, baby. We're just getting started. I hope you didn't think that round one was it. Let me clean you off, and then I'll uncuff you."

Jay looked skeptical for a second, and then he nodded his head in approval. "A'ight, just hurry up. Now that it's over, I don't like the feeling of being restrained."

I ignored him and threw my dress back on before I went to the bathroom. When I walked in there, I saw Cha-Cha standing outside of the window about to come in. We made eye contact with each other, and I nodded my head to let her know the time was now. I put my finger to my lips to signal her to be quiet as possible, wet the wash cloths with warm water, and returned to the bedroom.

"Took you long enough!" Jay complained as soon as I came in the room. "Get the key and unlock these shits. They're starting to cut off my circulation."

I smirked wickedly as I slowly walked toward him. "Uh-uh. You had your fun. Now it's time for me to have mine." I picked my purse up off the floor, pulled out my gun, and pointed it directly at him.

When he saw me aiming my weapon at him, his mouth flew agape and beads of sweat started to form on his forehead. "You stupid bitch! You set me up!" He started violently tugging at the handcuffs, determined to break free.

I shook my head at him and chuckled. "Give it up, chump. You ain't getting out. Seems to me like you're the stupid one. Rule number one in the streets: never shit where you sleep. Rule number two: don't bring strangers to your house, especially if that's where you keep your stash. You broke two of the cardinal rules because you were blinded by a pretty face with a fat ass. Now you have to pay."

On cue, Cha-Cha busted into the room with her gun drawn. I knew that she had already checked the house to make sure we were alone, so it was time to grab and go.

"Who the fuck is this ho? Y'all bitches bold enough to try to rob me? Y'all better run and hide when y'all leave here, because y'all are good as dead!" Jay ranted, spit flying from his mouth. He was so angry that his skin started to flush.

I eased closer to the bed until I was right up on him with my gun touching his forehead. "A man in your position shouldn't be giving out any threats. Who's to say that you'll even make it out alive?"

An angry scowl etched across his face, and he rose up like he was going to do something, but the handcuffs stopped him. "Bitch, y—"

I cut his statement short when I smashed the butt of my gun into the side of his head. The force busted his forehead open on contact, and blood started pouring from the fresh wound. Jay was already out cold, but I smacked him with the gun one more time for good measure. I didn't know if he was dead, but if he wasn't, he wouldn't be waking up anytime soon.

"It's in a floorboard inside his closet. Follow me," I instructed Cha-Cha.

We moved quickly as we rushed into the closet. I went to the exact spot that I saw Jay go, threw all the shoeboxes out of the closet, and searched the floor until I found a loose board.

"Jackpot!" I said as I lifted the panel and exposed more money than I had ever seen in my life. "This shit was too fuckin' easy!" I exclaimed as we started throwing the money in our bags.

"Let's hurry up and get the fuck out of here! We've already spent too much time in here," Cha-Cha said as we cleaned out every dime of the money.

Once our purses were filled to the brim and there wasn't anything left, we hauled ass out the front door and never looked back.

Chapter Six

"I can't believe we came up on two hundred thousand that easily!" Cha-Cha exclaimed as she threw money up in the air and started twerking.

We were back at the hotel with the money spread across the bed. There was so much of it that I wanted to jump on top of the pile and roll around in it, but I refrained.

"And to think that fucker tried to give me two hundred dollars for the pussy. Shit, I got that million-dollar like Nicki Minaj say. He had me fucked up!"

Cha-Cha and I both busted out laughing, and then her expression suddenly changed. She had a serious look on her face with a hint of sadness. "So, what are you gonna do now that you have all the money that you need?"

"Well, as soon as school starts, I'm gonna be snatching Jason up out of there and we're hitting the road," I informed her. Cha-Cha had a little cousin that went to the same elementary school with my brother, and she told Cha-Cha that he was still attending school there. That presented me with the perfect opportunity to get Jason without anyone knowing. "You know what? Why don't y'all just come with us? I mean, there's enough room in that big-ass truck for all of us to load up in there and be out. There's nothing here for either one of us. We've both fucked over a lot of people, so I think it's time that we get the fuck out of dodge."

Cha-Cha sat up straighter, and her eyes brightened. "You would really want us to come with y'all?"

"Why not, Charlene? You're my best friend, and I love your kids, too. Even though your fake ass didn't come see me at the hospital, I wouldn't be able to live with myself if something happened to you. We did all of our dirt together, so if it comes back to bite one of us, then they're gonna have to come after us both. We don't even have to pack anything. We have enough money to have a fresh start somewhere else. I was thinking we could start over in Arizona. I heard that it never gets cold there, and that shit is on the other side of the U.S. No one would find us there."

"What about school? You don't think they'll put out an APB for Jason after we kidnap him from school?" she asked.

"I'm not worried about that. As long as I have my brother with me, they'd have to kill me before they take him away again. We'll figure out a way to create new identities for ourselves, and if we have to, we can homeschool the kids. I don't know how things will play out once we get there; I just know we gotta go. You don't have to leave if you don't want to, but come ten a.m., I'm out!"

"I didn't say that I didn't want to go. I just want to make sure that when you leave, you won't regret it. People might get suspicious if you don't show up to Kenan's funeral. And what about your mom?"

"What about that bitch? She's the reason why I had to do all of this in the first place. If her careless ass hadn't left my brother home alone, he would be with me right now. The only thing she'll be worried about when she gets out of jail is getting high, so she probably won't even notice we're gone. My mind is made up! I'm not staying for the funeral; I won't be waiting for my mom to get out of jail, and as far as I'm concerned, Jason and I just disappeared without a trace. It's either you're gonna come with us, or you're not. I'm not up for any more of your questions, because you're pissing me off."

Cha-Cha threw her hands up in surrender. "Okay, girl. Let me get all my important things and the kids together, because this time tomorrow, we'll be crossing state lines."

"By this time tomorrow, we'll be more than halfway there. You only have two more hours to pack. I'm about to shower and take a quick nap to get my mind right. You can take the truck to do what you need to do and pick up the kids. Just make sure that you're out front by nine thirty a.m. Don't be late, Cha!" I warned.

"I won't be late, girl. It won't even take me a full two hours. And Naima?"

"What you want, girl?" I asked jokingly.

"I love you, girl!" Cha-Cha's sentimental ass said before she leaned down and threw her arms around my neck. "We did it, and now you and Jason will be reunited in a couple of hours."

I wasn't usually the mushy type, but I hugged her back. "I love you too, Cha. I know I told you that you weren't my real friend, but you've really shown me that you got a bitch back. Now, get the hell out of here!"

Cha chuckled as she grabbed the keys and left the room. I lay back on the bed, but I couldn't fall asleep because I was too excited to see Jason. It had been an excruciating month and a half without my brother, and I knew that no one could take care of him like I could. With me was where my baby brother belonged.

Chapter Seven

As the fourth-grade students started to file outside for recess, I kept a close eye on the door. Cha-Cha had parked the truck right beside their playground so I could get a good view. A few minutes had passed before my eyes landed on my baby brother. I couldn't control the tears that started to slide down my face. I was grinning like a Cheshire cat and crying at the same damn time. I was so elated to see him that my emotions were all over the place. He looked clean and healthy, but that was where it ended. The smile that he always wore was replaced with a look of sadness. I noticed that he wasn't interacting with any of the students, and he was usually one of the most outgoing kids you'd ever meet.

I wanted to jump out of the truck and snatch him up as soon as I saw him, but I had to wait for the right opportunity. I observed him for a few more minutes and noticed that he didn't go play with the other kids. He was sitting on a bench all by himself with his back facing us. The bench was literally only a few feet away from us, but I needed a distraction so the teachers wouldn't see me leaving with him.

God must've been on my side, because a fight broke out between two kids at the basketball court. They were out there fighting like grown-ass men, and it took all of the teachers outside to break them up. I used that opportunity to jump out of the truck and approach the bench. I jogged up behind Jason and covered his eyes with my hands.

"Peek-a-boo, I see you!" I sang.

"Naima?" He turned around, and when he saw that it was me, his eyes lit up like Christmas trees. "Naima! Naima!" He just about tackled me to the ground when he jumped up and hugged me.

"Jason, I'm taking you with me. I need you to hold my hand and don't let go. When I say go, run as fast as you can and don't look back. We're going to that truck right there, just a few feet away." I pointed.

Jason nodded his head, and as soon as I grabbed his hand, we took off. Cha-Cha already had the passenger door open, so I lifted Jason off his feet and threw him into the front seat. When I jumped in behind him and slammed the door shut, Cha-Cha was already speeding off. I looked back and saw teachers chasing after the truck, but they weren't fast enough.

"We did it!" Cha-Cha squealed with excitement as she put the pedal to the metal and headed toward the interstate.

I pulled Jason into my lap and squeezed him so hard that I was probably smothering him. I showered his cheek and forehead with all the kisses that I'd missed out on when we were separated.

"I've missed you so much, Jason. Who were you with while I was gone? Were them people treating you right?"

"They were nice, but they weren't my family. I kept trying to tell those people that I didn't want to go with them and that they needed to take me to my sister. They had me in a group home with a bunch of other kids, and some days

I had to share my bed with somebody else because there wasn't enough room. Please don't make me go back there," he pleaded, eyes pooling with tears.

My heart started to ache just thinking about the emotional turmoil that my brother had to endure. "Jason, you never have to worry about any of that ever again. You're gonna live with me now, and we're going to travel to a new state to live. Have you heard about Arizona?"

Jason raised his eyebrows. "Yeah, I heard that there's a lot of desert there. Are we about to be living in the desert?"

I laughed at his observation. "You're right, Jason. There is a lot of desert in Arizona. It isn't all desert, though. They have cities too, and we will be living in the city. Once you get used to it, it won't be any different than living here."

"What about Mom?" he asked.

"Well, Mom did something really bad, so she had to get punished for it. We won't be seeing her for a while," I explained to him.

"Good, because I only want to live with you. Mom is nice sometimes, but most of the time she only cares about herself. When you were at the hospital, Mom didn't even feed me every day because she was hardly home. I thought you were dead, so I cried every day. I can't live with Mom by myself ever again. Only if you're there."

I was seething after hearing how neglectful that bitch had been to my brother. If she wasn't locked up, I probably would've killed her. "You don't have to worry about any of that bad stuff anymore. When Mom is finished doing her time and you want to see her, I promise you that I'll be right by your side. I won't allow anybody to harm you ever again. Do you hear me?"

Jason finally displayed that smile that I loved. "Yes, I hear you. I love you, Naima. I'm glad that you're not dead and that you came to get me."

"As long as I'm alive, Jason, I'll always come for you."

I made a mental note to get my brother in therapy once we got settled. He had been through a traumatic experience watching somebody that he knew as family shoot his sister. Not to mention that he was born to a crack-addicted mother that sent him too many mixed messages. If I didn't want my brother growing up fucked up like I was, I needed to do something about it while he was still young. Now that we were back together, I was going to raise him like he was mine and make sure that he made something of himself. There would be no hood struggles for my brother. I was going to make sure that he grew up to become a powerful black man that made a difference in the world.

"Sunny Arizona, here we come!" Cha-Cha shouted as we tore up the interstate on our way to our new home and our new lives.

About the Author

Jasmine M. Williams, born and raised in Virginia Beach, VA, is a mother of two with a passion for writing. Her knack for writing started in middle school when she and a classmate would compete over who could write the best short stories. Reading the novel *The Coldest Winter Ever* by Sista Souljah inspired her to want to write a story of her own. All the obstacles that life threw her way and becoming a mother at an early age didn't deter her dreams; it made her fight harder to make them a reality. She aspires to become a full-time author and to see one or more of her books hit the silver screen. While writing and being a full-time mother, she is also working on getting her bachelor's degree in business management.

Other titles by Jasmine Williams

Bad, But Perfectly Good At It 1–3
May the Baddest Bitch Win 1–3
Would You Ride For Me 1–2
Us Over Everything 1–2
Let Me Show You Real Love 1–2
Beautiful Vengeance
(Collaboration with Author Perri Forrest)

Honor Among Boss Chicks

by

Niyah Moore

Juju

"We need to hit another lick 'cause I gotsta get some more money," Tah said after she downed a double shot of Hennessy.

"We both could use some more money," I said, raising my hand toward the bartender for a refill of Jack Daniel's with honey. "The pot is getting low."

We were used to coming up on money no matter where we were. Whether we jacked it, hustled it, or bartered for it, we were the queens of hittin' licks. Tah was my best friend. She was a rider who had been down through all the hard times. She was there when we ain't have nothing. She never switched up and even stayed through all the fights and arguments. It didn't matter that she was Indian and I was Black. Tah was real and never changed after all these years. And we for damn sure never let no nigga come between us.

That night, we were back home in Las Vegas after we had been on the run for a few weeks. We had almost got caught in D.C. with a stolen car. We couldn't wait to get back home, but we had to let things cool down a little bit. In Vegas, there was always a lick to pull, but it was becoming harder to stay off the police's radar.

I drank my drink and scanned Caesar's Palace. I was looking for the right target. I happened to notice two tall, dark-skinned kings walking up to the bar. Now usually, when we were working, I didn't pay attention to anyone I found attractive because I didn't want to catch feelings. Catching feelings was the worst thing to do when you were trying to rob someone.

I elbowed Tah to see if she saw them too. "What about them?"

She shook her head. "What makes you think they got some money? They look like some wannabe Migos."

"They're way cuter, though."

The one on the right stood at six feet one inch. He was wearing a Versace shirt and an expensive pair of what looked like Embellish jeans. He had long dreadlocks that hung down to the middle of his back. The other one on the right was six foot four. He wore similar attire. His haircut made him look like a pretty boy. When he cracked a smile at his friend, I caught a glimpse of his gold grill.

I thought about what Tah said about them being wannabes. We met plenty of posers, and it always ended up being a waste of our time. I went back to scanning other areas of the casino to see what else might work.

"Hey, my name is Dom," a lovely deep voice said.

We turned around to face the taller one with the fade and the gold teeth. His boy was a few feet back as if he were afraid we were going to bite.

He continued, "We want y'all to join us. What's ya names?"

Reluctantly I replied, "I'm JuJu."

"JuJu. You bad! Chocolate goddess. We walked through this way a couple of times. You ain't see us?"

I smirked. "No." I didn't see him or his friend. I was too busy talking to Tah about our next move. Playing with my long, thick French braid that hung over my shoulder, I looked him up and down with my chestnut brown eyes. I didn't know what it was about him, but I could tell that this night was about to get interesting.

He chuckled a little as he said, "It's cool. We saw y'all, and I had to say something."

"Okay. Well, this is my best friend, Tah."

"Tahlia," she corrected with a slight attitude.

She wasn't feeling him. She tossed her long, curly brown hair away from her face and rolled her almond-shaped hazel eyes that shadowed a touch of green.

"Nice to meet you." Dom put out his hand to shake my hand as he flashed his diamond-encrusted watch.

Tah didn't look impressed at all as she stared him down. "All right now, while you stuntin', don't get mad when ya watch gets snatched."

I threw my lips to my drink and sipped. He did flash his wrist like he was showing off. Tah had read my mind.

Dom laughed, thinking she was playing. He had no idea that she was serious as fuck. It was cute how he didn't look the least bit worried about getting his watch snatched. *Cocky*, I thought. That was what intrigued me even more.

Tah said rudely, "Now, what you should've started with is that smile rather than that watch, but uh, how can we help you, Dom?"

He licked his lips. "Come hang out with me and my boy."

"Hmmm . . . we'll see. Where y'all from?" I asked with my left eyebrow raised.

"We're from L.A."

"Where? Like, Compton?" Tah quizzed with a scowl. Then, she threw me this look to say they *indeed* didn't have no money.

"Hell nah," he said with a frown. "Not dissing Compton or nothing like that, but we're from Long Beach."

"So . . . what y'all doing here in Sin City?" I questioned.

"We decided to spend a few nights out here. This is our last night. You joining us or not?" he asked, growing impatient.

"Let me talk to my girl and I'll let you know," I answered. "Where can we find you?"

"We'll be on the other side of the bar, getting a drink," he said.

"Cool. Give us a few minutes."

Dom walked back to his friend so they could go to the other side of the bar.

Tah shook her head. "We wastin' our time, JuJu."

"Just chill. I'm telling you now, there's something. I feel it in my bones. I call first dibs on Dom." I handed a credit card to the bartender to close our tab.

"Now, hold on, JuJu. You done lost your mind—"

I eased off the stool, pulling my dress down, and went their way. She followed behind me.

Dom turned to face us as soon as we reached them. "Hey, that didn't take long at all. This is my boy, C. Millionaire. This is JuJu and Tahlia."

"Nice to meet you both," C. Millionaire said as he gazed at us, but his eyes were glued to Tah.

He went by C. Millionaire. *Now, why they call him that?* My wheels were turning. Were they rappers?

"What y'all trying to get into tonight?" I asked.

"We just wingin' it," C. Millionaire said. As he smiled, he flashed a pair of deep dimples.

Shit, they might've been the most attractive targets we ever had. Typically, we hit the pockets of some old, wrinkled-up men. I had to clear my throat to remind myself that this was business. Pleasure was out of the question. As fine as they were, I had to ignore the attraction, but how else was I going to find out what they were working with?

We strolled over with them to a high rollers Poker table. We watched as C. Millionaire and Dom place their bets. Tah and I ordered a drink from a waitress walking by, and Dom paid for it.

I was feeling myself up until I felt a hand go up my dress and rub my ass. I turned to see that it wasn't Dom or C. Millionaire who got a quick feel. It was some oversized Pillsbury Dough Boy.

I shouted, "Watch yo' motherfucking hands, dude!"

This overstuffed white punk did it again as if I was to be played with. I tossed my drink into the fat man's face. The man stood there with his mouth parted open in the shape of an *O* as my drink dripped from his head to his cheap-ass suit.

He grabbed hold of my arm, pulling my body too close to his. "Hey now, sweetheart, you didn't have to throw your drink all over me. A nice kiss would've been better."

"Fuck you!" I spit in his face.

He wouldn't let me go as he pulled my arm rougher.

"Hold the fuck up! Didn't she just tell yo' ass not to touch her?" Tah shouted. She was right behind me with the same screwed-up expression on her face.

I was trying to pull away, but he wouldn't take his slimy hands off me. He was all up on me as if he were getting some sick pleasure out of me resisting.

Dom stood over him. "Aye, yo, check this out. She said to step!"

The fat man let me go as if he were suddenly scared.

I smiled at Dom for a second, thinking I could play the damsel in distress role for a little while longer, but then I went back to staring at the fat man as if he had lost his mind.

"Bitch," the man murmured under his breath as he turned to walk away from the Poker table.

I pulled the back of his suit jacket roughly before he could get away. Putting my fingers stiffly into his back as if it were a gun, I uttered, "I'll shoot you right here in this fucking casino, you stupid muthafucka. Now, who's the real bitch, bitch?"

The man put his hands up and pissed his pants.

I let him go. "Yeah, that's what I thought, pussy."

He bolted out of the casino, bumping into a waitress on his way out, tripping over himself.

We laughed hysterically.

Dom caught a glimpse of the way I was holding my hand as if it were a gun, and it amused him. He even had to laugh. "That was a good one. I need someone like you at home with me."

My flawlessly arched eyebrows were raised, and my cold brown eyes were wide. "I'll go anywhere with yo' fine ass."

Dom smiled. "Let me order you another drink."

I smiled right back, but I couldn't help but notice that Tah still had a funny look on her face. She still wasn't feeling them. I ignored her.

Dom and C. Millionaire finished up a couple of hands and collected their winnings.

Dom placed a purple chip in the palm of my hand and said, "Let's go."

"Where we going?" I asked, pretending as if that chip were no big deal.

C. Millionaire handed Tah one, too. She looked at me with a smirk. I nodded.

Purple chips in Vegas were worth five hundred apiece. We had five hundred dollars each in under one hour just talking to them. Oh yeah, I knew I had a good feeling.

I eyed the black, purple, white, and green chips that Dom had sitting nicely on a handheld rack. He had more than $350,000 worth of chips. Instantly, my panties got wet.

C. Millionaire lit a cigar as he paid attention to how beautiful Tah was. His eyes never left her ass as she walked in front of him with a sashay.

Tah wasted no time. She went straight to the window to cash out her chip.

I looked at Dom as he counted the chips. "You win enough tonight?" I asked.

"Hardly. If we didn't have y'all here, I would still be at that table. It's like I feel so damn lucky right now, you know. I can stand to win a little more."

"Is that right? What was your biggest gain in one night?"

"At what? Poker?"

"Yeah," I replied.

"Six hundred eighty thousand," he said without blinking.

"Damn. Seriously?"

He shrugged a little. "Yeah, but I mean, that's nothing."

That's nothing? Who the fuck are these guys? I thought to myself.

Tah

JuJu seemed to be enjoying the company of these phony-ass niggas a little too much. She knew our get-down, and this wasn't even our style. It was typical to make a nigga give up everything he had for some pussy. We weren't prostitutes, and we vowed to never get that desperate, so what the fuck was we doing? Real boss bitches didn't need to open their legs to get what they wanted. They had other skills for that.

However, I had to give it to her. Her senses were on point. These weren't some aspiring rappers. Without us knowing them for more than an hour, C. Millionaire wasted no time telling me exactly who they were.

They owned a multi-million-dollar diamond store and were running an empire of some sort. I found that hard to believe because they didn't dress as if they had millions, but I had to chill because they were in Vegas on vacation, and this was Sin City, the number one place that catered to various vices.

C. Millionaire seemed to pride himself on being a jeweler of the highest quality of diamonds and rare gems. They serviced the Los Angeles elite. Their custom pieces graced the necks, ears, fingers, and wrists of rappers and ballers alike. They were specific in the choosing of carat weight, anatomy, cut, color, and clarity in their diamonds. The company was highly recommended, and the waiting list for custom jewelry had some A-list names begging for more. The size of the bank account determined how long someone would be on the list. Dom and C. Millionaire were at the top of the food chain. They worked hard, but they played harder.

Out of the corner of my eye, I could see Dom checking JuJu out. That night, she was wearing a short black-and-gold dress from a custom boutique that highlighted her dark skin. My girl had always been gorgeous. She could have any man she wanted, so she didn't need to settle for anything. She deserved the fucking best.

"So, what we about to do now?" Dom asked. "I'm tired of gambling."

C. Millionaire stated, "I'm done. What about y'all?"

I answered, "We rollin' with y'all."

JuJu was down no matter what these niggas said. All that money sitting in Dom's tray was what had her giddy. I had already cashed out the purple chip just in case they wanted to take the shit back. I still didn't trust them or believe their unbelievable story.

"You can invite us to y'all's room. Where y'all staying?" JuJu asked.

"We got a room here. Penthouse suite," C. Millionaire replied.

JuJu should've consulted with me first, but she wanted to get them in a more intimate and undisclosed setting to snatch those chips.

"Perfect," Juju said. "We'll follow you."

I tried to give her the eye to say let's move on to something else, but she refused to make eye contact with me.

We made our way toward the elevators through the buzzing casino. The slot machines and the sounds of the clicking and clanging rang in our ears.

JuJu linked arms with me and whispered in my ear, "You down, right?"

"I'm riding as always, JuJu, but I don't know. . . ."

"It's Gucci. Trust me."

C. Millionaire and Dom walked casually behind us, clueless.

Once inside the elevator, C. Millionaire stood close to me, and Juju stood underneath Dom.

"I don't mean to come off like I'm doing too much," C. Millionaire whispered gently into my ear. "But damn, you're fine."

"Thank you."

"You carry yourself well. I like that. What's your nationality?" he asked with fascination.

"I'm Persian and royalty," I responded. "You're looking at a real-life Persian princess." Well, that was my infamous story. I wasn't Persian. I was Indian and certainly not anyone's royalty. I had told it so much that it just rolled out of my mouth.

He looked as if he bought my story, and I didn't even have to sell it that hard. I thought to myself, *Maybe JuJu is right.* I needed to lighten up and chill. I leaned in closer to him, pressing myself against him. He flashed me that dimpled grin. Shit, he was cute.

The elevator reached its floor, and JuJu spilled out like a teenage girl excited about prom night. As we walked the long hallway, I was thinking about going to L.A. to see if this jewelry store even existed.

C. Millionaire stopped abruptly in front of Suite 812 and reached into his pocket to retrieve the keycard. He stepped back and allowed everyone to walk inside. He flipped on the lights and welcomed us into their temporary luxury suite.

Although we lived in Las Vegas, we checked into hotels to make it look like we were on vacation. We didn't need to look obvious. We weren't new to the penthouse suite life at all, but this suite was plusher and more lavish than the ones we were used to.

JuJu turned on Spotify from her phone and used Bluetooth to connect to the sound system. Future's song "Rich Sex" blared through the Bose surround sound.

I tossed my Lana Marks Cleopatra clutch onto one of the chaises and released the pins in my hair, letting the curls cascade down my back.

JuJu opened the mini bar and peered over the choice of liquor. "Okay, lady and gents, we have brandy, vodka, cognac, gin, rum, champagne, wine, whiskey, tequila, and bourbon."

Dom put the tray of chips in a safe and closed it. JuJu noticed and gave me this look to say, *Fuck*!

When no one answered JuJu about what they wanted to drink, she filled two glasses with ice and poured vodka. She danced a cup over to Dom, and they headed to the balcony.

I walked around the suite, scanning.

C. Millionaire followed me to the bedroom. "What you lookin' for?" he asked.

"The phone."

"Why?"

"Room service. Is that a problem?"

He shook his head with a smile. "Not at all."

He flopped down on the bed and watched me as I ordered food. He was watching my ass like a hawk.

Juju

Bzzzz. Bzzzz. Bzzzz.

The sound of my phone vibrating from the nightstand woke me up. I sat up as flashbacks from the night ran through my mind. I was still in a penthouse suite in Caesar's Palace. Last night wasn't a dream. I drank too much and couldn't remember if I'd carried out anything other than fucking. Once Tah disappeared into the room with C. Millionaire for the night, I took my opportunity to get some much-needed dick. I hadn't fucked in weeks. Being on the run put a severe damper on my sex life.

With my phone buzzing like crazy, I wondered who was blowing me up. I reached over to grab it. When I picked it up, it didn't ask for my lock code, and I realized that it wasn't even my phone. It was Dom's.

We had the same exact rose gold iPhone. I set it down and picked up mine, which was right next to his. I had a text message from Tah.

Tah: Meet me in the bathroom now.

I looked over at Dom. He was naked, lying on his back with the covers pulled up to his waist. I pulled the covers back to see if it was the alcohol that had me thinking his dick was big. My eyes widened as soon as I saw it. Oh, it wasn't the alcohol. I pulled the covers back over him and got out of bed.

Struggling to find my panties, I looked back at Dom's sexy ass to see if my movement had awakened him. It hadn't. Unable to find my panties, I grabbed Dom's shirt and threw it on. I tiptoed toward the bathroom.

As I neared the door, I could smell a hint of Granddaddy Purp coming from the bathroom. Brain, aka Tah, was undoubtedly in there devising a plan for Pinky, aka me. I walked into the bathroom and closed the door quietly behind me before locking it. Tah immediately passed me the blunt. I hit it long and slow.

Blowing out smoke through my nose, I asked, "What's the plan? 'Cause I know you got one. I can't think of shit right now."

Tah rolled her eyes and neck at me with a threatening look. "Bitch, I hope you ain't dickmatized or no shit like that. I know you gave him some pussy."

I laughed. "I think I got too drunk."

"Don't blame it on the alcohol. You wanted to fuck him the moment he walked up to us. I'm going to say this shit one time, so I hope you're listening. Don't go falling for that nigga, JuJu. You already know that fallin' in love only gets shit fucked up."

I smacked my lips. "Bihhh, you got me fucked up. The only muthafucka I'm falling for is the bag. It's us against the world, baby. Why you fucking with me this early, Tah?" I passed the blunt back to her.

She gave me another hard look. "Let's get to Los Angeles and I'll figure out how it will all go down. Just be ready to play your part."

"I stay ready. Dick don't do nothing but keep me energized. My heart ain't in shit, and you know that."

Loyal to one another, we were tighter than blood sisters, and at times, we called one another sister. We had two different personalities but were so much alike at the same time.

Growing up in the same foster home, Tah and I rebelled and ran away together often. She always had a swindle or a plan, whether it was setting up and getting over on the clueless weed dealer or stealing liquor. We stayed having a good time with our middle fingers to the world. We learned that we couldn't get far in life with that cheap-ass penny-pinching shit, so we started taking high-end shit from Macy's, Nordstrom, Neiman Marcus, Bloomingdale's, and Saks Fifth Avenue. We wanted the good shit.

We made a pact to stay on top of the world by any means necessary and live our dreams to the fullest together. Since our parents had turned their backs on us, we would never forsake one another or our sisterhood. We would honor one another no matter what.

Knock! Knock! Knock!

The loud knocks startled me so much that I dropped the blunt on the marble floor. "Shit." I picked it up quickly.

"Yeah?" Tah answered.

"Is everything good in there?" Dom questioned from the other side.

Tah replied, "Umm, yeah . . ."

"I was just checking. Y'all blazing in there? You ain't sharing?"

"Aw, damn, we smoked that shit up. We'll be right out," I said, taking one last puff of what was now a doobie.

"Well, hurry up. Y'all rollin' back to L.A. with us or nah?" he asked.

"Hell yeah, we rollin'," I said.

"A'ight. Come on."

We waited a few more minutes for him to walk away before we started talking again.

"Girl, I had Dom's ass speaking another language. Now, I don't remember much, but I *do* remember that, and that big-ass dick—" I coughed from the smoke.

"Well, I ain't give up shit. You know me."

"I don't know how you do it," I replied. "Maybe if you got some dick, you would loosen up."

Tah threw up her hands and stretched. "Keep your mind off the dick. We can't afford to fuck this up."

I agreed. I had to put my head back in the game.

Tah

"JuJu! Wake up! We're here." I shook her hard.

JuJu woke up and looked around. The private jet had landed after a quick thirty-minute flight. We had never been on a private plane before, and the comfort of it had JuJu taking a quick nap. She grabbed her Coach purse, and we followed them off the jet.

The seventy-nine degree weather felt so lovely, and the sun was shining brightly. The sky was clear, and the humidity was much more tolerable than in Vegas as we hopped into a stretch Escalade.

"Where we headed?" JuJu asked.

"To the Four Seasons," Dom replied. "You have a good nap?"

"Yeah." Juju smiled and then covered her mouth as she yawned. "I still feel tired."

"Well, I hope all your batteries are charged, 'cause we have hella shit to do."

What kind of shit? I wondered.

The pit of my stomach turned as small knots formed. I never liked to be in a situation where we had no control. We didn't know these niggas, and we only knew what they told us. They could've been taking us somewhere to kill us. I would've packed my Mace, but I thought we were flying commercial.

It had taken about forty-five minutes from the airport before we pulled up in front of the Four Seasons hotel. They checked us into a two-bedroom master king suite.

Dom handed JuJu the keycard and said, “Go on up. We’ll come up in a sec.”

“Okay,” she said as if it were no big deal.

All the while, my mind was racing. What was going on? They were acting weird suddenly.

I was silent all the way up to the room, and so was JuJu. She wasn’t thinking about how weird they were acting, though. She was daydreaming. I rolled my eyes because her head was not in the game.

Inside the room, a gorgeous view of Los Angeles greeted us.

“This is too fly,” JuJu said and then whistled.

I sucked my teeth while looking over the room.

“You know this had to cost some serious dough,” she continued.

“All this is cool and everything, but what are we going to do about some weed? ’Cause we don’t know nobody out here,” I asked, feeling irritated.

“Bitch, what? You know I found out we were flying by private jet, so I brought the weed,” she said with a slight grin. “I got enough in my bag to get us through.”

“Cool. We only plan to be here for one night, so we don’t have a lot of time,” I reminded her.

“That’s all we need,” she replied.

Suddenly, we heard the door open. We got quiet as Dom and C. Millionaire entered the room.

“You ladies want to get some food?” Dom asked.

“Yeah, I’m starving. Can we go to Roscoe’s Chicken and Waffles? I’ve always wanted to go there,” JuJu said.

"No problem. We gotta handle some business. One of our drivers will take you out," Dom replied. "After that, you're going shopping." He handed JuJu a black American Express card.

JuJu's eyes lit up. I rolled mine as I turned my back to face the view. Either JuJu was a damned good actress, or she was really excited about shopping. I couldn't wait to get this shit over with because they were trying to sweep us off our feet. It might've been working on JuJu, but it wasn't working on me.

I was hard to impress, so shopping around town, buying whatever the fuck we wanted with that black AMEX didn't move me. At the seasoned level I was, nothing ever impressed me. The sights, sounds, and the smell of being somewhere new usually helped me to breathe a little. We were in Los Angeles with these complete strangers, so I couldn't relax. JuJu, on the other hand, was having a blast.

"We did it this time," JuJu said as we stood in line outside of Roscoe's on the corner of Sunset and Gower. The restaurant was packed. The line was to the corner, but we were next to be seated.

"All I know is that this food better be smackin', 'cause I ain't feelin' this line at all." I scowled.

As we were seated, the scent of chicken frying made my stomach growl like a baby tiger. The waiter handed us some menus. After looking it over, we ordered two sunsets, lemonade and cherry punch.

"Tah, I was thinking. . . . Well, you know that Dom is straight feeling me, and I want to use that to our advantage. Dom has the same exact phone as I do. This morning, he left it on the nightstand next to mine. I grabbed it, thinking it was mine, and he didn't even have a lock code on it. . . ."

She paused as if she were thinking of what to say next.

I barked, "Bitch, hurry up! Get to the point!"

"I am! So, I went through his phone. I've been excited because their shit is legit with this jewelry store. Everything is done over his phone, like their banking shit. I don't know why he wouldn't keep the shit locked."

It was like a light bulb went off in my head. JuJu had access to everything at her fingertips.

The waiter returned with our drinks. We placed our orders of chicken, waffles, greens, and smothered potatoes. After he left, we went back to thinking of what we could get from Dom's phone the next time JuJu could get it. After about twenty minutes of talking quietly, the waiter brought the food and set it on the table.

As soon as he left, JuJu said, "Whatever we come up with has to be good and slick."

"You already know. We got this," I assured. "This is all about timing, but we don't have much time."

"I know. Let's finish this food and go burn this credit card up. Momma needs a new pair of shoes and a bag to match," JuJu said.

C. Millionaire

We had an important business meeting at the jewelry store to discuss Los Angeles' annual jewelry showcase. It was going to be huge, and anybody who was somebody was going to attend. As soon as the meeting was over, I noticed that Dom was checking his phone continuously.

"Hey, where the fuck is your mind right now? I need you to keep your eyes open and stay sharp. We got major moves happening right now."

Dom responded, "I'm just keeping track of how much these bitches are spending. I mean, the pussy was good, but uh . . . I'm not quite sure why you thought it was a good idea to give them the black AMEX."

"You worry too much," I said. "They can't spend all that money. Plus, how else we gonna get them to trust us? Right now, Tahlia's guard is still up."

"True."

"When these bitches are done, we'll give them a li'l private tour of the store and let them pick something out. That should seal the deal, and they'll do whatever we need them to do," I said.

"Don't you think that will make them think we're tricks or something?" Dom asked.

"They already think that, but who the fuck cares? Rappers do the shit all the time, and don't act like you don't know why we're doing it in the first place."

"I know why we're doing it, but this is going overboard. Why you wanna do it like *this*, with these hoes?"

"They ain't hoes, 'cause I ain't get no pussy," I said.

"I got some pussy, though," Dom bragged, smiling with those gold teeth gleaming.

"Yeah, but you didn't pay for it."

"Didn't I?" Dom asked sarcastically. "She got five hundred dollars."

"Yeah, but she didn't ask for it. We gotta see if what we heard about these bitches is true. Right now, they think we're targets, and that's perfect."

Dom nodded.

Juju

"Blue and Co. Diamonds." I read the gold lettering aloud as we stood outside of the jewelry store. "Who the fuck is Blue?"

Tah shrugged. "Your guess is as good as mine."

We had shopping bags galore at our feet and lining each arm. They were heavy. We could've left everything in the Escalade, but we didn't know what the next plan was. We bought shoes, handbags, clothes from chill wear and party wear down to panties and bras.

"Damn, this store is nice," I said. "I ain't ever seen a jewelry store owned by black folks like this before."

"Yeah, especially two black men that nobody's ever heard of," Tah stated.

While we were out shopping, we did some asking around in the streets about them, and nobody had heard of them. Now, they did bring up the name Blue, but who was Blue? How were they one of the largest jewelry stores in the city and nobody had heard of them? Tah felt like something wasn't right, but I didn't see what the big deal was. We were popping tags on their dime, so who cared if nobody knew who they were?

"I bet they keep everything tight. This ain't gonna be easy. Look how many people are up in there buying stuff," Tah noted. "We may have bitten off more than we can chew."

"When has anything ever been more than we can chew? I told you I felt like something was special about them. You bitchin' up on me now?" My lips curled up into a snarl.

"Me? Bitchin' up? Hell nah! You know that ain't me."

Two guards stood in front of the door with their hands clasped in front of them. The place reeked of luxury and high style. The diamonds and exotic stones in that place clearly cost a fortune.

Dom came outside with a smile on his face.

I immediately straightened up and pretended as if I wasn't gawking at the building.

"Welcome. Come inside."

We picked up our bags, and he grabbed the ones we couldn't carry.

"Blue and Company Diamonds is worth millions. We have nothing but high-end jewelry. We manufacture everything in-house, and we're one of the top distributors in Los Angeles."

The presentation of the store was incredible. I couldn't even front. There were individual pieces in five-foot cases of their own. The lighting made everything look sparkly and shiny.

Dom led us down a long hallway to the back of the store, where we put our bags down.

"You can't come to Los Angeles without seeing how we get down," Dom stated.

C. Millionaire entered the room. "How was shopping?" he asked with a raised eyebrow. "Y'all fuck the stores up or nah?"

"We grabbed a few things," I replied.

"Good. Did you eat?" he questioned.

"Yeah," Tah quickly answered.

"The chicken and waffles were the best I've ever had," I said.

Tah added while looking around, "It definitely lived up to the hype."

"Cool, cool. Come with me, JuJu," Dom said. "Tahlia, you go with C."

We splitting up? I screamed in my head. Now, what kind of shit was this? I looked at Tah, and she didn't look nervous, so I went along with it.

Dom linked arms with me as he escorted me out of the room. Walking down the hall, he led me to a section of necklaces that had rubies, sapphires, and emeralds embedded in the pieces.

"Whoa," I gasped.

"Have a seat," he said in a lightweight demanding tone.

I sat in front of the case. "These are beautiful."

He smiled proudly as he signaled for a young white woman with blond hair to come over to the case.

"Open this case and have her try on the one with the rubies."

I nearly wanted to dance in my seat. It was like boom, we met them at the casino, we spent the night in their luxurious-ass suite, and now we were in Los Angeles trying on their jewels. I was hyped. I couldn't play it cool if I wanted to.

The young woman set the necklace on a dark blue velvet–covered tray and handed him the white gold necklace that looked much like a dangly chandelier with all the layers of rubies and diamonds. I turned my back toward him and used my hand to lift my hair out of the way. He gently placed the necklace around my neck and fastened it on. He took my hand as we stood up, and he led me to a large gold mirror.

I gasped when I saw the way it decorated my neck.

"It's a ruby and diamond fringe necklace with a total of thirty-eight carats of internally flawless diamonds. You can wear pieces straight like this every day if you fuck with me."

I wanted to ask how much something like this would cost but didn't want to seem thirsty. Hell, I was used to stealing and boosting expensive things, but this right here was some *Ocean's Eleven* type shit.

"I love it."

He removed it from my neck and handed it back to the woman before I could get too used to the way it looked.

"If you could have one piece of jewelry in this store, what would it be?"

I investigated the cases and stopped when I came to a pair of diamond hoop earrings.

"I've always wanted a pair of earrings like these." I pointed.

He signaled to the woman again to get the earrings.

I was excited as I put them on my ears. Looking at them in the mirror, the way those bad boys sparkled, I felt like this was the best day of my life. I knew the retail price of earrings like this at Tiffany & Co was about $5,200, and I was sure that these were worth much more.

"Now, I would wear these every damned day. I love them."

"Twenty-four karat white gold with round brilliant one-carat diamonds. You can have them. Consider it a gift from me."

He was showing off now. This nigga was straight up trickin', but I guess he was taking notes from the rapper T.I., 'cause it wasn't trickin' if he had it.

"Can I ask you something?" I asked, feeling a little suspicious suddenly. This was now becoming a fairytale.

"What's up?"

"Why y'all doing all of this? I mean, do we look like some needy-ass hoes?"

"Nah, I know you or Tah don't need men to do anything for you. I can tell that you two handle your own business. But, I mean, if you can't handle it, let me know. I'm sure someone else can handle it."

"Cut the bullshit. What is it that you *really* want from us, Dom?"

He bit his lower lip, stared into my eyes, and said, "I don't want shit, but . . . we do have some unfinished business in the bedroom. You passed out last night before I could finish. You down to take another ride or what?"

I nearly melted looking at this fine-ass nigga. I felt my heart throb just as hard as my pussy. I wanted to fuck him right there.

Tah

As if planned, C. Millionaire took this as his opportunity to try his hardest to impress me. He showed me the entire store, and I wasn't moved by none of that bling. Yeah, I knew the jewels were real, but who in their right mind would invite complete strangers into their world like this?

"You sure you don't want anything?" he asked.

"I said I'm good. You've done enough," I said.

He thought for a moment. "Follow me." It almost sounded like a demand.

I followed him as he led me down a long corridor until we reached the front of their vault. Jackpot! As we stood in front of the vault, he placed his hand on the screen. The system scanned his fingertips, a slot opened, and he put his face close for a retinal scan. His identity was confirmed, and the vault doors opened.

C. Millionaire looked into my eyes as he said, "Tahlia, what I'm about to show you is very precious, and access isn't just granted to anyone, but I want to show you something."

"Okay."

We walked into the vault. The door closed behind us, and my eyes scanned the room. This was their secure space where their money, valuables, and documents were stored. Vaults were made to protect their contents from theft, and he didn't know me from a can of paint, so why was he showing me? Was he stupid, or was this a setup?

He started moving cases of exotic jewelry ever so gently with care and ease from in front of a door. He punched in a code, and the door opened. Piles and piles of neatly stacked cash almost touched the ceiling of the room. All that money reminded me of some Pablo Escobar shit. Now, this was more like it.

He took a stack of cash from one of the piles and asked, "Is this what you like?"

I was so caught up in the moment that he could've been the devil asking me to sign over my soul. "You gon' give it to me?" I asked, keeping a straight face.

C. Millionaire led me to the front of the jewelry store where the Escalade was waiting to take us back to the Four Seasons. They instructed us to get dressed in something beautiful for dinner. With that cash in my purse, I was willing to see what was next.

JuJu was already there when I got in.

As soon as the door closed, she asked, "What took you so long?" She took a good look at me and paused before she said, "Wait, you gave him some?"

I tilted my head back and laughed as the car pulled away from the curb. "No. His ass took me to the vault and gave me five thousand dollars." I pulled it out of my purse and waved it in her face.

"Damn! Shit, look what I got." JuJu flashed her new diamond hoops.

"All of this is so damn confusing," I said. "I don't know what to think." I lowered my voice so the driver couldn't hear. "How can we steal anything when they're just giving it to us? Hell, we didn't ask for any of this shit."

"Maybe it's time that we let our good looks do all the work for once," JuJu said. "Beats having to worry about getting arrested or watching our backs. We're already treading the thin line of being on Crime Stoppers."

I leaned back and sighed, feeling like I was in a dream. "I hope this ain't some bogus-ass shit."

"Seems like the real deal to me, Tah," she said with a smile.

I nodded, but still, something seemed a little off. I was going to keep playing their game for now.

Juju

Dom and C. Millionaire wanted to split us up again for dinner. Tah was pissed about that, but honestly, I wanted to be alone with Dom again. I knew the rules, but there was something about him that had me feeling tingly inside. A black Phantom took me to some big fancy house. When I got out, Dom was waiting for me in the driveway.

I was wearing a red dress that hugged my body precisely right. His eyes approved of my attire as he took my hand. We walked to the front door and walked inside.

"Welcome to my crib."

"This is your spot?" My eyes dazzled underneath the grand chandelier of the entrance hall of his home.

"Yes. This is where I lay my head."

I sashayed in, working the hell out of that dress.

"Come to the living room and have a seat."

I sat on the couch and looked around. I didn't smell any food cooking, so I wasn't sure what was going on. I eyed the place, looking to see if anything was lying around; some critical information to report to Tah. So far, I didn't see anything worth mentioning. Even though they had given us so much more than what we thought we could get, we needed to finish this shit up so we could get on.

Dom was just staring at me. It was as if he were looking through me.

"What's up?" I asked.

"I'm trying to figure out why a woman like you would trust someone you don't know."

"Who said I trusted you?"

"I'm just saying . . . You're so beautiful. You can have any man you want." He cracked a smile, and I noticed he wasn't wearing his gold teeth. He had perfect white teeth.

How could I ignore the fact that if I were looking for a man, he would be perfect? He was fine and wealthy, two things that I needed in my life. Hell, I didn't want to scam people for the rest of my life. I was close to my thirties, and it was time to settle down. Why couldn't I settle down with someone like him?

Thunder and lightning struck out of nowhere, and I hopped off that couch. I held my chest as my heart beat hard and fast. "This damn weather is bipolar like a muthafucka."

"I know. It was such a beautiful day today, and now a storm is coming. Don't worry, though. I'll get you back to the hotel nice and dry. That is, if you're not afraid of getting a little wet." He winked and poured two glasses of red wine. "Relax while we wait for dinner to be served. I have some of the best chefs up in there."

"What are they cooking?" I inquired, sitting back down.

"Lobster, filet mignon, shrimp pasta, and some other yummy things."

"Sounds good." My stomach liked the sound of that. "So, do y'all do this for a lot of women?"

He laughed at my way of prying. His smile was infectious, and to me, his response was honest.

He handed me the wine, and I drank. My eyes gazed out of his massive windows to see the rain pouring down. "I'm glad we're in here instead of out there. That rain ain't no joke," I said.

"It would make more sense to be in here instead of out there."

I kept sipping, trying to play off just how hot and bothered I had become from just looking at his fine ass. I caught him looking down at my breasts. I *knew* the girls were sitting up just right.

He hit a button on the wall and suddenly, the lights changed colors and flashed to the rhythm of the music playing throughout the house. That was when I noticed that the floor-to-ceiling wine cabinet was fully stocked. This was what I called living. I had pictured myself living like this plenty of times.

"You mind if I look around?" I asked, kicking off my stiletto heels. I didn't wait for him to reply as I walked around his house.

He watched me without saying anything as I thoroughly inspected whatever my eyes could see down to the tiniest details. I dissected him as well, but I was looking for anything that would help us rob them blind.

I didn't know Dom had walked up behind me until he spoke. "You hungry? Because I am."

I was startled by the amount of bass in his voice buzzing in my ear. "Yeah, I'm starving. Is dinner done?"

Seduction was supposed to be part of my plan, yet I was the one being seduced. As my heart sped up, my thoughts raced. More thunder clapped loudly, and lightning struck, shining brightly through the windows. Suddenly, the power went out, and everything shut off.

He walked calmly toward the hall closet. I was right on his heels because it was too dark to be left alone. He reached in and handed me a small box of foot-long matches. "We'll just have to eat by candlelight." He took out long candles in candlesticks and lit them. "Dinner is ready. Let's go eat."

As we got closer to the dining room, the aroma of the food teased my nose. I sat down at the table. Our plates were beautiful. It almost looked too cute to eat. I noticed he prayed over his food, so I pretended to do the same.

"So, what's the deal with you and Tahlia?"

I took my fork to the pasta. "What you mean?"

"Like, why y'all still single? Two badasses with no men?"

"Life is like that, you know. I can't explain it. But we aren't looking, either."

"I see. Well, I told you a lot about me, but you haven't told me anything about you. What kind of work you do?"

"I'm in retail," I lied smoothly.

"Retail? Nah, that ain't true."

"Why it ain't?"

"First of all, the dress you had on last night cost more than what someone in retail would be able to afford."

"How you know it wasn't a gift from a man?"

He laughed as he ate. "Baby, let's just say I know more about you than you think. You honestly believe we met you on some fluke? Nah."

I dropped my fork against the plate and stiffened up, not sure what he was trying to get at.

"Relax. There's no need to panic. We aren't exactly who we said we are, but you aren't who you said you are, so that makes us even. I need you to do something for me."

"What you want?" I asked, looking straight at the candle. I was going to grab that bitch and burn him with it if it got too crazy.

"I have a job for you, and I want to know if you're down. It will pay you more money than you've ever had. But you can't tell Tah or C. Millionaire. This is my thing."

I shook my head vigorously. "No deal. Tah is my partner. We don't do shit without each other. I don't know how you and C. get down, but uh, we don't roll like that."

"So, you mean to tell me that you are willing to pass up a million dollars for her?"

I swallowed hard. *Did he just say a million dollars?*

"I'll let you think about it. If you're in, then I'll tell you what the job is. For now, let's just enjoy one another. I'm in the mood for something else."

"What you in the mood for?" I asked, paying close attention to the way he said it.

Dom got up and walked to me. He bit his bottom lip and looked into my eyes. His fingers found their way to the straps of my dress. He slid his hand to my bare breasts. I wasn't wearing a bra. The feel of him excited me, and although what he had just asked me was out of pocket, I wanted him.

"Tell me what you want," I said.

He smiled but didn't answer with words. He lifted me from that chair, pushed the food up the table, and sat me on it. I ripped his shirt off as buttons popped and went flying everywhere. Our tongues danced as the built-up sexual tension between us was released. His fingers traveled up my thighs and found their way to my wet center. I wasn't wearing panties either. As he was playing with my clit gently, I moaned.

I sucked his lips feverishly. Fumbling with his pants, I wanted to get him out fast. I needed to feel him inside me. Within seconds, he plunged into me, and I gushed all over him. He turned me around roughly, so he could hit it from the back. He fucked me so hard that all I could do was scream in ecstasy. I was coming, and an orgasm was beyond my control. I held that table to keep from falling over.

"Don't stop, Dom! Fuck!"

He was grunting, and his sounds of pure bliss sounded so good. I wasn't thinking about Tah. I wasn't thinking about what he wanted me to do. I was only thinking about the way his dick made my pussy feel.

Tah

"Don't fall, bitch. Don't fall," I repeatedly recited, drilling the words into my brain as I stared at myself in the mirror. I was attracted to C. Millionaire, and it was taking everything in me to tell myself otherwise.

I snapped out of my trance and double-checked my freshly painted face. Not as much as a single hair was out of place, but I checked anyway. Tonight, I had to get a real plan in motion, and I still didn't have a clue.

JuJu was enjoying being showered with attention and lavish gifts as if that was a plan. That was far from a plan. Something had to jump off soon if we wanted our own dollars. Fuck their money.

A knock on the door jolted me from my thoughts. With a million-dollar smile, I answered the door. There he stood, as refreshing as a tall drink of lemonade on a hot summer's day. C. Millionaire allowed his dreads to flow freely, and they showcased their true length and glory. Good Gawd! Whoever twisted him did an incredible job at keeping them healthy.

I stood silently in the doorway for a moment at a loss for words. He finally got the reaction he had been looking for, so he smiled.

"You ready?"

"Yeah," I answered, walking out of the hotel room.

C. Millionaire had told me to dress comfortably, so I wore a loose-fitting top with three-quarter sleeves and a pair of Roberto Cavalli jewel-encrusted jeans. On my feet was a cute pair of Alexander McQueen suede flats. Not only did I look fly, but I was comfortable.

"I gotta be honest with you; it's not every day I get to go on a date," C. Millionaire said, revealing his vulnerable side.

I checked him out. His style was different, but it was sexy nonetheless. He wore a Burberry V-neck sweater with straight leg jeans and a clean pair of matching Burberry trainers.

"You look good," I admitted.

"Thank you. You look perfect!" he said as he held his hand out to escort me into the elevator.

"Thank you. What's on the itinerary for tonight?"

"I want to do something I've never done as an adult. Are you ready to scream?"

"You want to make me scream?"

"Yes. Are you ready for all of C. Millionaire?"

Before I could reply with some witty comeback or get lost in his hypnotizing aura, his cell rang. As he viewed the caller ID, he decided it was best he didn't ignore this call. Business always came first, even in his downtime.

As we walked out of the elevator, he answered, "Hello?"

I tried to pretend as if I wasn't listening as he led me to the car. He was listening. Once inside of the Escalade, he poured me a glass of chilled champagne.

I slowly sipped while the car pulled off. I gazed out of the window, pretending to take in the sights, but my ears were waiting for him to talk to the person on the phone.

"Yeah, I'm here. Okay, so what's the problem? Okay, look, I'll hire extra security. Just a small team to escort the jewels straight from the vault. Our regular security guards can be there as an extra helping hand to watch over them. Problem solved? Okay, I'll get Dom to make some arrangements." He ended the call and said to me, "Hey, my bad. Business can sometimes be demanding."

"It's okay." I looked beyond him through the tinted window as the car was coming to a stop. That was a quick ride. I could see a large neon-lit Ferris wheel.

"We're here," he said.

We were at a carnival.

"What? Are you serious?"

"I asked if you were ready to scream."

I laughed a little.

"Come on," he said.

I got out of the car and followed his lead. We strolled the fairgrounds, and as the night went on, we pigged out on burgers, garlic fries, cotton candy, and soft serve ice cream. We rode every roller coaster and extreme ride in the park. Thunder and lightning cracked loudly, and the raindrops began drizzling down.

"I completely forgot about the storm," C. Millionaire admitted.

"Damn it! These are suede shoes," I expressed as I dashed to take cover.

I ran into the house of mirrors. I darted down the corridor of wobbly mirrors as my images bent and changed my frame from short to tall and slim to wide. At first, C. Millionaire just stayed in place to give me a head start, but he eventually took after me. I sprinted behind corners and ducked into weird hiding spots all while the mirrors made me appear and reappear in places I was not. C. Millionaire reached out his hand to touch me only to be trapped in a mirage.

He whisked around quickly, trying to figure out how to get to me, but these mirrors had him confused. Each time he turned a corner, believing I was right in front of him, his dream was shattered by only the touch of another mirror.

I laughed hysterically.

As he made his way to the exit, I came up behind him and said, “Hey.”

He scooped me up in his arms, picking me up off my feet. He held me firmly as he said, “I know you’re not a Persian princess, Tahlia Patel.”

My smile immediately left, and I tried to break free.

“I need you to do a job for me.”

“What?” I scowled at him. “You knew who we were this whole time?”

He put me on my feet. “Yeah. Hey, we’ve been looking for the best of the best. Your boy Fernando told us that you were someone who could help me.”

“So, why didn’t you just come out and say that Fernando sent you, instead of playing games?”

“Because we had to test you out first.”

“I don’t understand. Why couldn’t you be straight up to me and JuJu last night?”

“Because we don’t want JuJu on the job. She’s not as focused as you are. You’re the one with the brains, and we need this shit to be seamless.”

“Well, I ain’t doing it. Not without JuJu.”

“Is that the only way you’ll get down?”

“The *only* way,” I asserted.

He nodded his head. “Good, I like that. Shows you’re loyal. The shit we need to be executed is risky. I know you two are already on the run, so don't get fuckin' caught."

This shit just did a whole 360. We had them all wrong. We were trying to find a way to figure them out, but they already had us figured out.

"How much you paying?"

"One million."

"What you want us to do?" I asked, curious.

Juju

Dom's cell rang as I was giving him some grade-A head. To know that he was into scheming and scamming like me, shit, that made his ass even sexier.

"Shit, baby, give me a second." Dom tapped on the screen of his phone, replying to the message before he set it back down on the end table. "Okay, now I gotta go piss." He climbed out of bed and walked to the bathroom, closing the door behind him.

I reached over and grabbed his phone from the table. I swiped across the screen to unlock it and then went straight to his text messages.

C. Milli: Did you get everything taken care of?

Dom: Not yet. Working on it as we speak.

So, this nigga lied about C. Milli not being in on the job. These two were in this together. I put his phone down and went to mine. I texted Tah and let her know that we needed to talk.

Dom returned, and I put my phone back in my purse. Thunder sounded, and a quick flicker of lightning flashed. The storm wasn't about to let up anytime soon.

"Since you're going back to Las Vegas in the morning, I want some more."

I looked down at his hard dick pointing at me. Why was he so irresistible?

"We can do that. Come here."

***

I knocked on the hotel door the next morning with my heels in my hand. There was no answer, so I called Tah's phone. I had accidentally left my keycard inside the room. Just when I thought that she hadn't made it back yet, Tah snatched the door open.

"Damn, Ju, you just had to spend the night, didn't you? Then you sent me that janky-ass text talking about we need to talk. Yeah, we definitely gotta talk, bitch. They know who we are."

"I know! This nigga Dom was talking about he wants to work with just me, but I told him that shit was out. He even said he didn't want C. in on it, but I went through his phone and C. was asking him if everything was good," I said.

"Girl, I can't wait to talk to Fernando's ass. He told them everything about us without giving us a heads up."

"How do we even know this job is cool?" I asked.

"It sounds cool. He told me the idea, but I'm thinking of a way to cut these bozos out of their own deal and do what we do. Shit, I don't like getting played," Tah replied. "And I can't help but feel like they want to screw us over in the end."

"At least you got more info than I did. I couldn't get Dom to say shit."

"That's 'cause all he cares about is fucking you. Sit down so I can tell you what's up."

I flopped down on the couch.

"They got this big-time international jeweler coming from Dubai. These cats are interested in buying these rare diamonds and gems from C. Millionaire and Dom's vault." She pulled out her phone and showed it to me. "These are pictures and descriptions of the jewels. The thing is, they don't want to sell them because they are so rare. Instead of just telling them no, they want us to switch out the jewels for fakes, so that way they can retain the jewels and get the money at the same time."

"Why won't they just sell them the fake jewels themselves?" I asked, feeling confused.

"See, when the Dubai guys find out they're fake, they gotta be able to blame somebody. They want to blame the security company that will be transporting them for swapping them."

"Oooooh, gotcha. They already got the fakes ready?" I asked.

"No, but Fernando already agreed to do that part. They just don't want to be the ones to interact with Fernando. They don't want their rich hands dirty whatsoever."

"I see."

"You know I already came up with another plan, though. We're not just going to hand those jewels over to them for only a million dollars. Nah, those rare and exotic jewels are worth fifty times that. They thought that wining, dining, and splurging shit would make us loyal to them. Fuck them niggas! We are taking all that shit," Tah asserted.

I busted out laughing and started jumping up and down with excitement. "See, this is why I love you!"

"I'll think more on this plan on the way home."

Tah

We ended up taking a commercial flight because I didn't know if C. Millionaire and Dom had cameras with audio on their jet. We politely declined their ride and said we had already booked a flight.

JuJu had the window seat, and thankfully, no one was sitting in the third seat near the aisle. I took a good look at JuJu. Even though she was dressed for the day, the bags under her eyes looked as if she'd had a rough night.

"Um, looks like he kept you up all night."

"Let's just say my ass was hollering and screaming for hours like I've never had good dick in my life."

I shook my head. "You're fucking up, Ju."

"Stop. It ain't that deep, Tah. I know what I'm doing."

"It don't sound like it. Sounds to me like you're distracted. They already tested us once with asking us to cut one another out."

"Relax. This is all a part of my plan."

"I notice you say *your* plan. Now isn't the time to veer off and start doing your own thing. We gotta be in sync. In this email C. sent me, they're hiring security to transport the jewels from the store to us for the switch and then to the venue. . . . Well, what if *we're* security? We gotta eliminate the middle people."

JuJu scowled. "What? They'll recognize us."

"Does Valentino still owe you a favor?"

"Yeah."

"Valentino has to pull off one of the biggest makeup jobs of his life. If we do this shit right, we'll have a shitload of money to do whatever we want." I cleared my throat once the stewardess walked down the aisle, checking to see if everyone had their seatbelts on. Once she was gone, I said, "Right now, I'm going to create a fake security company." I unlocked my phone to get busy.

"All right." JuJu closed her eyes to get ready for takeoff.

"Boom, they fell for it," I hummed in a song, coming into the living room of our apartment.

JuJu hurried out of her room to hear the update on the plan. "What happened?"

"The security company is a go. Dom just hired our little fake company. He liked that our prices were better than the other quotes he received. He even paid an extra two hundred fifty dollars for insurance in case something was to happen. I made the contract look real professional."

"You did all of that from your iPhone?" JuJu asked in awe.

"Yeah, you know I will make anything happen with this phone. And I found out that they weren't honest with us. These jewels are worth close to eighty million dollars."

"And they only wanted to break us off a milli?" JuJu smirked.

"That part."

JuJu whistled. "That's a lot of fucking money, Tah."

"Yeah, and it will be ours. Call Fernando so we can go over there right now. When we get there, don't say shit about what we're trying to do. Let's just make him think we're going with C. and Dom's plan, because we really don't know if he's on their team. After that, we'll go to LINQ to pay Valentino a li'l visit."

"Valentino needs to get us some free tickets for tonight."

"We don't have time to watch the full show, JuJu. Since you're the one he owes a favor, you gotta go backstage to holler at him. I gotta get in this shower." I sauntered into my bathroom.

JuJu followed me. "You think we will make good security? Hell, I walk like a woman."

"You'll be fine. We don't have to get out of the car. Plus, if Valentino's ass can make those men look just like female celebrities, then you know he can make us look like believable men."

She rolled her hips and started twerking.

"All that damn twerking. You dance for Dom?"

"No . . . but I might when we go back." JuJu chuckled and walked into her room to start unpacking.

Juju

I dug my cell out of my purse and dialed Fernando. He was a short Filipino nerd with glasses that knew all the ins and outs of how to cheat the Vegas casinos. He was so good that he hadn't been caught like the rookies.

He picked up on the first ring. "JuJu, I was just about to text. I heard you met C. Millionaire and Dom. Is everything a go?"

"Yeah. You available tonight?"

"I'm pretty much home alone. The wife and kid just left."

"A'ight. We will be there within the next hour."

"Cool."

In Fernando's garage, Tah spread out the pictures of the thirteen pieces of jewelry that the boys were planning to display at this gala. She had printed them up before we left the house.

"Can you duplicate these?" she asked.

He looked at them, pulling the papers close to his face. "Hell yeah, but it won't be cheap. I already told C. Millionaire that. The glass and crystals I gotta use will cost a pretty penny."

"C. said whatever your price is, he will wire you the money," Tahlia said. "By the way, why the fuck you didn't tell us you were sendin' muthafuckas our way?"

"My bad. I didn't think you would trip, especially after hearing how much they were cashing out. See, once they came to me, I knew you two would be able to execute this shit."

"It's good, Fernando," Tah replied. "Let's just get this shit over with."

He went into his cabinet and pulled out a small brown cardboard box. He handed it to Tah. "Oh yeah, before I forget, here are your chips. These are for Treasure Island. Be careful, though, because I heard they've been watching everybody like a hawk. I know you ladies know how to get away with anything, but be chill, you know."

Tah opened the box, and we inspected the multi-colored chips. She shook her head. "Nah, it's good. We don't need them right now, but maybe some other time."

He nodded. "Hey, don't cross these cats. They may not look like it, but they'll bury you alive in the fuckin' desert."

I wasn't sure why he felt the need to throw that out there. I looked at Tah, but she looked unbothered by his statement.

"You act like we haven't been known to body a few niggas ourselves," she reminded him.

"Oh, I know. I'm just letting you know not to underestimate them. These aren't some rich dudes just trying to get over on some international buyer. It's deeper than you think."

"Well, tell us just how deep, Fernando, since you were the one that plugged them with us. Who the fuck are we really working with?" Tah asked.

"I just know what I told you."

Tah narrowed her eyes as she said, "Yeah, okay. How long will it take to get the phonies?"

"I told them two weeks, give or take a few days."

Tah shook her head vigorously. "We can't wait that long. The gala is in two weeks."

Fernando scratched his head. "Uh, okay, I guess they'll have to be done the day before you leave. Is that okay?"

"That's pushing it really close, but if you can make sure that they are perfect by then, all we have to do is pack them up and go, but you have to work double and overtime on it."

He sighed before he said, "Fine. I'll get the materials no later than tomorrow and get to work as soon as possible."

"Good."

LINQ was one of the newer hotels on the Las Vegas Strip that sat between the Flamingo and the Venetian.

Tah had one thing on her mind, and that was business. Her eyes and ears were scanning the place. The show had already started, and Frank Marino was dressed as Joan Rivers, doing his comedy schtick as the host. The audience was laughing.

"Hey, JuJu, go talk to Valentino," she said. "I'll wait right here."

"Okay, and after that, do I get to see the show?"

Tah rolled her eyes. "Yeah, so hurry up."

I made my way toward the backstage area and stopped when I came to a big buff Caucasian security guard with slicked-back brown hair.

"What you need, li'l lady?" he asked as if he didn't know who I was.

"You know I'm here to see Valentino."

The buff guy took a good look at me before he let me through.

The men in drag were rushing between sets to change wardrobes. They had a hell of a wardrobe collection, very over the top and very Vegas. Valentino did most of those elaborate wigs and makeup.

When I walked into the main dressing room, Valentino was putting his final additions on Tina Turner's makeup. As soon as he saw me, he cooed, "JuJu daaaahhhling."

"Valé baaaaabbyy," I replied.

We embraced and gave one another a kiss on each cheek.

Valentino was 42 years old with jet-black wavy hair. Not a hair was out of place, and he was a very feminine-acting male. He apparently preferred to date men. His Italian accent made him sound more like a woman from New Jersey than a man from Italy.

"Let me just get Miss Tina on stage, and then I'm free to talk," he said.

"No problem, boo. I'll be right here. No rush." I took a seat on the other side of the room where I wasn't in anyone's way.

The dressing room was always so busy. I was used to seeing the men tuck their dicks to put on thongs, and men with tits, nice tits, as they squeezed into shimmery dresses. Dealing with Valentino had been an experience. Some of these men worked it better than some women I knew.

Valentino adjusted Tina's wig and nodded his head for me to follow him to his small personal office on the other side of the dressing rooms.

"So, what brings you down here, gorgeous? Where's Tah?" he asked.

"Tah's watching the show. I'm here to cash in on that favor you owe me."

"Oh, yeah? I was wondering when you were going to hit me up finally. What's up? What you need?"

"All right, I need to know if you're free, not this weekend, but next weekend to go to Los Angeles."

He grinned. "Los Angeles? What's going on in Los Angeles, and is this a free trip? I'm always down for free anything."

"Yeah, we'll cover your airfare and hotel if you can make us look like men. We have something important that we need to get a hold of in Los Angeles, and we need disguises. I'm talking mustaches and beards. Like, really transform us. I would go into more detail, but I won't do it back here. Just know that we'll break you off with big cash."

Valentino didn't give it much thought. "Hell, I need a vacation, and I've never been to Los Angeles. I will think on some looks for the both of you. This will be fun. Shit, I could use some L.A. dick." He clapped his hands.

Just like that, Valentino was in.

Tah

Fernando came through on those fake jewels as promised in a week and a half. They were flawless and looked exactly like the pictures.

On schedule, JuJu and I boarded C. Millionaire and Dom's private jet with three Louis Vuitton trunks, drinking champagne and laughing the whole flight. Valentino confirmed that he had boarded his first-class flight. I texted him the information about the hotel we would be staying at. I was able to get him a room adjoining ours.

When we got off the jet, we arranged to pick up our own rental car and van. We didn't need their driver to pick us up. I drove the black van, and JuJu drove the white Toyota. While driving, I made the first contact with C. Millionaire.

"Hey, you."

"You in town?" he asked.

"Yeah, we just touched down. What time should we meet you?"

"The event starts at seven p.m. Security is supposed to be at the shop at five to transport the jewels to you guys. Make the switch. Then, they'll deliver the fake jewels to the event. In the meantime, you'll bring the real jewels to us when you come to the event. Got it?"

"Yeah, I got it."

We had our own plan. We would take the real jewels all right, but we weren't taking them where he wanted us to take them. I was able to find another guy to make another set of fake jewels because we didn't trust Fernando. We were going to deliver the second phony set to C. Millionaire and Dom. That way, they wouldn't have a clue that we took their real jewels.

"Perfect," he replied. "I can't wait to see you."

"I can't wait to see you either," I replied with a devilish grin and ended the call.

As soon as I parked in the hotel's parking lot next to the Toyota, I hopped out and attached the security logo magnets I had made in Vegas.

"Century Security," I announced.

JuJu stepped back to look at how official the van looked. "Damn, bitch, we're good."

"It looks believable?"

"Hell yeah."

"Good. Let's rock."

"Valentino just arrived, so we can get into makeup," she said.

"Perfect. We gotta be at Blue and Co. at five. We'll drive back here with the real jewels, get dressed, and meet up with our boys with the other fake ones before seven."

"Let's get it."

We headed to the hotel and into the lobby. We checked in under aliases and went up the elevator to our room. As soon as we were inside, JuJu knocked on the adjoining door, and Valentino let us in.

"Heeeeeeey," he said.

"Heeeeeeeey," we replied in unison.

"I know this is going to take a while, so let's get started," I said.

"Who's first?"

"Oh my fuckin' God! Look at us," JuJu gasped as we stood in the mirror.

We wore full navy blue suits with yellow ties and shiny dress shoes. JuJu had on a tiny afro wig with a thick mustache, looking like Isaac from *The Love Boat*. I looked like a Mexican with my hair slicked back, thick eyebrows, and a shadow beard.

"We won't talk much because our voices will surely give us away," I said. "We'll nod and give short answers when asked anything."

"Yup," JuJu said.

"Valentino, we'll be back in about an hour."

"I'll be right here. Can I order room service?"

"Knock yourself out," JuJu said.

We went down to the lobby, exited the hotel, and got into the van.

When we arrived at Blue & Co. Diamonds, we backed up into their loading dock. Two muscular men loaded the jewels in glass cases into the back of the van. Dom came around to the driver's side. I almost started sweating because I wasn't expecting to see him. He knocked on the window so JuJu could roll it down.

He asked, "You have the directions?"

"Yes, sir," JuJu replied in her deepest voice, avoiding eye contact.

"Someone will be at your next location to unload and re-load. Leave from there and drive to the second location. Drive to the front gate. You don't need to touch the cases because someone will take them out of the van at each drop. You got that?" Dom said.

We nodded.

He backed away from the window.

JuJu rolled it up and pulled away.

"Well, that went well," I said, looking in the mirror to make sure my disguise was on properly. Nothing had budged. I got in the back to start switching out the jewelry, but there was a problem. The cases had locks on them.

"Shit! They didn't say shit about locks!"

"We were supposed to switch the cases out with the other ones, not take the jewels out."

"Shit," I said, nearly panicking. I didn't need this shit to get fucked up right now. I hadn't gotten another set of cases. "Bet you they put locks on here to stop us from stealing them. Clever bastards!"

"They ain't cleverer than us," JuJu said, reaching into her wig and pulling out a bobby pin. "I know you can pick any lock with one of these."

I took the bobby pin with a smile. "You right about that. How much time do we have?"

"You gotta work fast. I'll be pulling up to the hotel in five minutes. Don't stall, 'cause they're timing us. Any delays will make them suspect us."

I picked the locks on all five cases in no time and switched them out with the fake jewels I had in the bag. I took the locks and put them in the bag so we could lock up the counterfeit jewels in some identical cases. By the time JuJu pulled up to the hotel, I was done.

Valentino was waiting outside with a suitcase. He opened the back and took the bag of real jewels from me. We pulled off, and I hopped back into the front seat.

We arrived at the venue on time, and someone unloaded the cases as planned. As soon as we were done, we were on our way back to the hotel.

"This can't be this easy, can it?" JuJu asked.

"Don't jinx it," I said.

We parked the van two blocks away from the hotel, ripped the magnets off the van, and hurried to the hotel.

We took off the costumes in Valentino's room.

"You secured the jewels?" I asked him.

"Yeah, I put them in a suitcase in your room like you said," he replied.

"Perfect." I took the second set of fake jewels and placed them in the replica cases. I attached the locks to each case.

"What you guys going to do with the jewels? They're too exotic to sell on the street."

He was right, but I was already ten steps ahead.

"I'm making a connection with a buyer at the gala tonight. There will be plenty of rich folks up in there. We'll meet up with them in the morning, and the deal will be done."

We removed the wigs and facial hair, washed our faces, and put on our gowns.

Juju

We had the second set of fake jewels in the trunk. We pulled up to where they wanted us. Dom took the cases into a tent off to the side that had been closed off.

C. Millionaire smiled. "Thanks, ladies. I must say, y'all did the damned thing tonight. Our international buyers couldn't tell the difference."

And neither can you, I said in my head with a snicker. I looked at Tah, and she grinned.

Dom instructed one of their men to take the cases away.

C. Millionaire opened a briefcase and said, "Here's the money we promised."

"Wait," Tah said. "You want me and JuJu to split the million, while you two just got all that money for selling those fake jewels?"

C. Millionaire cocked his head to the side. "That was the deal. You can't be worried about our profit. That ain't how this works, sweetheart. We don't have a problem, do we?" He lifted his jacket to show that he was packing some heat.

Tah cleared her throat. "You're right. That was the deal. I just thought maybe we could negotiate something."

"Nah, ain't no negotiating shit."

Tah nodded and looked at me. I didn't say a word.

C. closed the briefcase and handed it to Tah. "You guys staying for the gala, right?"

"Yeah. I'll go put this in the car." Tah took the briefcase.

Dom was staring at me. "Hey," he said when we made eye contact.

"Hey."

"So, will I see you again after tonight, or is this it?"

C. Millionaire flashed Dom this weird look. I felt a little tugging at my heart, and I didn't know if it was because of the way he was asking me. Tah already said that after tonight we could never see them again. They were going to find out the jewels were fake, and they would kill us.

"Yeah, we'll link up, baby," I said.

He flashed me that grin I was growing fond of. "Good, 'cause I really like you, JuJu."

"I really like you too, Dom." It was the truth. I liked him, but I liked him a little too much.

Once Tah returned, we walked into the gala on their arms.

This event was like no other we'd ever attended. A live band played music as everyone socialized. Champagne was served by waitresses. White and gold décor filled the place. It was classy.

Tah and I stood out amongst the crowd. My dress exposed all my back and my cleavage with a plunging neckline. Tah's legs were exposed by a split that ran up to her hips. Our hair was straight. Tah worked the room, mingling and mixing. We knew we were too sexy to go unnoticed. The attention of every man in the room was on us.

"Damn, they can't take their eyes off you," Dom said.

"And what about you?" I asked.

"Excuse me?" He was smiling with that charming smile that made me weak in the knees.

"What about you? Where are your eyes?"

He gazed at my body. "My eyes are the same place they've been all night. On you. I can't wait—"

"Shhhh," I said, placing my finger to his lips. "Tell me later."

I wanted to hear what he had to say, but now wasn't the time. Tah was watching us. She had already warned me about getting too emotionally involved. I didn't want her to know that I was falling in love with Dom. Tah was looking straight at me, so I straightened up and cleared my throat as I reached for some champagne from a nearby table.

Tah whispered in my ear as soon as Dom walked away. "What's the fuckin' deal? We should be leaving right now."

"No. This is all a part of my game."

"What game? The game is fucking over. We got the shit, so let's go."

"It's not over until we're gone."

"You're choosing him over me?" Tah asked.

"You think I'm gonna turn my back on you for him? We made a pact, remember? *Honor among boss chicks*, a sisterhood. I'll never go against you."

"You want everything you can't have. Once we leave here, they can never hear from us again."

I downed the champagne. "I got it."

Tah gritted her teeth and said through them, "You love him, don't you?"

I sighed. "It ain't like that. It's just I don't know. . . . It's different this time. Everybody that we've ever robbed or scammed had it coming. They've been nothing but good to us. Okay, so what if I want to fuck Dom one last time tonight? That just means the sex is good. I'm not falling in love."

Tah was furious, but she kept her cool. "He may be feeling you, but as soon as they find out that we crossed them, we're fucking dead. I don't want you to get caught up in some fairytale. We're family, and we all we got," she said.

She was right. It was time to go.

I clutched my stomach and pretended to faint. Tah caught me.

Dom saw and rushed over. "JuJu, you okay?"

"I don't feel so good. I shouldn't have had that champagne after taking my medication," I lied.

"We should go," Tah said. "She needs to go lay down."

"Do you need anything?" Dom asked.

"No, no, no. I'll be fine. I just need to lie down."

Tah helped me as we walked toward where our car was parked. C. Millionaire stepped in front of us. We halted, but I kept clutching my stomach.

"Thank you again, ladies. We'll be in touch if we need you again."

"Okay," Tah said, taking me to step around him. "I'll let you know when we land safely."

"Okay. Hope you feel better."

"Call me," Dom called to me.

I smiled on the inside as we went to the car.

We got inside of our hotel room and started cleaning everything up.

"We ain't taking their private jet home tonight, are we?" I asked.

"Fuck no. That's too predictable. You never know if they're checking those jewels after the way we just left," she said. "We're going to stay the night since we're checked in under an alias. We'll meet the buyers first thing in the morning and sell those jewels. Then, we're ditching the car, picking up another one to drive to Mexico for those fake IDs and passports. Last, we'll drive to San Diego and catch a flight from there."

"How will we get on the plane with all that money?"

"We'll take it into a bank in Mexico and transfer the funds to an overseas account."

"You really thought this one out, Tah."

"I had to. We ain't ever did anything on this scale, so the shit has to be perfect."

Dom

"Where are they, David and Charles?" Lead Federal Agent Sully interrogated me and C. Millionaire.

We were federal agents working undercover to finally get JuJu and Tah. The jewelry store was real, but it didn't belong to us. It belonged to this guy who went by the name Blue. The money wasn't ours, either. It belonged to the federal government. The Dubai buyers were even fake. This whole thing was a setup to catch them, and we fucked up.

"How the hell do we know?" I shrugged.

"I thought you said they would be at the Las Vegas airport tonight. We searched everywhere, and no record of two women traveling together. You don't think they're still in Los Angeles, do you?"

"They just might be," Charles stated.

"These petty thieves managed to pull a major heist with our goddamn help! You know that, right?" he barked.

"I realize that," I said, speaking up for Charles and me. "We honestly didn't think they would show up to the gala with another fake set of jewels. We thought they would take the real jewels and catch a flight immediately. When they showed up at the gala, it shocked the hell out of us. That's why we had agents waiting at the airport."

"You should've had some agents waiting for them when they first got the jewels in their possession. Did you know that they posed as security to transport the jewels?"

Charles and I looked at one another and shook our heads.

"What?" Charles asked in disbelief.

"That's right, you idiots! You hired them. They were dressed like men right under your noses, and you had no clue!"

This shit was crazy. We were hustled in every way. They got away with the million dollars, which was real, and the jewels, which were real. Hell, we even paid their fake-ass security company insurance money. Now, they'd vanished like magicians. I thought JuJu was feeling me, but I got played like a game of chess.

"We'll find them. We won't stop until we do," I said.

"You better. This was supposed to be our big bust, and you blew it." The agent walked out and left us there to think.

"I don't believe this shit." I sulked. "Fernando didn't say shit about making a second set of fake jewels. He baited them to save his own ass from prison, and he played us too."

Charles shook his head. "Nah, I bet you he didn't create them. They didn't trust him. These bitches are much smarter than we thought. We gotta hand it to them."

"You think we should just let this go?" I asked, feeling like he was giving up.

"No, I'm not saying that. We'll catch them. We'll keep our ears and eyes at attention. Their game has just been elevated, so they're not going to stop now."

Tah

The morning after the gala, Valentino texted JuJu and told her that the police were waiting for him at the airport when he arrived. They arrested him but didn't hold him because they couldn't prove shit. He told us that C. Millionaire and Dom were undercover Feds, setting our asses up, and Fernando had sold us out to save his own ass from prison.

We threw our phones in the trash right after those text messages. We met up with the buyers as planned, and they wired eighty million to our overseas account, which worked out better.

JuJu dyed her hair honey blonde. I shaved my hair bald and put that fake beard back on. We picked up some fake IDs and passports in Mexico, and we traveled around the world as Mr. and Mrs. Michaelson like some tourists.

We were now chilling on a secluded island where we felt safe for the time being. The temperature was about eighty degrees or so. The flower-perfumed air was alive with the song of birds. A gentle splash was nearby, and when I sat up, I could see the massive waterfall of perfectly clear water running over rocks. Although the island couldn't have been more than a half-mile wide, the sea had disappeared, lost behind an impenetrable screen of vegetation. The water looked ridiculously beautiful as every Caribbean island, and the colors were too intense to be true.

"I can't believe I almost fell for him." JuJu sighed.

I laughed. "What you mean, *almost*? You did, and if I didn't talk some sense into you, he would've handcuffed you to a bed and let the police take you away."

She shook her head. "It felt so real, Tah. Like, his feelings just seemed real."

"Yeah, I bet. It's good. One day, the right one will come."

"Same for you."

"I know."

"How long you think we gonna stay here?" she asked.

I shrugged. "Seems safe here, but let's play it by ear."

"With all this money, we don't need to scheme anymore. We can find our husbands and retire. Maybe have a couple of kids."

I laughed. "Girl, please. We can't shake this shit. It's in our blood."

JuJu thought about it. "Damn, you ain't ever lied!"

About the Author

Niyah Moore is an award-winning author with more than twenty-five published works to her credit. A Sacramento, California native, Niyah's love affair with the written word began early. By the age of nine, she was fully immersed in the possibilities of prose. Under the subtle urging and guidance of her literary mentors, Niyah embarked on a professional writing career.

A true contemporary artist, Niyah's foray into the literary world began in 2007 with the social media platform Myspace, where she submitted her writing to be included in select anthologies. Niyah has since secured multiple independent publishing deals, as well as having been involved in several collections such as *Zane's Busy Bodies: Chocolate Flava 4* and *Anna J's Lies Told in the Bedroom*.

Niyah has a way with words, which keeps her romance readers, as well as her contemporary fiction fans, anticipating new arrivals. Her noteworthy novels include: *Tell Yo Bitch* series, *Nobody's Side Piece* series, and *Guilty Pleasures* to name a few. Niyah was an honoree for the 2013 Exceptional Women of Color Award of Northern California. She is a two-time recipient of the African American Literary Award for Best Anthology and named among UBAWA's top 100 urban authors of 2017.

In 2014, Niyah signed her first major two-book publishing deal with Simon & Schuster, under *New York Times* Bestselling Author Zane's imprint, Strebor Books. Niyah's first release under Strebor Books was *Pigalle Palace*, which was featured by Ebony.com, and her highly anticipated follow-up, *Thunderstorm.*

Niyah's journey has been paved with determination and drive. Her latest novel, *She Loves the Savage in Me,* is available wherever fine books are sold.

Dishonorable

by

INDIA

Prologue

BLAH! BLAH! BLAH!

The sound of gunfire ripped through the townhouse like booming thunder. Kita could hear her friends in the living room screaming out for help as bullets pierced their bodies. Quickly, she stepped back into the bedroom and locked the door.

"Fuck!" She panicked. There was no way out, and to make matters worse, she was trapped in a room with no weapons. Her heart raced erratically as she put her ear to the door and listened.

"Where is the fucking cash at?" a man's voice bellowed from the living room.

"I ain't got no fuckin' money in here!" Alexis screamed.

"I'm going to ask you one more fuckin' time. Lie to me again, and you won't like what happens next."

Thinking fast, Kita fumbled with her cell phone to dial for help.

"Nine-one-one, what's the emergency?" The operator sounded more like a robot than an actual person.

"We're at 906 Chene. Unit number three. Send the police and a few ambulances."

"What seems to be the emergency?"

"Oh my God!" Kita could hear someone headed in her direction. The pattern of their footsteps matched the beating in her heart; she was ready to pass out. "I'm at my friend's house. Someone just came in shooting!" She tried to whisper.

"Do you know how many assailants there are, or what they look like?" The operator bombarded her with questions.

Frustrated and afraid, Kita dropped the phone onto the bed when she saw the knob on the door jiggle. It was over, and she knew it—or so she thought, until the window called her name. Alexis's townhouse was set up with the front door on the first floor and the rest of the house on the second floor. Kita didn't want to jump two stories, but desperate times called for desperate measures.

After prying the window open, she kicked out the screen. With one leg dangling over the edge, she looked back just in time to see the room door open. Before the person had the chance to enter, Kita closed her eyes and jumped. Thankfully, she landed on her knees instead of her stomach or back.

BLAH! BLAH!

Two shots whizzed past her head. Without hesitation, she picked herself up and frantically tried to reach a neighbor's house.

BLAH!

The next shot tore through her calf, which dropped her where she stood like it was nothing. Yet and still, with one good leg, Kita willed herself to keep pushing. She had to fight for her child if nothing else.

BLAH!

The fourth blast was the shot that put Kita down. The bullet had entered her back and exited through her chest. It was like something from a movie the way pieces of her flesh opened and flew out in front of her. Kita felt a burning sensation so hot she wondered if she was on fire. The pain was unbearable. She wanted to scream, but her lungs were full of something—blood, perhaps. She tried twice to get up, but it was useless. Her limbs were not listening to her brain.

As she lay there, she could hear the sound of neighbors, and possibly an ambulance, too. Thank God help was coming, although she doubted she could hold on for much longer. Her body was growing cold. Her eyes opened and closed. The world was losing Markita Antoinette Jones.

As she lay there dying on the sidewalk, Kita wondered how her mother would react to the news. She was Jackie's only living child. Her brother, Marlowe, had died a few years ago. Now who would care for her mother? What about Rico? At the thought of him, a tear gathered in the corners of her eyes. She wondered if he would be mad at her once he found out about her double life. The police would definitely report the incident as being drug related. Kita knew Rico would hate her for losing their child, and she wondered how long it would take him to move on.

Damn! Kita wanted to make things right. She wanted to start over, but in life, she knew there were no second chances. It was time to meet her maker and face judgment for the way she had been living lately. She wondered if Alexis and Kenya would be there too. With her friends in mind, she managed to muster a faint smile. How did three innocent girls from the hood get caught up in a life of crime? This simple question triggered a movie to begin playing in Kita's head. With her eyes closed, she began to relax and allow herself to be transported through the imagery of her life.

The flashes began with pictures of a much simpler time. Back then, the only hard decisions Markita had to make revolved around which shoes to wear with what outfit. Soon the flashes escalated and painted a much more vivid picture of a harsher time. After losing Marlowe, Markita stepped up to the plate and took over the family business with the help of her girls. Although they had done well for themselves, it was at the height of their game that Markita began to see the end of their reign. She knew all good things had to come to an end, but she didn't expect their story to stop here. How could she die like this on the cold, dirty concrete?

As she fought with all she had to stay alive, the thought of who was behind the hit weighed heavy on her heart. Was it a disgruntled customer from the past, a jealous rival, or had someone in her circle become dishonorable?

Chapter One

Several Years Earlier

"*Wobble baby, wobble baby, wobble baby. . . .*"

The music blared through the speakers strategically placed around the courtyard of the Chambers apartment complex while the parking lot served as a dance floor. Several women were already out there shaking and gyrating their ample frames, trying to outdo one another.

"Come on, Kita, let's dance. That's my shit!" Alexis tugged on the tail of her friend's shirt.

"Nah, you go ahead. I'll be right here handling this rib tip sandwich." Kita took a bite of the flavorsome meal and got barbeque sauce all over her luscious lips.

"Your mom was nice enough to organize this block party for our graduation, and all you wanna do is sit here and eat?" Alexis folded her arms across her lanky body. She probably weighed a buck fifteen at best. Kita, on the other hand, was thick and curvy. Be that as it may, neither of them had issues when it came to boys. Alexis was a chocolate girl with high check-bones and naturally curly hair. Markita was more of a caramel color with deep dimples on her full face.

"Girl, you don't need me to dance. Go ahead!" Kita shooed her friend away before taking another bite of the sandwich. Mr. P, her mother's boyfriend, was manning the grill and, as usual, his BBQ was on point. Besides, Kita wasn't much of a dancer anyway. She just liked to watch and laugh as other people made fools of themselves.

"Forget you, then." Alexis flicked her tongue out and headed over to the parking lot to join the other women. The wobble was coming to an end, but the DJ kept up the momentum by transitioning into the cha-cha slide.

"Bye." Markita waved before surveying the area with a huge smile.

Her mother, Jackie, had truly outdone herself with the party. There were two large banners with CLASS OF 2007 hanging from light poles for the whole apartment complex to see. Jackie also had streamers and balloons everywhere. Everyone was in attendance, too, except for Kita's brother, Marlowe. He was older than her by five years and was always busy running the streets. Markita didn't normally complain when Marlowe missed events because she knew he was busy; however, this was different. She wanted her big brother there to celebrate with her. It wasn't every day that a girl from the ghetto graduated with honors, was class valedictorian, and received a partial scholarship to college.

"What's wrong, Kita?" Jackie stepped out onto the patio carrying a large container filled with Kool-Aid. She was still wearing the dress from the graduation ceremony but had exchanged the heels for a pair of Crocs. Kita, on the other hand, had ditched her ceremony attire the moment she arrived home. She was now rocking a white skirt and halter-top with the red commencement cap and tassel. It was a symbol of accomplishment that she, along with the other graduates, would rock proudly that day.

"Have you heard from Marlowe?" Kita finished the last of her food and stood to assist her mother.

"This morning he called and promised to be here." Jackie handed the container over to Markita. "Don't worry. Knowing your brother, he's probably out trying to purchase you some elaborate gift or something."

"I hope it's a new car!" Kita squealed. She had been circling ads in the *Auto Trader* magazine for weeks. *Maybe Marlowe saw the cars I circled and is going to surprise me after all*, she thought.

He spoiled his little sister rotten with the money he made in the streets as a drug dealer. Most people frowned upon people like him, but Jackie and Markita loved Marlowe to death. Sure, Jackie would've preferred her son find a better profession, but he was what he was, and she knew she couldn't change him. Besides, he was a godsend in her eyes. Not only was he a good son, but he was an all-around great person. Marlowe took care of people in the neighborhood. For the elderly citizens, he would pay a team of youngsters to assist them with odds and ends around the house like shoveling snow, raking leaves, and running errands. For the homeless people, Marlowe would have Jackie make about fifty dinners, then he would drive around the city all day and pass them out. He did this once a month. People really loved the Jones family; they had become a staple of the community.

"He better show up before the party dies down and nobody gets to see my car." Markita pouted.

"He'll be here. Don't worry." Jackie winked.

Two hours passed, and Marlowe still hadn't arrived. Markita called his cell phone over thirty times, and each call went to voicemail. "Something isn't right." Markita paced the living room floor. Her spirit told her that her brother was in trouble.

Jackie wanted to calm her daughter's nerves, but she knew Markita had been having accurate premonitions since childhood. Her grandmother, Lynette, once told her it was something that ran deep in their Creole blood and only passed to one child every other generation. Lynette knew her granddaughter had the gift; therefore, she deemed her the gifted one. Kita, on the other hand, thought it was more of a curse because it totally consumed her mind, body, and spirit.

Grabbing the phone, Kita dialed one last time. Before the phone could even ring, she heard Alexis yell inside the apartment, "Marlowe just pulled up!" A sense of relief came over both Kita and Jackie.

"Thank God!" Jackie shouted.

Kita ended the call and flew outside to see what surprise he had waiting on her. However, the minute she stepped foot onto the patio, her whole world shattered. Marlowe's brand-new black Yukon Denali had rolled onto the sidewalk and collided with a green electrical box. From her position, she could see that the body of the vehicle had been riddled with bullets. Several people standing outside started screaming.

"He's been shot!"

"Somebody call the ambulance!"

Markita screamed for her mother to come before running over to the vehicle, which was now smoking. She pulled on the door, but it was locked. Thinking fast, she grabbed a rock near her feet to break the glass. The windows were tinted, so it wasn't until the glass shattered that Markita saw her brother slumped over toward the passenger seat. Frantically, she reached in, unlocked the door, and pulled him out. The gray Versace T-shirt Marlowe was wearing had turned bright red. The face on the Jesus piece around his neck had been broken from one of the bullets that hit his chest.

"Dammit, don't die! Please don't die!" Kita screamed. "Marlowe, what happened?"

"Never mind that." He coughed. "I got some work in the back. Grab that shit and hide it for me, Kita." Marlowe spoke in a hushed tone. Kita was elated to see that her brother was alive.

"Marlowe, baby, what happened?" Jackie ran up to the SUV and dropped down to cradle her son. One of her worst fears had come true. She never thought she would have to bury one of her children. Staring down at her first born covered in blood was unreal. "Where are you hurt, baby?" she cried.

"Kita, handle that shit." Marlowe ignored his mother. If the police found all the drugs in the trunk of his whip, he would surely be going upstate for a very long time.

"Okay. Okay, I got you." Kita wiped off her tears and went to the back of the vehicle to retrieve the drugs.

After popping the trunk, she was faced with three large duffle bags. One by one, she removed them, closed the trunk, and dragged the bags into the house. Several people were gathered around, but no one was paying her any attention.

Once inside the house, her mind raced. *What if the police raid the apartment? Should I flush the dope?* She knew enough to know that police would have to have a warrant to search her mother's house; therefore, Kita decided to hide the bags instead of flushing them. Flying to the closet like a mad woman, she grabbed two of the large Rubbermaid containers her mother used to store Christmas stuff and winter blankets. After dumping the contents to the ground, she tossed the bags inside, fixed the closet back up, and then headed back outside to check on her brother.

By now, the ambulance and one squad car were present. Kita was relieved. Normally the police took forever to respond, but she later found out that Marlowe had called them on his way home, before crashing into the electrical box.

"Is he going to be all right?" she asked her mother as they were closing the ambulance door. Jackie was being consoled by Mr. P, her on-again/off-again boyfriend.

"He took a bullet to the chest, Kita," Mr. P responded in a low tone. "I'm going to take your mother to the hospital. Are you coming with us?"

"No. I can't." Kita began to cry. She didn't care for hospitals, and she couldn't stand the thought of losing her brother. "Just call me and keep me posted."

Chapter Two

"I can't believe this bullshit!" Alexis paced back and forth. She couldn't believe how tragic the day had turned.

"Me either." Kita stared down at her blood-covered hands. Silently, she wondered why anyone would want to harm such a loving, generous creature. Whoever did it would probably turn up dead tonight. Marlowe was a well-loved individual. Once word got out about what happened to him, his friends would most likely comb every inch of Detroit until the perpetrator was found.

"Have you heard anything from your mother?"

"No," Kita replied. She wanted to remind Alexis that she had been sitting there with her for the whole hour her mother had been gone but decided against it. It was no use starting an argument with Alexis, who was just as concerned as she was.

Just as Kita reached for the phone, there was a knock at the door. She wasn't in the mood to speak with any nosey neighbors, so Alexis went to open it. It was Kenya, the third piece of the trio. She sashayed in wearing a frightened expression.

"Is he all right?"

"I don't know, girl." Kita shrugged.

"How did you find out?" Alexis asked. She knew news traveled fast, but damn! Kenya had just come back from the airport, where she'd dropped her father off after leaving the graduation ceremony.

"You know I keep my ears to the streets." Kenya flopped down on the couch beside Kita. "I hear everything."

"Well, what did you hear happened?" Kita knew Kenya was a very reliable resource. The girl stayed in the streets, running behind some dope boy all day, every day. If anybody had the 411, it was Kenya.

"Marlowe and Man-Man was at the spot earlier and got into it. They started fighting on the lawn and, supposedly, Man-Man went in the house and got the blower. Marlowe jumped in the whip, but Man-Man took fire on the truck."

"Man-Man?" both Kita and Alexis asked. Bernard "Man-Man" Frasier was one of Marlowe's childhood friends. The two boys were like brothers at one point. It wasn't until Marlowe started making more money and getting more shine that their friendship took a turn for the worse. After noticing the tension and jealousy, Marlowe began to distance himself from Bernard. Apparently, Bernard wasn't too happy.

"Girl, if I'm lying, I'm flying, and as you can see, I'm still ten toes down." Kenya raised her right hand as if she were taking an oath and pointed at her feet.

"That bitch!" Kita was pissed. She couldn't recall the number of times Man-Man's ass had eaten at their table, spent the night at their house, and wore her brother's hand-me-down clothes when his crackhead mother couldn't afford to buy him things that fit. The Jones family had taken him in, and this was the way he did Marlowe?

"You want me to call my cousins?" Alexis already had the phone in her hand. She was ready to have this nigga dealt with.

"No, fuck that!" Kita smacked her lips. "I'm going to deal with that bitch my damn self."

"Girl, are you crazy?" Kenya asked with a raised brow. Markita was no killer! She was just a pretty girl with book smarts. That's it, and that's all.

"He got my brother on his deathbed, so hell fuck yeah, I'm crazy!" Kita snapped. A person never knew what they were capable of until they were pushed to the limit, and today, Markita had been pushed.

"Call me crazy too, then, 'cause I'm in!" Alexis added. Although she was tall and skinny, baby girl was a pit bull. She could definitely lay hands. Marlowe was like a brother to her, so she wanted to ride for him.

"Fuck it, then. I guess my ass is in too." Kenya sighed. If her girls had beef with a nigga, then she did as well. "Let me put in a call to get some guns and shit." She didn't know what Kita had planned, but Man-Man definitely had to pay for his actions.

"No need for all that. I know where my brother keeps his." Kita got up and went to the back of the apartment. Marlowe no longer lived there, but he did keep a safe in the back of Kita's closet. She knew by peeking many times that the combination was her birthday. Without faltering, she plugged in the numbers and opened the door. Inside were two handguns and three small stacks of money. Kita didn't care what the guns were called; she was just glad to see them. After checking to ensure they were loaded, she returned to the living room and handed one to Alexis.

"What about me?" Kenya asked.

"You're driving." Kita already had things figured out.

As the girls put the final touches on their plan, they were startled by a knock on the door. Quickly, they stashed the weapons underneath the couch cushions. Kenya and Alexis tried to look natural while Kita unlocked the door.

"Hello, miss. My name is Traci Knox, and this is my partner, Brice Walters." The plainclothes female officer smiled. "We're here investigating the shooting of Marlowe Jones. It's my understanding he was your brother, right?"

"He *is* my brother, bitch!" Kita corrected her. How dare this bitch use past tense like Marlowe was dead?

"My apologies. May we come in?"

"Why?" Kita folded her arms. She wasn't letting anybody in without a warrant.

"To discuss what happened to your brother?" Traci looked irritated.

"Lady, I don't know what happened, so you're barking up the wrong tree." With those words, Kita slammed the door. She didn't care for the police anyway. In her opinion, they never did much but get all up in your business.

Chapter Three

Four hours after Marlowe pulled into his mother's apartment complex, the police were finally wrapping up the crime scene. They towed his Denali away and pulled down the yellow tape.

After making sure the coast was clear, Kita and her girls were about to head out when the phone rang.

"Hello?" She almost didn't want to answer because she wasn't ready for any bad news.

"Hey, Kita. It's Paul." Mr. P's voice was unreadable, so Kita held her stomach.

"Did my brother die?" She swallowed hard.

"No, baby girl." Mr. P sighed. "Thank God, Marlowe is still with us, but he's not out of the woods yet. He lost a significant amount of blood, and doctors are worried that he may have mobility issues."

"Thank you, Jesus!" With a smile, Kita looked over at Kenya and Alexis. They, too, began smiling.

"Your mom is going to stay overnight. I was just calling to update you and ask if you wanted me to swing by and pick you up."

"No, thank you. Just stay with my mom and keep me posted." Kita was on a mission. The longer her mother stayed gone, the better.

"Okay, baby girl, I'll call you later." Paul ended the call.

Kita was elated about the good news but still determined to make Man-Man pay. Quickly, she dialed his cell phone, prepared to put her plan in motion.

"What's up, Kita? You good?" Man-Man pretended to be concerned.

"Yeah, I'm good. I just can't believe Low was shot, though." Kita played along.

"I swear on my mama I'm going to find whoever did this and close-casket that nigga!" Man-Man was going for an Oscar with the performance.

She wanted to tell him to shut the fuck up, but instead she remained silent.

"Have you got word from the hospital yet?" he asked.

"No, I haven't heard anything." Kita knew better than to tell him that Marlowe was still alive. For all she knew, his crazy ass might've tried to go up there and finish what he started.

"Damn, man, this shit is so fucked up." Man-Man sighed heavily into the phone.

"I know. I feel so scared and alone." Kita paused. "Where are you? Can I come over? I just want to be around some family right now."

"I'm at the spot right now, shorty, but—" Man-Man hesitated like he was about to tell Kita to take a rain check. She peeped game, so she kicked it up a notch by pretending to cry. "Look, why don't you slide through for a little bit? Ain't nobody here but me anyway. But you can't stay here all day. It ain't safe."

"Thanks, bro." She already knew the address, so she told him she was on the way and ended the call.

"Y'all ready?" Kita slipped the phone into her back pocket, grabbed the gun, and then her purse.

"Let's do this!" Alexis responded. Kenya nodded.

Thirty minutes later, the women pulled onto Woodlawn Street and cut the engine. They agreed that Kita should enter the house alone and leave the door unlocked. Alexis would come in five minutes later and back her up if needed. Each girl was nervous, but they had come too far to back down now.

"Watch the house. If anybody show up, y'all better come in and get me," Kita instructed before stepping out of the black Ford Focus. With the gun tucked into the small of her back, she strutted down the block and up to the house before knocking lightly on the door.

It took Man-Man only a second to answer. When he did, he stepped his five-foot-ten, medium-build frame onto the porch and peered down the block. This was something he did out of habit. Luckily, Kenya's car was too far away for him to see Kita's friends sitting inside.

"What's up, sis? How are you holding up?" He hugged Kita before turning and heading toward the living room. Kita closed the door but left it unlocked as planned.

"I'm sick about what happened, Man-Man." She swallowed hard. The churning in her stomach was intensifying. "I just hope he don't die." With every step, Kita could feel her heart leaping from her chest. For a second, she started to call the whole thing off and let the streets handle him, but Marlowe was her brother! It was only right that she obtained justice.

"I know, Kita. I can't lose that nigga. We're like brothers." Man-Man sat down on the couch and began bagging up a white, rock-like substance from the coffee table. Kita recognized it as crack cocaine. She had seen Marlowe doing the same thing many times.

"I'm just wondering what he did to deserve this." Kita looked around the scarcely decorated trap house with chipped paint, torn carpet, and several pieces of mismatched furniture. "Have you heard anything?" She took a seat on the recliner across from him.

"Nope." Man-Man never looked up from what he was doing.

"Well, the police came to our door, talking about they got a witness that saw what happened. They also said it was someone very close to my brother." Kita's lie made the nerves in Man-Man's eye twitch.

"Witness?" This time, Man-Man looked up like he was worried.

"That's what they said, bro." Kita shrugged nonchalantly.

"They name any names?" Man-Man stopped what he was doing to glance at her. Suddenly, he felt uncomfortable.

"The streets are talking, and they said it was *you,* nigga." With a French-tipped finger, she pointed at his guilty ass. Her words had shaken Man-Man to his core. Although his poker face was tight, inside he was shaking like a leaf on a tree.

"Me?" He looked offended.

"Yeah, what did Marlowe do to you?" Kita was not backing down.

"I'll be right back." Man-Man stood from the sofa just in time for the front door to open. In walked Alexis, and he looked back at Kita for clarity. "What she doing here?"

"Bernard, just tell me why." Kita casually removed the gun and pointed it at her target. Fear no longer consumed her. Her hand was steady. She was calm. "My mother fed your ungrateful ass! My brother treated you like family, and this is what you do?"

"So, you gon' shoot me?" Man-Man had the nerve to ask. The bastard even sported a smirk because he knew Kita wouldn't bust a grape if Mr. Welch himself asked her to.

"You shot my fuckin' brother, right?" she screamed.

Alexis stood silently with her gun raised. If this nigga so much as moved an inch, she would blow him into next lifetime.

"You and your little friend ain't got the balls to play this game." Man-Man laughed. Who did Kita think she was to walk up in his trap, toting a pistol? "Y'all got two seconds to get the fuck on before I body y'all bitches just like I did Marlowe."

That was all it took to push Kita to the point of no return. *POP! POP! POP!* She closed her eyes and let off three shots. When she reopened her eyes, Man-Man had fallen backward and was sliding down the wall, holding his chest. Her eyes widened in surprise. Neither Man-Man nor Kita could believe she had actually pulled the trigger. Alexis looked on in disbelief as well. She thought Kita would've bitched up.

"Are you okay?" Alexis walked over to Kita, who was standing there in a daze.

"I did what I came to do. Now I'm good." She watched as Man-Man bled profusely just as Marlowe had done. The sight gave Kita brief satisfaction, but then it was time to finish the job.

With a confident glide, Kita walked up to Bernard and slid her gun into his mouth, between his teeth. He wanted to plead with her not to pull the trigger, but he knew his fate was sealed. Karma was a bitch! In the game, if you live by the gun, you will inevitably die by one as well.

"Just do it!" he mumbled.

POP! One shot caused the back of his head to explode. Brain matter flew everywhere.

"Let's get the fuck out of here." Alexis nervously looked around the room as the realization hit her that she had just taken part in a homicide.

"Grab the dope first!" Kita didn't know why she was concerned with the cocaine, but she felt it was necessary to make the scene look like a robbery. Quickly, Alexis grabbed the dope off the table while Kita checked the house to make sure no one else was there. The place was empty, but she struck gold when she entered the kitchen. Sitting on the table were two medium-sized moving boxes. Inside of both boxes were at least six perfectly wrapped bricks of pure white, uncut cocaine. Kita didn't know what exactly to do with the dope, but she did know a lick when she saw one.

"Hot damn!" Alexis yelled when she entered the kitchen.

"Help me grab this." Kita grabbed one box and headed toward the door.

Just then, there was a knocking sound. Her heart damn near leaped from her body. Alexis clutched her pistol and proceeded toward the door. Of all the girls, she was the 'bout-it one. Standing on her tiptoes, she looked through the peephole. A young girl with a little boy at her side stood there looking crazy. Alexis knew she was a fiend trying to get served.

"What'chu need?" Alexis spoke loud enough to be heard without opening the door. Kita could've shitted a brick.

"Let me get a dime," the girl replied.

Honestly, Alexis had no idea how much crack ten dollars could get you, but she knew it couldn't have been much. Quickly, she fumbled in her pocket for the bags she'd just taken off Man-Man's table. After finding one of the smaller bags, she cracked the door, waited for the money, and then she handed the product to the girl.

"What was that?" Kita asked after the door was closed.

"That's what you call hustling." Alexis was quite proud of her ten-dollar transaction.

"Girl, let's grab this shit and go."

"What about him?" Alexis pointed to Man-Man's dead body.

"Leave that nigga here stankin'. Someone will find him eventually." Kita sashayed past him, wiped her prints from the doorknob, and walked right out the front door like nothing had happened.

Chapter Four

Almost a week had gone by, and the hood was still buzzing about both Marlowe and Man-Man. People speculated that the shooter was the same in both situations, so no one suspected Kita and her crew. For the first few days, the girls laid low, but after realizing the heat was nowhere near them, things went back to normal.

Kita finally willed herself to go and visit her brother. He was still in intensive care with tubes all over his body. His mobility was limited to hand and neck movement. He was paralyzed from the waist down. The bullet had entered through his ribcage and exited his back, severing his spinal cord. The doctors worked hours to repair it, but in the end, their efforts weren't successful.

"Hey, bro." Kita smiled upon entrance into the private hospital room.

"About damn time you came to see a nigga." Marlowe looked his sister over with a fake grimace before smiling back. "I was beginning to think you had wrote me off or something."

"Boy, stop!" Kita leaned in and kissed his forehead. "I could never do that."

"So, what took you so fuckin' long then?"

"I had shit to do." She laughed before taking a seat beside the bed. The room was filled with every type of flower, balloon, and card you could've imagined.

"What you lookin' all sad for?" Marlowe didn't like the sympathy. Kita was staring down at him like he was in a casket or something.

"I never thought I would see you like this, that's all." She choked back a few tears.

"I'm going to be all right, believe that!" Marlowe was a soldier. It would take more than this to put him under. "How is Mama holding up? When she come visit, she try to act strong, but I can tell by the stains near her eyes that she be crying on her way up here."

"It's hard, Marlowe, but Mama will be all right as long as you're all right." Kita could feel the tears sliding down her face although she tried hard to hold them back. "That day when you pulled up, bleeding and shit, I thought you was dead."

"Me too." Marlowe chuckled lightly. He had been out minding his business, and in the blink of an eye, his whole world had changed. "I can't believe that ho-ass nigga Man-Man shot me. If it wasn't for the fact that someone took his ass out already, I would've put all the bread I got on his head. Karma is a bitch, though. I wonder who did me the favor."

"You're welcome," Kita spoke softly, relieved to lay the burden down. She knew if she could trust anyone with her secrets, she could always trust her brother.

"You say what?" Marlowe thought he was trippin'.

"I heard it was him, so I went over to the spot and handled that nigga. I took his dope, too." Kita stared at Marlowe without so much as batting an eyelash.

"Shit." Marlowe rubbed a hand across his goatee. Never could he imagine his baby sister doing some shit like this. "Anybody see you?"

"Nope. Niggas think the same person that came for you went for him too."

"Good. What about the gun?" He didn't bother asking where she had gotten one because he knew she knew where his was.

"I tossed them."

"You used two?" Marlowe looked confused.

Kita wasn't going to implicate Alexis, so she lied. "I took two just in case. I only used one, but I tossed them both."

"Cool." Marlowe had taught his sister well. "What about his dope?"

"It's in the Rubbermaid container with yours. I was just holding it until you told me what to do next." Kita stopped talking when the door opened. In walked two men; both were Italian or something.

Marlowe recognized his company and tried to sit up, although he knew it was useless. "Kita, go grab me some lunch from the cafeteria." He could've just had the nurse send the dietary aide up, but Kita knew it was a hint to get lost for a few.

"I'll be back in fifteen minutes." She stood and eyed the men before exiting. Quite naturally, she didn't leave. Instead, she stood right near the door and ear-hustled the conversation taking place inside the room.

"Marlowe, it's good to see you, son." Chino, the head of the Lopez family, leaned down and kissed both sides of Marlowe's face.

He didn't like to have a man kissing on him, but this was the customary greeting amongst the Lopez family—a family he had been a part of ever since he was fourteen. Chino and his brother Marco had taken Marlowe in when he was just a pup running reckless on the streets of Detroit. They saw the fire in his eyes and could feel the hustle pumping through his veins. The kid was something special, which was why they took him under their wings and trained him to be a kingpin should they ever retire. Neither man had a son; therefore, Marlowe was the closest thing. People in their organization questioned their moves and were pissed that a nigga was chosen over an Italian, but no one said anything aloud.

"That fuck nigga caught me slippin'." Marlowe felt the need to explain. "I thought he was my friend."

"Tsk. Tsk." Chino wagged his finger. "The first thing I ever taught you, young Marlowe, was that there are no friends in this game."

"Friends are only enemies in disguise. Remember that?" Marco added. "The only thing that you can rely on most of the time is family, and even half of them can't be trusted." The brothers shared a laugh, but Marlowe remained silent.

"I hate to see you like this, son." Chino patted Marlowe's shoulder. "It's obvious you're out of the game. You may not want to hear this, but we're going to have to replace you."

They had just given Marlowe control over the entire cities of Detroit, Royal Oak, Hazel, and Highland Park. He supplied everyone with Grade A product. Marlowe was the man in his city. No one made any moves without his say so.

"Bullshit!" Marlowe barked. He had worked too hard for his spot and his reputation just to watch that shit crumble like his legs. "I built my clientele from the ground up, man! I'm eating off this shit." There was no way Marlowe could part with his lifestyle. He couldn't go from eating lobster to some damn Spam.

"Look at you, Marlowe. How can you get out there and hustle?" Marco asked with his arms folded.

Marlowe paused before replying. Honestly, he hadn't thought about it, but he would figure something out. There was no way he could go back to being broke.

"Don't count me out just yet. Have a little faith in ya boy." Marlowe sounded more confident than he actually felt.

"Okay, son." Chino patted Marlowe's shoulder again before standing. He knew how hard this must be for his protégé; however, for the Lopez brothers, it was business as usual. If Marlowe didn't come up with a solution soon, they would have to find someone to replace him.

After the men said their goodbyes, Kita returned to the room. She could see her brother deep in contemplation. "What was that about?"

"Kita, this doesn't concern you." Marlowe was angry with his sister for being nosey.

"Is that your supplier?" She knew her brother was top secret with his connection.

"Why?" He peered at her.

"Just curious." Kita smiled.

"Well, don't be!" Marlowe shook his head. He didn't want his sister involved with any of his street dealings. She was on her way to college to really make something of herself.

"When do you leave for school anyway?" He switched the subject.

"I ain't leaving until you're back to your old self."

"I told you I'm good. Your ass better be on that plane headed to college real soon, or me and you will have a problem." Marlowe used his serious voice.

"I was thinking about staying here for the first year, until you get on your feet."

"Markita, Detroit has nothing to offer you. Baby girl, take this opportunity and run with it!" Marlowe stared at his sister. "If I was half as smart as you, I would've made some very different decisions with my life."

"Don't talk like your life is bad. Besides this, you're doing damn good if you ask me." Kita didn't have time for the lectures.

"You think I'm proud to be selling drugs? You think I like constantly having to look over my fucking shoulder? You think I wanted to become a cripple?" He wasn't trying to raise his voice, but he was passionate about what he was saying. "Look at what my lifestyle did to me, sis."

Kita didn't say anything. How could she? Everything her brother was saying hit home. After a few seconds of silence, she finally found the courage to ask, "Why didn't you stop?"

"It ain't easy." Marlowe looked away. "The longer you do it, the deeper you get. I wanted to walk away, but I had people depending on me."

Years ago, things had gotten tough for the Jones family after their father left. With nowhere to turn, Jackie and her children ended up piss-poor and living in a shelter. Tired of wiping his mother's tears and feeding his baby sister with the food he had to steal day in and day out, young Marlowe made a conscious effort to bring change. He jumped feet first into the belly of the beast.

"In life, we may not always do what's right, but as the head of the family, you always do what's necessary."

Marlowe's words resonated with Markita for several reasons, the main reason being that this was the final conversation she would ever hold with her beloved brother. Hours after she left the hospital, Marlowe began bleeding internally. He was rushed to emergency surgery, where he died on the operating table.

Chapter Five

It had been six months since the death of Marlowe, and Kita was in a funk. After his funeral, she boarded a flight to Washington, D.C. and prepared to start school at Howard University. Things there were an epic fail, and she couldn't concentrate. She missed home, and she missed her brother. Without a word, one day she packed an overnight bag, left her dorm room, and boarded the Greyhound bus back home.

Jackie wasn't surprised when Kita showed up on her doorstep. Actually, she was happy to see her.

"Although we've come to the end of the road . . ." Boyz II Men crooned over the sound system in Kita's room. She had been playing the song nonstop since she'd been home. It was hard to believe that her brother was gone. If her tears could've built a stairwell to heaven, she'd be able to see him daily.

"Kita, please play something else, baby." Jackie poked her head into her daughter's room. The song was wearing her out. She knew this was a part of her daughter's grieving process, but Jackie couldn't take it. Losing her dear son had damn near killed her. She was tired of being reminded of the pain day in and day out.

Closing the bedroom door, Jackie returned to the dining room table. She was sitting there, sorting out bills. Almost all of them were past due or shut-off notices.

"Damn!" Jackie rubbed her forehead. This was something she'd never had to do when Marlowe was alive. He paid for everything and even gave his mother spending money every Friday. After using all she had saved to bury her child, she was left with practically nothing. Mr. P helped as much as he could, but the majority of his check was being garnished by the IRS for back taxes. Jackie went and applied for various jobs, but no one called her back. Once again, times were tough for the Jones family, but she had faith that things would soon change.

"What are you doing, Mama?" Kita entered the dining room and took a seat. She felt bad that she hadn't been able to help her mother with any bills. While away at college, she used every dime she had to purchase textbooks and to eat.

"I'm just catching up on a few things," Jackie lied. She didn't want her daughter to worry. However, Kita had already snooped through the mail. She knew what was going on.

"How bad is it?" Kita asked.

"We'll be all right." Jackie had faith that something would work out.

"What happened to the money you saved up?" Kita wasn't trying to be all in her mother's business, but she was curious. Jackie forever preached about rainy days, and now it was a fuckin' thunderstorm.

"I used it to bury your brother." Marlowe didn't have any life insurance; therefore, Jackie had to fork over almost sixteen grand to lay her son to rest. She used the rest on bills and groceries.

"Don't worry. I'll figure something out." Suddenly, Kita remembered the work she had been holding for Marlowe, as well as what she took from Man-Man.

"Kita, I don't want you to consume yourself with this. Just concentrate on enrolling back in school next semester. Do you hear me?" Jackie didn't like the look in Kita's eyes.

"I got you." With a smile, Kita leaned in and kissed her mother's cheek.

Later that night, while Jackie was out with Mr. P, Kita called a meeting with her friends. She hadn't seen them at all since she had been back, and she couldn't wait to catch up, but right now, it was all about business.

As usual, Alexis was the last one to show up. "What's the emergency?" she asked after entering the room where her friends were.

"We've been waiting on you for almost an hour." Kita glanced at the digital clock near her bed.

"I was babysitting." During the day, Alexis was in charge of her little sister, Talia, who was ten. Their mother worked double shifts at an adult care home. "I'm here now, so let's get started."

"How would y'all like to earn some extra money?" Kita glanced around her bedroom at her friends. Kenya was sitting on the bed, and Alexis was now positioned Indian-style on the floor. They were all ears.

"Just let me know where to sign," Kenya answered while looking at her nails. It didn't matter what the job entailed. She was always down to put a few extra dollars in her pocket.

"Making money doing what?" Alexis was game, but she needed a little more information. If this job wasn't paying more than $8.75 like her current job, then she would have to decline.

"Selling dope," Kita replied. The room fell silent. "I've been holding some of Marlowe's bricks and what we stole from Man-Man. I was thinking we could sell that shit and split the profit. I don't know about y'all, but things have been tight around here lately." Kita hated to admit that her mother was struggling, but the truth was the truth.

"I don't know the first thing about the drug game, but I know together we could rock this shit!" She did her best to appeal to her friends, although she knew they really couldn't turn her proposition down. All of them had come from the same hood where good things came to those that hustled. "I don't know about y'all, but I'm hungry. I'm tired of watching everybody eat. It's time for us to grow the fuck up and get in the game."

Silently, each girl pondered over what their friend had proposed. Although they knew the game came with more downs than ups, Kita was right. Alexis was tired of seeing her mother work so damn hard to get nowhere. Kenya was exhausted as well. Her only taste of the good life came when she was the arm candy of a D-boy. Still, those relationships never lasted long before they'd be on to the next.

"So, are ya'll in or what?" Kita asked. She didn't have to hold her breath for long.

"You know the game has a funny way of ending friendships." Kenya extended her arm out in front of her. "So, I'm only in as long as we vow to always have each other's backs."

"And we can't let the money change who we are." Alexis extended her arm with Marlowe in mind. Had his friend not gotten jealous, he would still be alive.

"Friends forever!" With a smile, Kita placed her hand on top, and the deal was done.

Within a week, the girls were up and running. They had spent hours breaking down the coke, weighing it, and bagging it up into various sizes. Kenya hit the streets to promote, while Alexis and Kita searched the city for a trap house. Luckily, they didn't have to look very far. Alexis made an arrangement with her cousin, Shyla, to sell the potent narcotic out of her apartment in the projects. Shyla was an on-again/off-again dope fiend. All she wanted was a complimentary hit every day, and then the girls could do whatever they pleased with her apartment.

Things started off well. With Marlowe and Man-Man off the streets, there had been somewhat of a drought in the city. Once customers found out about the new location, they showed up in numbers. Kita, Alexis, and Kenya were overwhelmed by the response. Although they knew it wasn't safe, they had to split into three shifts just to keep up with the demand. The girls were getting money every hour on the hour for three weeks straight. Needless to say, life was good, until the first of many problems knocked on Shyla's front door one day.

"Who is it?" she asked without getting off the stained burgundy sofa. She was stretched out, watching a movie on Lifetime, courtesy of Alexis. Until her cousin started using her apartment, she didn't have cable. Had she known what luxury she'd been missing, she would've had someone steal it for her a long time ago.

BOOM! BOOM! The banging got louder.

Shyla sat up and turned down the television. "I said who the fuck is it?" This time when there was no reply, she got her skinny self up and went to check the peephole. That's when the door was kicked off the hinges and two masked men invaded her living room.

"Where is the dope?" the biggest one asked. He had a gun pointed at Shyla's head.

"What dope?" she nervously stuttered.

"Bitch!" He hit her with the butt of his weapon, causing blood to squirt from her head. "I don't have time for the games. Where is the dope?"

"There is no dope in here!" she screamed.

"I'm going to ask you one last time, and then I'm going to blow your fucking brains out!" He cocked the gun.

"Ain't nothing in here. She went to get some more," Shyla blurted out. "She'll be back in a few minutes." Shyla was so scared that she made a bowel movement in her pants.

"Good girl." The assailant patted her head like a dog.

Just then, Kita approached the door with a small knapsack. She was so busy texting on her phone that she didn't even see Shyla's door off the hinges until it was too late. "Fuck!"

"Get her!" the man instructed his partner.

Kita took off running through the housing projects like a track star, but the man was up on her in no time. He wrapped his arms around her and tackled her to the ground. *WHAP!* He landed a hard blow to the side of her face before snatching the bag off her shoulder. She tried to hold on to it as best she could, but when he sent another blow to her face, she was knocked out.

When she came to, Kenya and Alexis were staring down at her.

"What the fuck happened?" She grabbed her face, which was rocking with pain.

"We were robbed." Kenya extended a hand to help her friend to her feet.

"Is Shyla okay? They had a gun to her head," Kita recalled.

"That bitch is fine, just a little shaken up. Luckily, after taking the dope, they left."

"Did they take our money?" Kita's heart sank.

"No, it's still in the drawer in the refrigerator." Alexis had checked their hiding spot the moment she entered the apartment. Thankfully their assailants weren't smart enough to look for it. However, it was a valuable lesson for the girls to never keep the money and the product in the same place.

"I wonder who it was?" Kita asked. "It had to be someone from around these projects."

"I say we put some bread out on these niggas! The streets will definitely start talking then," Alexis suggested.

"I say we chalk it up as a loss and just move the fuck on," Kenya countered. After all, everyone had to take a loss at some point in the game. She was just glad theirs happened sooner than later. Now they knew they had to tighten up.

"Fuck that!" Kita snapped. "If we let this ride, then we become a target for everybody else." She knew letting shit slide was a no-no. This had to be handled immediately. As women in this treacherous industry, they had to move faster, think smarter, and go harder than their male counterparts.

"Okay, I'm with it, if that's what y'all want," Kenya relented. "I'll put the word out. Meanwhile, we need to close up shop and find a new location."

After dividing their earnings from the day, each girl headed off into different directions. Kita had a splitting headache, so she headed home, where she was flooded with a ton of questions from her mother.

"What the hell happened to your face?"

"I got into a fight, nothing major."

"A fight with who, Mike Tyson?" Jackie stared at her daughter's bruised and swollen face.

"Some chick from the projects." Kita shrugged. "Like I said, it's nothing."

Jackie didn't believe that a girl could pack such a punch. She knew there was more to the story, so she continued to pry.

"Why were you fighting in the first place?"

"Ma, can we please talk about this tomorrow?" Kita tried to bypass Jackie, who was blocking the path to her bedroom.

"Does this have anything to do with the baggies of cocaine I found in the closet?" Jackie watched the expression on her daughter's face turn from annoyed to embarrassed. It was the same expression Marlowe had worn years before. "Markita, are you telling me what I think you're telling me?"

"I haven't said anything, so how could I be telling you something?"

"Then answer my question!" Jackie demanded.

"The cocaine is Marlowe's. I've been selling it to—" Kita never got to finish her sentence.

WHAP! Jackie backhanded her daughter on the other side of her face without so much as a second thought.

"Are you out of your mind? Do you know what just happened to your brother due to this very thing?" Jackie couldn't believe Markita could be so damn stupid.

"In life, we may not always do what's right, but as the head of the family, you always do what's necessary." Markita repeated the words her brother had spoken on that fateful day at the hospital. To her, it was a confirmation that she was doing the right thing.

"Baby, you don't have to be the head of this house. I'll figure something out." Jackie was now in tears.

"Ma, there was an eviction notice on the door this morning." Kita had removed the red note from the door on her way out earlier. She didn't want anyone to see it, especially Jackie. It just would've been one more thing to worry about.

"I'll call somebody. Don't worry."

"I paid it already." Kita's eyes met her mother's. "Things will be okay for us from here on out. Don't worry." She reached into the pocket of her jeans and held out four hundred-dollar bills.

Jackie wanted to put her foot down and turn the money away, but she couldn't. It had come at a time when she desperately needed it the most.

"I ain't getting money like Marlowe, but soon, just watch." Kita smiled.

"Markita."

"Mom, I got us."

"Please be careful." Jackie broke down sobbing. She felt like a bad mother who had failed to provide for the needs of her children.

"Don't worry. After a few months of this, I'll leave the streets and return to college." It was a promise that Kita had no intention of keeping.

Chapter Six

Days turned into weeks, weeks into months, and months turned into a full year. Kita's supply had emptied fast, but with a new supplier by the name of Breeze in their corner, the girls had been putting in work in and around their city, so much so that the locals had coined them the Get Money Girls. Currently, they were the only known team of female dealers in their city, which made them a big deal. The streets loved their product, and the rival dough boys loved them. It was hard for a nigga to hate on a bitch, especially a bad bitch.

Each girl had stepped her game up in a major way. Alexis's skinny ass went to see Dr. Curves in Atlanta to purchase a pair of DD breasts and a big, round ass. Kenya was pushing the latest 2008 Lexus RX 350 on all chrome. Markita wasn't much of a stunner. Aside from buying a sleek, yet simple, cocaine white BMW 745 and moving her mother to a condo in Ann Arbor, all she did was stack her ends. Occasionally, she found a reason to splurge, and tonight was one of them.

It was her brother's birthday, and Kita had rented out DUO's entire bar and restaurant. The place was packed, and at her request everyone, was dressed in blue, Marlowe's favorite color. Though it was still hard to see his face on the T-shirts and buttons, times like this made her feel his presence.

"Let's give it up for my nigga Marlowe one time!" the DJ yelled on the microphone, and the entire crowd began cheering and clapping.

Markita watched from her seat in the VIP because she wasn't in much of a social mood, but she did like being amongst people who loved her brother.

"Excuse me, young lady. Is this seat taken?" An older Italian man wearing vintage Armani slid into the booth beside her. She wanted to tell him to get on, but suddenly she remembered his face. He was one of the men who had visited Marlowe in the hospital.

"I'm Chino." He extended his hand. By the bezeled-out Rolex watch on his wrist, Kita knew he was well off.

"I'm Markita. Thanks for coming to celebrate the life of my brother." She smiled. For some reason, she felt comfortable with the man.

"You may not know this, but he was like my own, Markita." Chino sipped from the Heineken beer in his hand. "Young Marlowe has definitely been missed."

"You can say that again." Kita used her finger to trace the rim of her cup filled with orange juice. She wasn't old enough to be drinking yet, and she honestly had no desire to.

"Can I be frank with you?" Chino leaned in close to Kita. "I see what you and your friends have been doing lately, and I must say I admire your work. You remind me a lot of your brother." He paused. "If you're interested, I would love to have you on my team."

Kita didn't know if she should scream with excitement, hug him, or just play it cool. She chose the latter. The Lopez brothers were the alpha and the omega of the coke and heroin business in Michigan. She knew you could only join their organization by invitation.

"Mr. Lopez, I'm elated." Kita grinned.

"Please call me Chino." He winked, and just like that, the Get Money Girls had been catapulted up the food chain.

"Thank you so much for the opportunity." Kita was ecstatic at the thought of better quality products for a lower cost, larger domain, and supreme clientele. The girls would be making triple what they were making with Breeze. Ray Charles could see how sweet this deal was. The one stipulation of their agreement was that the Lopez brothers only wanted to do business directly with Kita. She knew her girls wouldn't care as long as they got paid. With that in mind, she extended her hand, and they shook in agreement.

The night after the party, Kita called a meeting to inform her friends about their proposition. When they asked who the new supplier would be, she told them he would rather remain nameless. Alexis didn't give her any grief about it, but Kenya was a different story. She didn't like the fact that her girl was keeping secrets, so she had a major attitude.

"I'll think about it."

"Think about what?" both Kita and Alexis asked in unison.

"I don't know if I like doing business with someone I don't know."

"Stop being dramatic." Kita rolled her eyes.

"Kenya, I feel where you're coming from, but this new arrangement is too good to pass up." Alexis pleaded with her girl, and after a few minutes of consideration, Kenya gave in.

After finishing up the last package, the women cut ties with Breeze. He didn't like it, but he had no choice; the girls had made up their minds. Losing associates had become a trend lately. Breeze had no idea where everyone was getting their work from, but whoever it was crossed the line by taking money out of his pocket. He was left with a bitter taste in his mouth, and sooner than later, he vowed, someone would pay!

Within a matter of four months, Kita, Alexis, and Kenya had really earned their keep. They were running circles around their male counterparts and making more money than anyone ever imagined. Things were looking good, and both Chino and Marco were impressed. After seeing the value in their new protégé, they began to put her on with more supreme clientele, such as lawyers, ball players, and entertainers.

"Where are we going?" Kenya asked Kita when they pulled off of the service drive. The trio had been riding in silence for more than twenty minutes because Kita didn't want to blow the surprise.

"I told you we're going to see a new client." She pulled the rented Cadillac into the valet lane of the Westin hotel in Southfield.

"Who is he?" Kenya hated being out of the loop. It was bad enough she wasn't allowed to know who their supplier was, but now Kita was obtaining new clients without her.

Without a word, Kita exited the car and retrieved a suitcase the size of a carry-on from the back seat.

"So, you're going to ignore me?" Kenya followed behind Kita, who sashayed into the hotel entrance like she owned that bitch.

"Just chill the fuck out, okay." Kita was starting to regret bringing her instead of Alexis. Kenya could really get under a person's skin.

"Fine!" Like a child, Kenya twisted her lips and folded her arms across her chest.

Kita approached the receptionist and asked that she call the penthouse to inform the hotel guest of her arrival.

While the girls waited in the swank lobby with ceramic tile, recessed lighting, and a baby grand piano, neither Kenya nor Kita said a word. Instead, they exchanged random glances at one another. Luckily, the stare-down didn't last long. The bronze elevators opened, and the girls were greeted by a white guy wearing a red blazer, white shirt, black tie, and black pants.

"Are you here for the penthouse?"

"Yes, we are. Are you Auzzie?" Kita asked in a lowered tone.

"Yes, I am. Right this way." He held the elevator door open, and the girls hopped on. "I'm glad you could make it on such a short notice."

"No problem," Kita replied while Kenya stood there trying to figure out what the hell was going on.

The elevator ride up was short. When the doors opened, both Kenya and Kita marveled at all the security guards standing their post.

"Shit!" Kenya counted four men right away. "Who's up in this bitch, Lil Wayne?"

"Close." Kita winked.

"Right this way." Auzzie bypassed the muscular men in plainclothes, leading the girls toward his client. "Silver Dollar is back here."

"Did he say Silver Dollar?" Kenya whispered. Kita nodded. "Oh my God!" she mumbled, trying hard to contain herself.

Silver Dollar was a rapper who turned mogul seemingly overnight. With hits like "Down for You" and "Girl Stop Playin'," he was arguably one of the best rappers alive. After his sophomore album, Silver Dollar began to apply his street knowledge to the boardroom. This proved to be a smart move that garnered several lucrative deals with major corporations. He had come a long way from his days on the streets of Harlem, or so everyone thought, but truth be told, this nigga was still up to no good.

"Who the fuck is this?" Dollar stared at the women with a grimace. He was sitting in a chair being massaged by a small Asian woman.

"They've got what you asked for." Auzzie shifted nervously. He didn't like being on the short end of his client's temper. Dollar had been known to rough a few people up from time to time.

"Oh, these bitches got the work?" Dollar looked from Kenya to Kita. Neither of them looked like dope dealers. As a matter of fact, these bitches looked like the arm candy he fucked before and after each performance. It was hard for him not to laugh.

"You can kill that bitch shit!" Kita bucked. "Your man called my people and said you needed four bricks of the good-good. With a stone-cold grimace, she unzipped the suitcase, removed its contents, and set the items down on the table, never removing her eyes from Dollar. He stared her down just the same.

"Let me see what you got." He motioned for the masseuse to take five.

"Let me see the money, my nigga," Kenya jumped in, not missing a beat.

Dollar liked these fiery bitches, but he still gave them a hard time. "I'm Silver Dollar, baby!" He laughed. "I'm good for it."

"Look, I ain't trying to be rude or no shit like that, but we got better things to do with our time. Show me the money or we're out." Kita looked annoyed.

Auzzie looked like he could've shit a brick, but Dollar was amused.

"All right, little mama. Relax." He licked his lips before reaching toward the floor.

On cue, both Kita and Kenya pulled pistols, prepared to pop off if need be. Dollar was caught off guard, so he dropped the briefcase onto the table and raised his hands in surrender.

"Damn, I was only grabbing the money. Y'all bitches don't play."

"Open it," Kenya instructed Auzzie, who nervously stepped up to the table. After he fumbled with the combination lock on the briefcase, the lid popped open. There were three rows of crisp, stacked, rubber-banded money all the way across—forty thousand dollars to be exact. Kita grabbed three of the stacks and flipped through them all to make sure there were no imposters in the bunch. She wasn't one for taking losses.

"Is everything okay? Can I put my fuckin' hands down now?" Dollar asked.

"Here's your shit." Kita slid the bricks across the table, and Dollar smiled.

He was like a kid in a candy store. "Have some?" he asked after removing a blade from his pocket and slicing one of the packages open. His tongue moistened in anticipation of the narcotic since he hadn't had a fix in almost a week.

The girls watched as he tested the product like a professional, snorting a small line straight up his nostril. It was then that Kenya lost all respect for the icon. Now in her eyes, he was just a fuckin' junkie.

"Hot damn!" Dollar blinked several times. This was some of the best cocaine he'd had in a very long time. During his tours, he always made it a point to sample some of the best coke in each city. Luckily for him, his boy had put him on to these girls.

"Thank you, ladies." Auzzie smiled. He always felt accomplished when his client was happy with his fix.

"Yes," Dollar added with powder residue on his nose. "Thank you, ladies." He gave the girls thumbs up and snorted another line.

Kenya began dumping the money from the briefcase into their piece of luggage.

"How long are you all in town?" Kita asked as they followed Auzzie back to the elevator.

"Two days." He stopped and pushed the button. "I'll call you if we need more."

"More?" Kenya and Kita replied. They had just given Dollar enough dope for an army.

"What can I say?" Auzzie shrugged as the elevator arrived. "He has a big appetite."

"Damn, who knew Silver Dollar was a dope fiend?" Kenya asked once the elevator doors closed.

"Don't judge him. Remember, his problem is our profit!" Kita extended her fist and Kenya bumped it with hers.

Little did they know, their meeting with Silver Dollar had just put them in a whole other league. Celebrities shared many things with one another, like who had the killer coke, for instance. Every time there was a concert, stage play, or star-studded event in or around the city of Detroit, the girls would get a call to supply some big names in the entertainment industry. Things couldn't have gotten any better—or could they?

Chapter Seven

In the blink of an eye, two years passed, and the girls were still going strong. Their clientele had damn near tripled, and the money was practically coming in dump trucks. It was time for the girls to go legit and clean up some of their dirty money. Collectively, they all agreed on opening a chain of hair salons as the initial front business. After tossing around a few names, they voted on Detroit Dolls. None of the ladies knew a thing about hair or nails; however, they had grown up with plenty of girls who did.

A month earlier, Kenya had hosted interviews at each of the three locations. Stylists showed up in numbers and showed out in true Detroit fashion. After careful consideration, the girls hired twelve stylists and three nail techs. That night was the grand opening of the first location on Meyers and Seven Mile Road. All the stops had been pulled for the event. There was a red carpet, photographers, a strobe light out front, and WJLB 97.9 was broadcasting live.

"I can't believe we did this shit!" Alexis peered out of the tinted limousine glass. The line outside of the salon extended almost two blocks down. "Finally, a business my mother can be proud of," she said with a laugh. Diane, Alexis's mother, didn't approve one bit of the lifestyle her daughter had chosen. However, she always allowed her children to make their own choices, be it good or bad.

"I know, right?" Kenya squealed. She beamed with a sense of accomplishment. It felt good to see something she had a hand in creating getting so much shine.

"Let's do this, ladies." Kita stepped out of the limo with her girls in tow. The crowd of family, friends, and supporters met them with a barrage of applause. Standing at the door to greet them were their mothers.

"We're so proud of you three." Jackie handed them all a pink carnation. Behind her smile was a combination of admiration and a twinge of sorrow. She wished her son was there to see the woman Kita had become. She knew Marlowe would've been proud.

"Thank you," Kita, Alexis, and Kenya replied in unison before Helen, Kenya's mother, went down the line and passed out hugs.

"This place is beautiful!" Diane wiped a tear from her eye as someone handed Kita a microphone.

"Thank you all for coming out to support us, our new salon, and our awesome team of stylists." She addressed the crowd and handed the mic over.

"It feels amazing to have a business in a community we love so much," Kenya added before passing the mic to Alexis.

"Now, let's go party!" Alexis waved the crowd inside to see all the hard work they had put into their salon.

Detroit Dolls hosted a color scheme of red and white with black accents. The 1,800-square-foot salon housed posh pieces of furniture, valuable wall art, as well as a six-foot fish tank. It was placed inside of the wall dividing the waiting area from the styling stations. Speaking of hair stations, those took the cake, with leather reclining chairs that massaged and mirrors lining the ceiling. The floor was custom made with marble tile to match the décor. The trio had spared no expense on their first baby, and it showed. The place was absolutely gorgeous.

As the guests waited for the miniature hair show to take place, they were served champagne and hors d'oeuvres. Kita was about to take a seat when the finest man she had ever laid eyes on tapped her shoulder.

"Hello, I'm Rico Richardson, a reporter from Channel 2. You're Markita Jones, right? I believe I spoke with you about giving us a brief interview." His teeth were perfectly aligned, and Kita was taken aback by the tall, baby-faced stranger, but she didn't let it show.

"Yes, I'm Markita." She smiled politely. "If you're ready for the interview, we can head right this way." Kita ushered the well-dressed man to the back of the salon, near one of the styling stations. With a quick wave, she caught the attention of her friends, who came over and joined her.

"Ladies, I'm Rico Richardson with Channel 2 News. Can I get a quick interview?"

"You can have whatever you like," Kenya teased.

Everyone laughed before the cameraman handed the microphone to Rico and counted them down for recording. The interview only lasted five minutes, but the impression he left on Kita was long-lasting. Going against her better judgment, she'd given him her phone number and prayed like hell he'd call.

The next day, Kita was still on cloud nine. She was extremely happy with the grand opening because they'd secured more than a dozen new clients. Today, the stylists and nail techs would actually begin working, or so she thought.

"Hello?" she sang into the phone. The number was foreign to her; therefore, she thought it could've been Rico.

"Hey, Kita, it's Chrissy." She was the manager at the salon. The tone in her voice was concerning.

"What's wrong?" Kita pondered over the millions of things it could've been, like loss of power or no hot water.

"I think you need to get down here." Chrissy's voice was unsteady. "There are two unwanted guests here refusing to leave until they speak with the owner," she whispered.

"Call the police!" Kita was frustrated. Chrissy needed to learn how to handle things without always calling her.

"They are the police."

"Okay. I'll be there in twenty minutes." Without hesitation, Kita ended the call and put on her shoes. On the way to the shop, Kita put in a call to her lawyer to keep him on standby, and then she called her girls.

Her stomach fluttered when she pulled up to the door of the salon. She didn't know why the police were there, but sure as shit, a squad car was parked in front. After calming herself, she hopped out and entered her place of business.

"What's up?" she asked aloud. Chrissy was standing with her arms folded. Both of the officers were sitting on her expensive salon chairs.

"Thank you for keeping us company, little lady, but you're excused." One of the cops dismissed Chrissy before addressing Kita. "This is a nice little spot you got here." Though he was smiling, something about him made her uneasy.

"What can I do for you gentlemen?"

"My name is Officer Douglas. My partner is Officer Brown. We're the welcoming committee." Officer Douglas stood from his seat.

"Welcoming committee?" Kita doubted this was true.

"You see," he began with a New York accent, "when new businesses open up in this neighborhood, we come to welcome you and remind you of the rules."

"Rules?" Kita folded her arms and shifted her weight to one foot.

"Yeah, the rules. No double parking to unload your vehicle. No loud noise after nine at night." He paused. "And don't forget to pay your association fees."

"That's the most important rule," his partner chimed in.

"What fees?" Kita snapped. This dude was talking like the salon was a condo instead of a place of business.

"See, when you open up shop on this block, you're responsible for paying three thousand a week in association fees. These fees protect you from vandalism, theft, and fire damage."

"No, thank you. I have insurance." Kita was about to show these lunatics the door.

"Sweetheart, these fees are non-negotiable. You gotta pay me to make money on my block." The officer was done being nice.

"I don't know who you think you are, but I ain't paying you shit!" Spit flew from Kita's lip she was so mad.

"Don't get beside yourself. I would hate to see a pretty little thing like you come up missing."

"What the fuck is that supposed to mean?" Kita was seconds away from going off the hinges.

"It means if you don't pay us, you will regret it." Officer Douglas nodded at his partner. "We'll be back on Friday to collect. You ladies have a good week."

"Are you going to pay him?" Chrissy came from behind the counter when she knew the cops were gone.

"I ain't paying shit!" Kita meant that, too.

These niggas don't know who they fucking with! she thought.

In honesty, the cops knew exactly who Markita, Alexis, and Kenya were. The girls had been on their radar for quite some time. The girls' budding empire was gaining a lot of attention on the streets, both good and bad. If Officer Douglas and his partner didn't get their cut of the salon profit, they would surely be back with warrants and handcuffs.

Chapter Eight

Kita watched from the window as the cops pulled away. She grabbed her phone to dial Alexis, but it started ringing.

"Hello?" she answered with an attitude. Her mood had definitely been spoiled.

"Hey, Markita, it's Rico. Are you busy?" The mellow, baritone voice sent chills down the nape of Kita's neck.

With a smile, she replied, "No, what's up?"

"I wanted to ask if you could meet me for lunch this afternoon."

"Um, sure." Kita blushed with excitement.

"I'm filling in today for the afternoon anchor before my shift at six. Do you mind coming to the station?" He hoped she would say yes because he had already placed a small catered order to be delivered at one.

"No, I don't mind as long as you plan on giving me a tour." Kita sat down in one of the styling chairs and swiveled in circles.

"Girl, I'll give you VIP treatment." He laughed. "See you at one."

"Okay, bye." Kita hit END on the phone.

"Damn. Was that the reporter?" Kenya turned Kita's chair around. She and Alexis had been eavesdropping.

"Why are you all up in my business?"

"Dude got you open already?" Alexis added her two cents.

"Anyway." Kita smacked her lips. "Y'all just missed two police officers who made it their business to demand three thousand dollars a week to run our salon on this block."

"Three thousand!" Kenya and Alexis said in unison.

"You heard me." Kita nodded.

"What did you say?" Alexis asked.

"I told them not to hold their breath, in so many words."

"What did they say?" Kenya asked.

"They said they would hate to see me come up missing." Kita looked from Kenya to Alexis. "How do y'all want to play this?"

"I ain't giving up no bread." Alexis shook her head.

Kenya nodded. "I agree. Just like you said a while back, Kita, if we roll over and take it, then every Tom, Dick, and Harry will try to hustle us." Kenya recalled the event in the projects. Kita had been adamant about standing their ground and not letting the niggas who robbed them get away with it. They handled that shit, and it had proved to be the best move they made. As females in a male-dominated industry, they constantly had to assert themselves, and this situation was no different. "I say fuck the police!" Kenya chanted, and the others agreed.

After putting the salon business to rest, Kita had just enough time to change, apply makeup, and flat-iron her hair. It was a few minutes before one when she pulled up to the news station. The guard asked who she was there to see. When she dropped Rico's name, he winked. Kita didn't know what that meant, but he lifted the gate and let her pass. She was about to call Rico to find out where to go after she parked, but she could see him standing out front, carrying a bouquet of flowers.

"Are these for me?" She blushed.

"Of course." He smiled. "My mother always told me a gentleman greets his lady with flowers."

"Your lady?" Kita smirked.

"Well, not yet, but just watch." He handed over the flowers then went to open the door. Rico was dressed in a custom gray Italian suit. It was tailored to fit every muscle on his body. Kita wanted to run a hand across his chest but restrained herself.

"This place is fascinating. How long have you worked here?" As they walked down the narrow corridor, she glanced at pictures of other reporters along with celebrities that had made guest appearances. Ironically, several of them were clients of hers.

"I've been on the air for six months. I was an entry-level journalist for three years prior, though." Rico led Kita into the company boardroom. He didn't have a private office yet; this was the best he could do.

Once inside, he pulled her chair out as she marveled over the feast before her. There were lobster tails, crab cakes, coleslaw, and a baked potato.

"How did you know I like seafood?" Kita grinned.

"I'm a journalist. It's my job to investigate."

"Good one." Kita giggled. "Thank you. Everything looks amazing."

"I wish I could've taken you out to a restaurant, though." Rico removed his suit jacket then tucked a handkerchief into his button-down shirt. Although he always kept an extra wardrobe in the car, he didn't want to mess up what he was wearing.

"This is perfect." Kita dove right into her plate. The girl loved food and was far from a shy eater.

Over lunch, they talked nonstop. Rico told her he was an only child, had gone to Eastern Michigan, and that his father had recently suffered a stroke. He was such an open book that Kita felt bad for not divulging half as much information about herself. How could she? However, Rico didn't seem to mind. Afterward, he took her on the VIP tour as promised. She got to meet a few of the top reporters and played around at the weather board.

Before long, it was time for Rico to go on the air. From the wing, she watched him do his thing. She could tell he really loved his job. He was a natural at it, sort of the way she was natural at pushing weight. Just the thought of that alone reminded her they came from different worlds. She then began second-guessing why a man like him could even be into a girl like her. He was polished and refined; she was from the ghetto.

Unbeknownst to her, Rico had fallen in love with her the day he first laid eyes on her, and it wouldn't have mattered to him what she did for a living or where she came from.

Chapter Nine

From that day forward, Rico did everything in his power to make Markita his lady. He spoiled her with his attention, lavish gifts, and random trips whenever time allowed. Quickly, they became a couple, and Jackie loved him to death. His mother, on the other hand, was a different story. She wanted Rico to return the hood rat back to the hood immediately. As time went on, his devotion to Kita and her devotion to him proved to be enough. They loved each other intensely; it was only right to move to the next step.

"It's almost midnight," Rico whispered into Kita's ear. It was New Year's Eve. The women had rented out a ballroom at the Rooster Tail for an elaborate celebration with close friends and family. Although the place was packed, the couple preferred to nestle up in a corner and pretend they were alone.

"I'm glad I get to bring in the new year with you." Kita planted a wet kiss on her man.

"Get a fuckin' room," Alexis teased. She had been drinking since eight, so by now she was wasted.

"Kita, if it's okay with you, I want to spend every new year together." Rico smiled.

"No problem, baby. I'll put it on my calendar." She laughed.

"I'm serious. I want to spend the rest of my life with you!" Rico had to scream the words because the crowd began yelling.

"Ten! Nine! Eight! Seven!"

"I'm not going anywhere!" Kita yelled back.

"Five! Four! Three!" the crowd continued.

"I'm not going anywhere either, so let's make it official!" Rico removed a Cartier box from his pocket and dropped to one knee. "Will you marry me?"

"Happy New Year!" The crowd drowned out Kita's answer, but the tears indicated that she had said yes. This was the best surprise she had ever received. By the smiling faces around the room, it was apparent that everyone was in on it. Nothing could've killed Kita's vibe that night.

The next day, however, was a completely different story.

"How could a year that started so right go wrong so fuckin' fast?" Kita asked no one in particular. She had received another emergency call from the salon. It was the third one that day. Chrissy informed her that the cops had made it a point to stop in every day and harass customers for the past week. The salon was losing business, and Kita couldn't have that.

Pulling up to the shop, she grunted. There was a big-ass police car double-parked in front of the door. Officer Douglas was writing a lady in a black Cadillac a ticket.

"This is some bullshit!" the lady spat.

"What's the problem?" Kita asked.

"It appears your customer parked at this meter for two hours instead of the hour and thirty minutes she paid for." Officer Douglas laughed.

"So, now you're the meter maid?" Kita was irritated.

"I'll be whatever I have to be until I get my fuckin' money," Douglas countered.

"I already told you not to expect shit from us." Kita stood her ground.

Douglas put the ticket into the lady's car before heading toward the salon. "You know what?" He stopped and looked back at his partner. "I think we should call our friends down at the DEA and tell them to come get a makeover here at the salon."

"I'm sure they would love to snag three dope dealers and get a mani/pedi at the same damn time," his partner joked, but his words weren't lost on Kita. She was smart enough to read between the lines.

"Look." She raised her hands in surrender. This was a battle she didn't want to fight. For years, the trio had managed to stay under the radar, and she wanted to keep it that way. "I'll get your money to you on Friday," she relented.

"Make sure you add ten grand on top of that for our troubles." Officer Douglas fist-bumped with his partner on the way back to their car.

Kita wanted to scream but held back. Retrieving her cell phone, she was prepared to call the girls, but a text came through from her mother.

Where are you?

"Shit!" Kita had totally forgotten she promised her mother they would start wedding planning that day. Since the proposal, Jackie hadn't wasted anytime getting into the details.

Quickly, Kita replied, On the way.

Several hours and event spaces later, they had selected and secured Kita's wedding venue. The place was grand and upscale with a spiral staircase, several oversized chandeliers, and the ballroom was magnificent. The venue was every girl's dream; however, Kita wasn't as excited as she should've been.

After hitting the locks on her whip, Kita got in and laid her head on the steering wheel.

"What's wrong?" Jackie asked before her daughter started up the engine. She noticed that Kita had been extremely quiet that day, although she was as happy as a kid in the candy store. From the moment Rico had called to ask Jackie for her daughter's hand in marriage, she had started planning for the big day. Besides, it was a welcomed distraction from thoughts about Marlowe.

"Nothing. I'm good. My stomach is just upset." Usually when this happened, Kita was having a premonition or her period was coming. Either one was bad news.

"Well, what does it feel like?" Jackie smiled like she knew something Kita didn't.

"It doesn't feel good, so why are you smiling?" Kita rolled.

"When was the last time you had your cycle?"

"I don't know. A while ago, I guess." Kita tried to remember, but she couldn't. Maybe it was a few weeks ago? Maybe it was a month ago? So much was going on that Kita barely kept up with it.

"Baby, have you been nauseous in the morning?" Jackie was so excited that she could barely contain herself.

"As a matter of fact, I have." Just the other day, Kita had met Rico for breakfast and damn near threw up at the table before even taking one bite. She thought it was the Chinese from the night before, but now it was all making sense.

"Child, I believe you're pregnant!" Jackie slapped the dashboard. "Let's go get a test." She was elated about the possibility of a grandchild. Before Kita could tell her mother to slow down, the phone buzzed.

"What's up, Alexis?"

"Somebody took my fucking sister!" she screamed.

"What do you mean? Somebody took Talia? Took her where?" Kita looked up at Jackie, who was all ears.

"My mother called and said she didn't come home from school today. We went up to the school, and they said she never showed up." Alexis was crying hysterically.

Kita felt awful. "Calm down, boo. Do you think Talia has a boyfriend or something?" She knew Talia was going on fourteen. Maybe she was just being fast and skipping school.

"No." Alexis sniffed. "I talked to a few of her friends. They said on the way to school this morning, she realized she left her project at home, so she turned around and headed back. They haven't seen her since."

"Did you call the police?"

"Yeah, but it was no use. She has to be missing for forty-eight hours before we can formally file a report." Alexis blew her nose. "Do you know what can happen in forty-eight fuckin' hours?"

"I know, boo." Kita wished she was there in person to comfort her friend. God only knew what she and her family were going through. "I'm going to drop my mother off, and I'll be right over." Silently, Markita prayed nothing happened to Talia before they could find her. Putting the pregnancy test on hold, Kita dropped Jackie off and sped over to comfort her girl.

Chapter Ten

The clock was just striking seven when Kita pulled up to Alexis's brand-new condo. Kenya's Nissan was parked in the driveway, which meant she was there too. Before Kita could cut the engine, her phone began to buzz. It was a text message from a foreign number with a picture attached. Kita's first instinct was to delete the message without reading it; she hated spam. However, curiosity got the best of her, and she opened it. It was a picture of Talia, gagged and bound to a chair.

"Oh my God!" She grabbed her chest. Although Talia didn't appear to be hurt, a tear gathered in the corner of Markita's eye. She wondered what the young girl was going through and if she was scared. The text below the picture was demanding $100,000 by midnight, or Talia would die.

Quickly, Kita grabbed her things and flew into Alexis's condo. She must've gotten the text as well, because she was holding her phone and sobbing uncontrollably.

"Don't worry. We're going to get her back." Kita patted her friend's shoulder.

"What if we get them the money and they still kill her?" Alexis had a valid point.

Kita shook her head. "You can't think like that."

"I'll call the number and see if I can get someone on the phone." Kenya hit SEND and placed the call on speaker. The phone rang three times before the call was answered.

"You must be calling about my fuckin' money." It sounded like the person on the other end was using a voice disguiser.

"You will get your money, but how do I know the girl is safe?" Kenya eyed Alexis while waiting for the answer. They could hear some shuffling before someone spoke again. This time it was Talia.

"Is my sister there?" Her voice shook like she had been crying.

"I'm right here," Alexis yelled. "Are you okay? Did they hurt you?"

"I'm okay. I'm just scared." The phone made another shuffling sound, and then the robot was back on the phone.

"I want my money in large bills. Bring it in a garbage bag to the school yard at Beaubien Middle School. When you get there, leave it in the middle of the field and leave," he instructed. "My shit better be there on time, too!"

"Where will my sister be?" Alexis screamed.

"Once the money has been collected, I will call you with a location to pick her up from."

Click! Just like that, he ended the call.

Alexis slammed her fist down hard on the glass table, causing it to crack from edge to edge. "That nigga is going to kill my sister."

"At this point, all we can do is what he asked." Kenya sighed.

"She's right, boo," Kita agreed. "I'd rather give it to him than to hold out and see what happens."

"I don't have that kind of money," Alexis admitted.

"What do you have?" Kita had always scolded her about not saving money, but tonight was not the time for a lecture.

"I got about ten Gs in a safe." Alexis had blown through countless stacks of money on unimportant things. Now that she needed it and didn't have it, she saw why Kita always saved for a rainy day.

"What about you?" Kita looked at Kenya.

"I probably got thirty." Kenya really had at least $80,000 saved, but she was not about to shell that much bread out for someone who wasn't related to her.

"What the fuck have y'all been doing with y'all money?" Kita was pissed. The fact that they were short meant she had to cough up $60,000 of her hard-earned money. It wasn't an easy decision, but she couldn't let Talia's death fall on her shoulders.

"I swear I'll pay y'all back." Alexis sniffed.

"You're damn right you'll pay me back!" Kita knew this bitch was crazy if she thought she didn't want her money back. They were friends and all, but money was money.

After putting their money together in a duffle bag, the girls headed to the drop-off location. The park was dark and deserted. They tried to see if anyone was lurking in the shadows, but it was of no use. Alexis wanted to stay and wait, but her girls advised her that the kidnapper probably had eyes on them too. It was best for Talia's sake that they head back home to wait for the call.

It was a silent ride. Everyone feared the worst, although no one said so. To break the ice, Kita blurted out, "I think I'm pregnant."

"Are you serious?" Kenya wrapped her arms around her friend as she drove.

Alexis was in the back seat. She wanted to be happy, but she couldn't get in the mood. Kita understood, so she didn't take it personally.

"Have you told Rico yet?" Kenya asked.

"Not until I take a test."

"I feel so special. You gave us the exclusive," Kenya squealed.

"Since we're talking, I just wanted y'all to know that in six months, I'm out." Leaving the game had been on Kita's mind for a long time now. Rico had come into her life and changed her outlook on things. There was so much more to living than selling dope. Sure, it put money in your pocket, but at what cost? More money almost always came with more problems. Kita was tired of hustling. She was ready to live the square life with her man and now their child.

"You're leaving?" Now Kenya had an attitude.

Alexis was taken aback as well, but still she remained silent.

"Yup, in six months I'm done," Kita replied.

"How are you going to leave us hangin', though?"

"Kenya, I didn't plan this. It just happened." Kita understood her friend's frustration, but it was what it was.

The remainder of the trip back to Alexis's house was mute, just like it had started. Kita wished she would've left it that way before opening her big mouth. Things were already tense enough.

Within thirty minutes, they were back at the condo, sitting around the phone.

"Why aren't they calling?" Alexis tossed her cell phone across the room.

"Maybe you should try to call back," Kita told Alexis. When she went to grab the phone, the sound of screeching tires outside caught their attention. They all bolted to the door to find Talia sprawled out on the front lawn. Aside from a few bumps and bruises, thank God, she was fine.

"Thank you, Jesus!" Alexis screamed, dropping to her knees.

"Are you okay?" Kenya asked the shaken little girl.

"Fuck that!" Kita snapped. Now that Talia was back home, only one thing mattered. "Who is this nigga?" Kita was angry that someone had the audacity to kidnap one of their own.

"Did you see his face?" Alexis questioned her baby sister, who was obviously upset.

"No, I didn't see his face." Talia shook her head. "But I did hear someone call him Breeze."

The trio looked at one another as the revelation that their old connect was responsible hit them like a ton of bricks. After getting Talia back home with Diane, it didn't take long for the girls to agree that Breeze had to pay, and that he had to pay that night!

The first stop of the evening was to one of their rented storage units, where they loaded up on guns and ammo. It was on! Each girl had blood in her eyes. Their adrenaline was on overdrive. Kita hadn't felt a rush like this since she bodied Man-Man. Although she tried to suppress the feeling, she loved the way a gun felt in her hand. She felt powerful and in control.

The second and final stop of the night was to Breeze's.

"Let's do this." Kita slid a ski mask over her face before securing two guns into the waist of her skinny jeans. With her friends in tow, they headed toward

Giants, a popular after-hours spot he was known to frequent.

Upon entrance into the petite space with dim lighting, all eyes were on them. However, only one pair of eyes mattered. Breeze was sitting at a table in the back when he spotted the masked intruders.

"Fuck!" He tried to get up and run, but it was too late.

BLAH! The first shot came from Kita's gun. It had caught him in the shoulder. Blood splattered across the wall behind him. *BLAH!* The second shot was from Kenya. It ripped through his torso.

"You thought you could cross me and get away with it, nigga?" Alexis barked.

"Look—" Breeze didn't have time to explain before the hot lead from her gun exploded in his face. The flash of bright fire was the last thing he ever saw.

In a matter of seconds, the trio left just as fast as they'd come. The best part was that no one even knew it was them, or so they thought. Unbeknownst to the ladies, the young man who'd been playing pool followed behind them to the door. He watched as they snatched off their masks and pulled away. His name was DeAngelo. He was Breeze's younger brother. Lo didn't know why the women had just killed his brother in cold blood, but he vowed to exact revenge as soon as the opportunity presented itself.

Chapter Eleven

They say you reap what you sow, and lately Kita had the feeling that God's wrath was coming for the things she'd done. Although months had gone by and they'd gotten away with murder for the second time, her soul hadn't been right lately. Both men deserved what they got, but the girls should've let God handle them. Kita once heard a pastor say, "Wrong is wrong, even if done for the right reason." Instead of trying to settle the score, they should've left it alone. In the street, retaliation is a vicious cycle that never ends, and the families on both sides lose.

After killing their old supplier, the women unintentionally drifted off into their own lanes. Alexis began spending more time at home, helping raise her sister. Kenya continued running the streets, and Markita started going back to church like she'd done as a child with her grandmother. It was a place she found peace and refuge.

Believing in a higher power, Kita knew she would ultimately be judged for the things she was guilty of; however, she wondered if she still had time to seek forgiveness. Her burdens were beginning to weigh her down, and she was tired. It was time for a change, and she knew it, so the night before, she had purchased a one-way ticket to Africa. She needed a new start, and what better place than the motherland to do that?

Things had been rough in Detroit, and she knew nothing was going to change. The game was becoming more treacherous. The bond with her friends seemed different, and although her relationship with Rico was still intact, she felt guilty every day for keeping secrets from him. That night, she planned on telling him as much as she could about her life, with the hopes that he would be willing to look past her lies and leave for Africa with her.

"Kita, did you hear me?" Alexis snapped her long, thin fingers. "I said I bet Kenya five thousand dollars you have the baby on August twelfth," she said while counting a large stack of money. "As a matter of fact, I bet another five thousand it's going to be a boy." This time she slammed the money down on the dining room table, disturbing Kita from her somber thoughts.

"Girl, bye!" Kenya hollered from the galley kitchen. "I bet you twenty thousand Kita have a baby girl on August twentieth." She countered the wager.

"I can't believe what I'm hearing. Y'all bitches are something else." Kita laughed lightly, unwilling to believe her friends had nothing else better to do with their time and money than to place bets on her child's gender and due date.

"You act like we're hurting for cash over here," Alexis stated as she continued thumbing through her wad of money.

"You will be hurting for cash pretty soon if you keep doing dumb shit with it."

"Ain't nobody trying to hear that." Kenya grabbed a piece of fried chicken from the platter. "Yolo!"

"Look, Kita, you need to get out of your funk and get in on the bet." Alexis turned to face Markita, who was sitting with her feet up on the couch and her head on the armrest. She'd been sulking all day, and Alexis was annoyed.

"I'm not in a funk. I'm good." With a modest smile, Kita tried to shrug off the ill vibes. Today was a good day, or at least should've been, since her friends had gone out of their way and had planned a baby shower for the new bundle of joy growing in her womb. Markita's baby was expected to make an entrance into the world in three months, and she was ecstatic. She couldn't wait to become a mother, and it didn't matter what the sex of the child was, as long as it was healthy.

"Why are you so quiet then?" With a deck of cards, Kenya walked over and took a seat at the black marble dining table across from Alexis. They were about to get a game of Spades in before the guests arrived for the shower.

"Honestly, I don't know." Markita sat up and sighed. "I just feel like something bad is about to happen."

"Girl, bye!" Alexis burst out laughing, but when she saw that Kita was serious, she stopped abruptly.

"What exactly do you think is about to happen?" Kenya never looked up while dealing out the cards. She knew her friend was always the paranoid one in the group, especially now that she was pregnant.

"I can't explain it. It's just a feeling." Kita knew her friends thought she was crazy.

"Girl, ain't nothing going to happen to us." Alexis shook her head adamantly.

It was no use having a conversation with people who wouldn't take you seriously, so Kita felt no need to argue.

"We got money, we got guns, and we got each other's back," Alexis stated as a matter of fact.

"That's right!" Kenya reached out and gave her girl a high-five. "Y'all my bitches until they lay me down."

Normally, Kita would've joined in on the moment, but she wasn't feeling it.

"So, you ain't down with us no more?" Alexis eyed Kita suspiciously.

"I'll always be down with y'all." Kita mustered a smile, but truth be told, her days for riding with her girls were over. Now that she was about to become a mom and a wife, she had to leave the street life alone. Sure, the money was good, but what about the consequences? Kita was tired of looking over her shoulders and living in fear. She was ready to enjoy life the right way, with her man and their child.

"So, if we wanted to flip one more shipment, you would be down, right?" Kenya asked after slapping an ace onto the table and taking the book.

"I already told you I'm out of the game." Kita raised her hands in surrender and shook her head. No matter how much her friends begged and pleaded, the answer would still be no. "What do I look like selling dope at six months pregnant?" Kita made a show of rubbing her belly.

"You would look like a pregnant dope dealer," Alexis joked.

"A fly, pregnant dope dealer," Kenya added.

"I'm out!" The women had been in the drug game for over five years strong.

"Why you gotta' leave us hangin', though?" Kenya was a little annoyed when her friend chose to leave the game. Although she had more money than she probably knew what to do with, she hated to see the cash stop.

"I told y'all six months ago that I was leaving. Don't start acting like I sprung this shit on you yesterday." The minute Kita had read the positive test results from the home pregnancy test, she knew it was time to gracefully bow out. The game had been good to her. She stacked her money carefully and had a nice nest egg to fall back on. If her girls hadn't been as frugal, it wasn't her fault.

"Kita, I understand why you're walking away. Trust me, I do." Alexis looked through her hand for the best card to pull. "What I don't understand is why me and Kenya have to shut down shop too."

"I told you I don't have anything to do with that." Markita stood from the couch. "My connect is adamant about only doing business with me, and y'all know that." If it were up to Markita, she would've put her girls on in a heartbeat; however, her suppliers, the Lopez brothers, kept their circle air tight and preferred to hand select who they did business with. Kita knew the same way they found her, they'd find Kenya and Alexis if they wanted to continue working with them.

"But we've been buying coke from *your* connect for years. That shit has to mean something!" Kenya was frustrated. Silently, she wondered if Kita was holding out on purpose. It was funny how the game had them second-guessing each other.

"Look, bitch, don't be raising your voice with me. It is what it is, and that's it. That's the *last* shipment." She pointed to the boxes neatly in the corner. "Once we sell that shit and split our ends, it's over." Kita grabbed her cell phone and headed down the hallway. She retreated into one of the guestrooms in Alexis's townhouse and slammed the door. She hated to fight with her friends, especially over something she couldn't change.

As soon as she entered the quaint spare bedroom, her cell phone started ringing. A quick glance at the screen let her know her boo was calling. With a smile, she said, "Hey, baby, how are you?"

"What's up, beautiful?" Rico's rich voice made Kita's heart melt.

"You always know when to call me, don't you?" She took a seat on the bed covered by several throw pillows.

"What's wrong?"

"I just got into it with Kenya, that's all." As Markita spoke, her eyes roamed every inch of the wall in the bedroom. Alexis had various pictures of the three friends all over the place. Some of the pictures were taken at the club. A few of the pictures were taken on the block, and several were pictures in class, back when they were in middle school and high school. Kita had to laugh at the hairstyles and clothing they wore. If nothing else was apparent, the women had definitely come a very long way since then.

"What did y'all get into it about?" Rico didn't really care to know about the cat fight; however, Markita always complained about him never listening to her, so he used the opportunity to prove her wrong.

"It was nothing major. Just business stuff." Kita was vague with her answers.

"Baby, I'm sure whatever it is will blow over soon." Rico spoke into his cell phone while Andy, the producer, wired him with a microphone. It was almost time for his segment at six o'clock.

"Five minutes, everybody!" Heather, the stage manager, yelled. "I need all phones off now!"

"Hey, baby, it's almost showtime. Let me hit you right back." Rico ended the call abruptly without a goodbye.

Kita started to call back and make a fuss, but the doorbell rang, indicating that her first shower guests had arrived. Standing from the bed, she walked over to the window and peeped out to see who it was. From her position, though, she couldn't see anything.

"I bet you that's Noel," she said aloud to no one as she put on a smile and walked toward the door. Her old friend, Noel Parker, was known for being prompt.

The minute she entered the hallway, shots rang out, confirming that her worst fears were about to come true.

Epilogue

"I guess it's true what they say: bad bitches do die slow!" Alexis stood over Markita's cold body as she faded in and out of consciousness on the concrete, where she lay riddled with bullets. "Kenya took a whole five minutes, but your ass is going on ten." Looking down at her blood-stained watch, she spat, "Just go ahead and die already!"

"Why did you do this?" Kita hated to waste any ounce of breath she had left, but she needed to know why her best friend would do her so dirty.

"Well, I figured since this was our last pack, it wasn't no need in splitting that shit three ways," Alexis admitted. "I need all that coke to myself to make up for the loss I'm going to take when I no longer have *your* supplier supplying me." She made air quotes to be sarcastic.

"Were you behind the Talia thing, too?" Markita coughed. She was beginning to put two and two together. Alexis had scammed them out of their money as well as their coke.

"Oh, yeah, that was me." She laughed wickedly. "How genius was it to have my own sister kidnapped for ransom? You bitches came through, though, and my pockets appreciated that shit."

"What about Bree . . . Breeze?" By now Markita was so cold she was trembling.

"I set that nigga up to take the fall for the whole thing." Alexis smiled at how easily her plan had come together. Unfortunately, it didn't last long.

POP! A single bullet to the back of her head blew half her face off. Instantly, her lifeless body fell on top of Kita. Standing in her place was DeAngelo, Breeze's little brother, holding a nickel-plated 9 mm. He'd heard about the baby shower through one of the girls he used to mess with and decided tonight would be the night. Fortunately for him, when he'd gotten to the condo, someone had already started the job.

"I'm . . . sor . . . sorry," Kita whispered as tears rolled down her face. There was no use in begging for her life. She knew DeAngelo was about to seal her fate the same way they'd done his brother. That was the law of the streets.

"Fuck!" DeAngelo paced back and forth for a second until he finally tossed the hood of his jacket over his head and ran away. He'd come there tonight with every intention of killing all three women, but for some reason, he couldn't bring himself to shoot Kita. Maybe because she was pregnant, or maybe it was Alexis's admission of guilt. Whatever it was, it made him decide to leave her be—but it didn't matter. Not even two minutes after he disappeared into the night, Markita lost her fight with the reaper, and just like that, the Get Money Girls were no more.

About the Author

Detroit native India Williams has always had a passion for literature and language arts. After being challenged by her friends in 2010 to write and release her own novel, she penned *Dope, Death and Deception*. Instantly, it became a hit within the urban community. In a male-dominated industry, readers loved her strong female lead and out-of-the box story-line. The response was so overwhelming that it ignited a flame in India. In 2011, she created Grade A Publications, her own publishing company, where she promised readers nothing but five-star bangers.

Not one to disappoint, India went on to pen twelve novels, which include *Gangstress* and *The Real Hoodwives of Detroit*. These series were deemed "hood classics" by the readers and earned India the national bestsellers rank several times on Amazon, as well media attention on local radio and television stations.

In the years following India's arrival into the literary world, she has worked as a creative writer for T. Styles, *Mean Girl* magazine, released an audio book, penned two short stories, and has been featured in five anthologies along with some of the industry's vets. With hopes of seeing her work on the big screen, India continues to put everything she has into all of her creations. Her goal is to one day be a household name!

Mental

by

Brandie Davis

Chapter 1

"I told them. I warned them. I told them they would not approve. They would be dismissed the second they stepped foot here, and chaos would break out." Laverne twisted in her seat, fighting for a comfortable position. After a few turns, she found her comfort zone. "I told them to wear their human suits; they could walk amongst us without a problem, but nooooo . . . they came all green and four-armed, thinking they could just fit right in. Damn, aliens always think they know it all."

Laverne flung one leg over the other. Tightly they crossed as her attention jumped to the instruments playing in her head. After the orchestra played their tune, she pushed herself up. From underneath her, her fingers searched for her forbidden item and, within seconds, exposed a metal nail file. To the far right side of the patients' recreational room was the nurse's desk, a few feet from the exit. They had a perfect view of all the patients and the craziness that resided inside. Their constant presence and ongoing stares made a number of patients, in need of help, feel like caged animals being watched from behind glass.

The flat screen smart television was nailed to the wall, giving the place a hint of class, and the shiny chessboard positioned in the far corner of the room made it possible for patients to think in peace and not be disturbed by the occasional songstress and nervous breakdown. A few books arranged alphabetically on the shelves by the authors' last names sat dustless. The arts and crafts table was supplied with patients' unfinished works, sprinkled with color and nature. The windows were small, oval, and pristine. The floor was scattered with blues and greens, which caused patients to kneel down, and with their fingers, trace its swirls. It was modern, unconventional, and certainly unheard of. It was a land where the mind could escape and recover from the days when therapy didn't go too well and homesickness found its way back into a person's thought process. For however long an individual was there, it was home—a pretty and mesmerizing place many fought to get into when in need of mental rescuing.

Nurse Adler stood draped over the desk, admiring pictures of one of the techs' newborn baby girls. When doctors weren't on site, the techs and orderlies reported to Adler. It was a welcomed atmosphere for the staff; they responded quite well to her upbeat, no nonsense professionalism that few nurses in the institution exhibited. A smile was stapled to her face, her head sweeping from left to right, scanning the room with urgency. An uncomfortable feeling surged through her senses, diverting her attention from the pictures and onto the floor. Her vision dived into Laverne, shaping her nails while having the occasional idle talk with her imaginary audience. Fixing her posture, Adler pushed the photographs across the desk; their thin, flat shape ice-skated on the wooden surface and cascaded in the new mother's lap.

"Laverne!" Adler hollered. Her voice squeaked throughout the room and banged against the furniture, which made it echo and travel far and wide. "How the hell do you keep getting things in here?" She snatched the nail file from Laverne, aggravation and pure wonder caked on her face.

The thin, seventy-year-old Caucasian woman turned away from Adler, her chin pointed North and her leg kicked up and down. "I keep telling you, it's the aliens. They give me whatever I want."

Adler was puzzled as to why she never understood Laverne's mumbled obscenities. After three four-letter words, Laverne looked down at Adler's hands, then up at her face. Laverne's gray eyes were young and expressive.

"Keep it," Laverne said. "You need it more than me." Folding her arms across her chest, she paid Adler no mind while giving her attention to the oval window inches from her. Gradually, the loss of her nail filer hopped out of her thoughts, and she looked at the woman sitting across from her.

"Tammy, how far is Earth from Mars? I know it's a long way, but if I have the aliens put a rush on my time-traveling machine, how much time do you think I will save?" Laverne looked at Tammy, but from the corner of her eye, she noticed Adler was back at the desk, laughing with the new mama tech about what new item she had confiscated from Laverne today.

Seconds later, she continued speaking with Tammy. "What do you say, Tammy? How much time do you think I will save?"

Tammy didn't answer. In fact, she never answered when Laverne asked her about aliens. Every day when in the patients' activity room, she sat across from Laverne, watching her and every other person's actions, but never did she speak. She only scouted for her next victim. Getting out of Peaceful wasn't her priority. That would happen soon. Her priority was getting back at predators and minding her business.

Tammy looked at Adler happily socializing, their eyes meeting after seconds of watching her. Tammy smiled, and Adler's joy folded. Adler couldn't stand working for Tammy. To her, Tammy snatched the sunshine out of whatever room she stepped in and replaced it with storm clouds. Adler whispered a few words to her co-workers then left the room, quickly removing herself from the tension. Tammy knew she despised of her making Peaceful into her meat market and Adler into another one of her workers forced into the occupation. Tammy chuckled, because if Adler didn't shape up, her organs would soon join her collection.

Tammy's gaze followed Adler as she stepped out of the room. Her large, thick box braids fell in front of her face and obstructed her view. The strands swayed back and forth, their jet-black hue shimmering against the lighting.

"You're just as fucked up as I am," Laverne proclaimed.

Tammy ignored her, and when Laverne pressed play on her excessive rambling, Tammy looked around to see a decrease in the room's population. Lost in the low number of people in an otherwise popular room and unaware of the time, Tammy heard a loud, deep voice tell her, "Ms. Ward, please come with me. You have a visitor."

Chapter 2

Hering was one of two orderlies whose main duties included caring for out of control patients. Peaceful Minds Psychiatric Hospital was tucked away in a secluded area surrounded by rows of hills and emerald green trees within the state of Pennsylvania. The institution was built in hopes of giving psychiatric hospitals a better reputation than the more stereotypical portrayal imagined by the public. Mental health services needed a new face, and Peaceful would be that face.

Tammy stood, her sweat pants and baggy short-sleeve shirt hanging off her thin frame. Hering stood in front of her. Facing the exit, he scanned his plastic badge and punched a code into the keypad for the door to open. Walking out, the pair was stopped by another door.

Before the door closed behind them, Tammy heard Laverne scream out, "Tell the aliens to sit tight! I'll be out there soon!"

There were four doors Hering had to deactivate in order to reach his destination. Normally, patients went into the visiting area together, but Hering purposely left her out of the group and escorted her alone. At the second door they reached, Hering took his time when entering the code.

"He's not happy," he told her, his fingers punching in numbers.

Tammy didn't comment. She only grabbed braids blocking her view and tied them together to the back of her head. The simple action created a transformation she'd done for the purpose of comfort versus style. They walked through the third door without a word being said.

Hering opened the last door, and the bright light from the visiting room splashed inside the doorway. Stainless steel furniture decorated the room, flashing Tammy back to a time when she used to frequent a particular diner on her free days. The buffed marble floors spit out sparks and glowed when the sunlight touched it. Thin dark blue stripes outlined the large room, and when Tammy stood in the doorway searching for her visitor, her fingertips rubbed the blue color seeped inside the building's cracks.

"He's in the back," Hering whispered. He pressed his badge against his palm, preparing to make his exit.

Tammy walked inside, observing the faces of family and friends. Guests eyed their loved ones and asked questions in order to dictate whether progress was being made and if their psyche was aligning with reality. It was a sad sight: the hope and anguish that filled their eyes, the response given by individuals whose progress remained stuck or declined each passing day. Forced cheerfulness sprayed across the faces of workers who stood by, supervising encouraged visitors to remain positive and help the member of their circle fight to find their way back into the lives they had lost track of.

Taking her time to head to her journey, Tammy never hid her nosiness. Her head dipped in every table she passed, and she took in every spoken word and formulated her own history between patient and guest. The world was one big book, a series of stories, and she wanted to know them all.

With only an hour for visitation, her brother's eyes dropped low, the irritation climbing inside his appearance while watching his sibling take her time and throw herself inside everyone else's business but her own. He cracked his knuckles, releasing the negative energy developing from his mind.

Pulling out the cold chair, Tammy sat comfortably. The dip in the seat seemed to fit her behind well and made her quickly adapt to the metal. Cory looked at the employee from Tammy's ward. He waited until he made his rounds around the semi-large room, ensuring everyone was on their best behavior and not trying to sneak unapproved items in the building.

Cory sat forward, trying to fix his face the best he could under the circumstances, and looked his older sister in the eye. There was no "How are you doing?" or "How do you feel?" or "How are they treating you?" or "Do you need anything?" There was no expression of any kind on his face.

His eyes bore through her like a laser through steel. "You took Ray out. Why the fuck did you take Ray out?"

Her prying eyes focused on her brother's slender face, trying to sort through his contempt. "Excuse me?"

Cory's eyes detoured, falling to the floor. They were no longer filled with disrespect and anger. Within an instant, his mind fell back in time to when he respected Tammy. Since they were teenagers, Tammy took care of Cory. Her wing covered him with the intention of making life seem more normal than it actually was. Their mother was bipolar, and her children never knew what they would get from her. She had her extreme highs and extreme lows, and it was depressing and confusing for children who knew nothing about the illness plaguing their mother.

Not knowing what to do to make her mother better, Tammy left it in her father's hands. During his wife's most troubling times, he took on the disorder as if it were his own and fought to make it right. Protecting her mother was out of Tammy's hands, but ensuring her younger brother didn't miss out on life was a challenge she felt capable of handling.

When their father took his wife to her appointments, or when he had her placed in mental hospitals, Tammy distracted Cory with trips to the park or whatever gifts her after-school job could afford. Their father was aware of how traumatizing that sort of situation could be on his children, but instead of ensuring they lived lives that were more befitting for children, he kept his focus on his wife. He reasoned that if he healed her disorder, everything else would fall into place.

Tammy put her own life on hold to concentrate on Cory. It was the sole reason why Cory respected her. Having a moment to himself to reflect, he took a deep breath to settle himself down.

Cory closed his eyes in an attempt to measure his words more carefully. "I'm sorry, but I need to know why you would make such a move and how."

"He was working with the enemy. He switched sides with the simple promise of dead presidents. Anyone who associates with the man trying to weasel in on my business is dead. And as for how I did it, you can do anything you put your mind to."

Cory's fists balled at his sides and red surfaced in his cheeks. "He was going to vouch for me, help make it so that I could sell my drug."

Tammy flung her arms onto the table, her head cocked to the right. "What are you talking about?"

Again, Cory took a deep breath, his ongoing ties with his emotions validating why even the ill could lead an illegal business better than him.

"I want to enter the drug business. Create my own drug that will become bigger than heroin, and all I need to do it is Baldwin." Cory tried not to sound fearful in expressing his desire for a change of pace. He practiced digging deep down within himself to formulate the courage Tammy had shown when it came to making tough decisions. He searched for the gene that pushed a person to fight when instincts told them it was better to give up and accept their position.

Tammy's lips poked out, her head nodding up and down while looking out the oval window at the deep green grass growing in the front yard. Steel benches lined the entrance, patients in need of air walked beside nurses, smiling at purple and blue flowers creating a pattern of beauty. Tammy planted her hands on the table and pushed herself up just enough for the furniture to support her upper body, and leaned forward.

"I must be crazier than you all think. Did I just hear you say that you want to work with the enemy, the reason why I'm in here? You want out of our business so that you can sell drugs? You want to be a dope boy?" Tammy laughed and fell back into her seat.

"You want to go from selling organs to selling drugs. What's wrong with this picture, Cory? You want to turn on me? Where's your loyalty?" She slammed the tip of her index finger into the table repeatedly, a need to release her frustration. She raised her voice just loud enough not to draw unwanted attention. "If this is what you want, they might as well make you my motherfucking roommate, because you lost your damn mind. No brother of mine will work with the enemy!"

For months, Cory had weighed his options on what he needed to do versus what he wanted to do. He wanted to pay his sister back for the life she gave him when her parents were too wrapped up in the bipolar disorder. Tammy kept the family intact when their mother succeeded with her suicide attempt and drove their father to become mute when Cory turned nineteen. So, using his career as a surgeon to illegally remove organs from the living and dead was the right thing to do.

Yet, two years into the organ harvesting business, Cory acknowledged needing to be in his own shadow. He did a majority of the work; he was the business, but Tammy was the commander-in-chief. Cory needed out. He needed a life he could call his own without the feeling of owing someone.

"If you would have just allowed Baldwin to harvest organs, this wouldn't be an issue. All he wanted was to expand from drugs to organs. There's enough to go around. But you started it. Once you got wind that he wanted in, you couldn't accept it and started killing his men."

Tammy leaned her elbows on the table and pointed her finger in his face. "He stepped on my toes when he woke up one day and thought he'd take a piece of my pie. There are rules to this shit, and he didn't follow them. He pushed his way in. No meeting, no nothing. So, I started killing. But I'll tell you one thing that will never happen." Tammy paused, seeing their hour was almost up and people were rushing to get in the last of their conversations. She got up, her chair screeching.

"You leaving?"

She walked away. She was the first to wait at the door that would lead her back to her world of make-believe. Seconds later, the orderly announced that everyone must disperse, starting with the patients. Some patients stood, saying farewell and walking to the line Tammy had started, while a few threw fits and latched onto loved ones, begging for them to take them home. Cory once again became uncomfortable. He feared what each patient he was surrounded by was capable of, including his sister.

Observing the chaos, he caught a glimpse of a young woman grabbing a chair, watching her hurl it toward the window behind him. He hit the floor, watching in horror as the red-haired, rosy-cheeked woman ran head first into the shatter-proof glass. Like a ball bouncing off the curb, her head crashed into the glass and sent her flying backward, dropping into an unconscious heap on the floor.

Additional employees rushed their way into the room, some escorting patients back into their rooms, while others ran to a patient who was in the midst of a bulimic episode, triggered by one of her multiple personalities rising to witness the chaos around her. Staff politely yet forcefully led the visitors away from the scene and out of the room.

Being pushed by a gang of strangers and medical personnel toward the exit, Cory looked back and made eye contact with Tammy seconds before she disappeared behind the door. He wished she understood his need to be on his own, but how could she when all they'd ever had was each other?

Chapter 3

Five months earlier: How Did I Get Here?

"There's no doubt in my mind you'll get off. Granted, I see them ordering you into a psychiatric hospital, but that's what you wanted, so, in my book, that's a win." Ronson folded his hands in front of him and smiled like a kid who had just been awarded a sticker. During his twenty-plus years as a defense attorney, he'd lost an incredibly low amount of cases; however, Tammy's case was the only one that stressed his mental and flustered his nerves. He owed it to her to win this case.

They had crossed paths when his nine-year-old son was in need of a liver. Waiting on the organ the legitimate way forced him and his wife to watch their son suffer. The passing of each day walked them closer to his demise. Witnessing their son slowly fade into history pushed them in the direction of the black market. The couple agreed that would never be an option, believing things would work swiftly for their child, but when it didn't and things got worse, their hearts told them they were in need of another alternative. Tammy supplied them with a healthy liver within a matter of days.

"Anything you need. Do you hear me? Anything you need, you let me know," Ronson had said as he shook

Tammy's hand, expressing his gratitude after his son's successful surgery.

"I'll remember that," she told him. Although paying an arm and a leg should have been enough, it wasn't. Saving his son's life was worth more to Tammy, and that price was him doing whatever it took to secure her freedom.

Sitting in her kitchen comfortably while out on bail, Tammy listened to her lawyers' run-down of her case.

"I think that war wound was the icing on the cake, if you ask me." Ronson pointed at her bandaged arm. He explicitly pointed out the dried blood damaging the cloth during the proceedings.

Her last appearance in court was a good one. Despite being on trial for murder, she made sure the jury perceived her as a model citizen, but she saved the best for last. Leaving the courthouse after jurors sympathized over the mentally unstable forty-year-old who was forced into adulthood at an early age, she turned in a performance worthy of any significant acting award.

Tammy was in the process of departing the courthouse and, to the surprise of everyone who bore witness to the horrific scene, she blocked a number of judges, lawyers, and victims from entering. Tears escaped her eyes as she slapped her hands against the sides of her head and moved from left to right, a series of incoherent mumbled words jumping from her mouth.

With caution, Ronson leaned into her from the side. "Tammy, are you okay?"

People were watching, forgetting about their own cases and problems. Tammy didn't answer as she continued her exaggerated gestures before she suddenly slammed her arms against her sides. Ronson looked at a police officer walking up the steps, heading to the scene, but by then, Tammy had grabbed her right arm and sunk her teeth into the flesh above her elbow. Like a rabid carnivore, she tore into her skin. Globs and chunks of flesh were ripped off her body and spit onto the ground. Long, stretched-out skin hung from her mouth, swinging whichever way the wind blew.

No one responded nor reacted. Ronson dropped his briefcase as others turned away, doing their best to fight off the oncoming nausea. The officer finally reached the scene, tackling Tammy and pinning her to prevent her from harming herself further. Tammy's skinless arm rubbed against the ground, slashing at her exposed, gooey skin. That incident had become a part of the case, a beautiful, well-orchestrated complement to her plea of not guilty by reason of insanity. When asked why she had harmed herself, Tammy's answer was simple: "I just wanted the voices to stop."

"It's going to happen," Tammy responded confidently. "And when it does, I will request being admitted here." Tammy pushed a brochure over to Ronson. Words written in green script read *Peaceful Minds Psychiatric Center*, a picture of a modern day mental hospital built out of glass sitting peacefully in the background.

Ronson opened the brochure. "I heard about this place. Top notch, and the ratings are great. They're the new face of psychiatric hospitals."

"Yes, but I don't want in there for the treatment. I want in there because of her." Tammy's index finger pointed to a photo of Layla Flat, founder of Peaceful, on the inside of the brochure. "She's a greedy bitch, and she'll give me whatever I want in there, including the institution in its entirety if I talk using dead presidents."

Ronson nodded his head.

"Cory will meet with her, make her an offer, and recruit the staff I need to run my business. This lovely facility is the perfect cover, and he knows the type of people I'll need." Tammy smiled. "So, make it happen. Make the world believe I am out of my mind and in need of the best help Peaceful has proven they can supply. Throw me in there. Going to prison is not an option."

"You got it." Ronson would not let Tammy go to prison. This was the only proper thank you he could give her for saving his son.

Dropping the brochure inside of his briefcase, Ronson asked what he'd been thinking. "Will it stop here?"

"What to do you mean?" Tammy asked. She perched her glasses on top of her nose, going over her to-do list, her pen checking off three accomplishments in a row.

"After you're in Peaceful . . . this battle between you and Baldwin, will it end?"

"When I enter Peaceful, that's when it starts. He weaseled his way inside a business he had no place being. He had my Delaware office raided and stole all of my files. Those files contained my clientele, my workers, everything I'd built, and tried making it his own." Tammy relived the memories of that day, refueling her rage. "What if the Delaware income was all I had, my only place of business? I would have been finished."

Ronson knew the story. He'd heard it dozens of times, so he allowed her to save her breath and tried finishing her sentence. "And let's not forget him taking the legit route and trying to have you thrown behind bars."

"He actually pointed the cops in my direction and tried to take me down on murder." Tammy fell deeper into her thoughts, scoffing at the audacity of it all. She had to admit it was a smart move for a drug dealer to have the system do his dirty work.

"He knew you'd lash out and lash out right away. I wouldn't be surprised if he set everything up, ensured word got back to you about the raid and who was behind it. I even believe he handed over the man you killed willingly, as bait to lure you in and eat you alive." Ronson sat back in Tammy's cushioned chair, one leg over the other. "You're not in the business he's in. He saw no need in making things ugly. He baited you, and you fell for it."

Tammy didn't like hearing that she was considered weak, let alone an unworthy opponent. But it all made sense, and all the dots connected when she thought back to the night that would lead her down the path into a mental hospital.

Ray texted Tammy while she was in New York expanding her business. He was the one who informed her about the raid and Baldwin being behind matters. And it was him who turned her rage into delight by telling her where she could find Baldwin's business partner, unaware that she was being set up the entire time.

It was all too easy, but this was her rationale through the benefit of hindsight. After stopping in Delaware to see the damage, Tammy found her target and followed him to his home. Finding the tip of the spare key sticking out from under the potted plant, she made her way inside and killed the man in the shower. His face looked shocked, caught off guard and frozen in time. It wasn't the look of a person who knew a storm was brewing, not the look of a man who knew to watch his back. It was the look of a victim, a person set up by his boss in order to deliver his competitor to the po-po. Neighbors poked their heads out their doors at the exact time sirens rang in front of her mark's building. Why depend on hallway cameras when eyewitnesses could do the trick?

Retreating from the building, Tammy saw police officers positioned behind their squad cars, guns drawn and aimed her way. Tammy canceled her steps and stopped in place. It was a night of red-and-blue lights filling the air and replacing the twinkle in her eye. Residents gawked from their windows, and bystanders on sidewalks took in the scene. Everyone provided her a few minutes of fame—except for one person.

Walking through the crowd stationed behind the officers, a homeless man waltzed on by with ease, despite a slight limp in his walk. He stopped a few times, yelling for a few seconds as he stomped his feet before he continued walking, and still no one noticed. He was a man in the open, lost in a sea of bodies.

It was the perfect plan.

"I just wanted them to stop!" Tears welled in Tammy's eyes, filled to the rim, a talent well made for being an actress. "The voices are my friends. They told me what to do, but now they won't stop. They lied to me! They're not my friends." Tammy's voice went from a sensible adult to a scared, hurt child. "I just want to make them stop. Please make them stop."

She held the gun to her head as the officers' postures became sharper and more focused.

"Lower your weapon!" one officer screamed. "Just put the gun down!"

"They won't stop!" Tammy told him, her face a fountain of water and her body a shaken blur.

"We'll make them stop!" another officer yelled out. "If you put down the gun, we'll make the voices stop!"

"You're lying! You're just like them!" Tammy pushed the gun directly to the side of her head, closed her eyes, and pulled the trigger.

And then nothing happened. The sound of an empty gun filled the air. Tammy's eyes shot open, trying again and again to shoot a gun she knew she'd emptied on her mark. She kept trying to shoot until one of the cops reached her and removed the gun from her hand.

"I just wanted them to stop," was all she said.

"He set me up," Tammy said out loud to Ronson. "He had someone in that building listen out for gunshots and call the police on cue."

Ronson gathered his belongings in preparation to leave.

"That has to be it. Before I go, why didn't you tell me you had a record?"

"Because I don't."

"No, not a criminal record. But why haven't you informed me that you've had dealings in the past with psychiatric wards and that you have been diagnosed with delusional disorder? That sort of thing does help, you know." Ronson stood from table.

Her case was going well. The scene she had caused the night of the murder, the scene in front of the courthouse, and the police officer who tried to save her testifying that due to experience he believed she was mentally defective, all put her in perfect positioning to be committed in lieu of prison. Her plan was well thought out, so, in her mind, her past had no reason to resurface.

"Bye, Ronson."

Ronson nodded his head and walked away without another word, but left wondering exactly who his client really was.

Chapter 4

The institution's library was where Tammy fit in best. It was a world of make believe meshed with reality. Whenever Tammy chose to ignore the facts of the world, she was allowed to without being chastised and looked at as mental. She sat at a hard, wooden table with key streaks of letters and pictures. The chair she sat on was once bark from a tree cut down five years ago. The library was the only room in Peaceful in need of a makeover. Patients' constant visitation wore down its bright appearance and withered away its quality. Today, however, the place was left abandoned by everyone except for Tammy and five others. A number of fiction books were scattered amongst the table and added color to the solid patched furniture. Shelves of non-fiction novels stood behind her.

"I want her." Tammy's thin, long finger pointed in front of her, her chipped fingernail on stage for everyone in the library to see.

"Bianca?"

"The redhead," Tammy told Hering. This woman had been in the hospital since Tammy first arrived, yet she didn't know her name and didn't care to, because her name wasn't what she was interested in.

"Yeah, that's Bianca, the one who ran into the wall weeks ago during visitation."

Tammy was searching for her next involuntary organ donor. She had been watching Bianca for weeks, examining her interaction with her family during their visits and progression during group sessions. Each day that passed, Bianca's mental status had deteriorated. Family members who once came in mobs dwindled and came in pairs, if at all. She was not trying to get better; she liked being free-minded, able to do and say as she pleased without society's judgment. She didn't listen to rules, broke several laws, and lived life by her mind's unrealistic standards. Whenever she was told she couldn't do something, she'd act out and trigger one of her violent personalities. Diane was the reason she was in Peaceful. Pauline was the one who denied visits for the past three weeks, forcing her family to give her some space. When her personalities spoke, they listened.

"She'll have no one checking on her. Since she's been denying her visits, her family has agreed to give her a few weeks to herself, 'some time to allow her personalities to rest' is how they put it."

"Did you check her charts and run tests?"

"Everything's clean."

"Take care of her and have everything set up and ready to go by midnight."

"Beautiful, just beautiful."

The palm of Tammy's left hand pressed against the surgical room's glass door. Her miniature nails clawed at its doorframe. When her right hand reached the doorknob, it shook from the inability to enter. She wanted to feel her skin, to hold it and dig into it, to rip it in two and mold it into a ball. She wanted to put it on a canvas and make art of meat. She wanted to win, but with victory came patience. So, Tammy's need to enter the room was repressed and neglected. Her medical team was only twenty minutes away from completely removing the skin from the back of Bianca's corpse. Surely, she could wait twenty minutes, and by the look in her eyes, her doctor knew to leave a piece of skin especially for her.

Listening to the sounds of the clock counting down, Tammy was torn from her biosphere when a sock was spit out and a scream released.

"Let us go!"

"Shut the fuck up!" Tammy shrieked.

A small group of naked people whose arms, legs, and mouths were duct-taped to perfection sat uneasy and distraught. An eruption of wiggling and squealing in their crowded corner sounded off when the adhesive wore down and fell from the mouth of one of the hostages and gave her the opportunity to yell.

"You're dead! Fuckin' dead!"

Grabbing an encyclopedia from the coffee table—Tammy's reading material while waiting for surgeries to conclude—she slapped the young woman across the face with the hard copy. And she didn't stop. Tammy kept swinging until the muscles in the girl's neck weakened and she could no longer hold her skull up, ultimately knocking the girl out. Tammy grinned as the girl comfortably slid down the wall into a puddle of her own blood.

The girl's workers, the people she and Baldwin employed, bucked. They wrestled in place, trying to rip themselves from the tape while speaking countless words that only emerged as mumbling. Foreheads wrinkled and eyes narrowed, every person directing their irritation and disgust Tammy's way. If Baldwin wanted in on Tammy's business, then a lot of his workers would donate body parts, including his girlfriend. Kidnapped and brought into a mental institution, Tammy was finishing a fight she was dragged into.

From inside the isolated room, Tammy's medical team collectively looked through the glass, their focus torn from their skinning. Tammy slammed an open palm against the glass her staff looked out of, and with every spoken word, followed it by a pound on the door.

"Get . . . back . . . to . . . work!"

Her screaming had given energy to her prisoners. They moved faster and with more intensity. The walls shook, and the person Tammy categorized as her liver started to rub his taped hands against the nail sticking from the wall. Tammy was so concerned with the surgical room she didn't notice his movements, nor the fact that the tape was slowly breaking.

Adler burst inside the room, angry and breathing heavily. The corner of people and the young unconscious woman were the first two things she noticed. The crowd of people tried to break free, gashes and bruises from being dragged in by Tammy's men forming a trail of blood their way.

"What are you doing?" Adler spewed. The mere sight before her caused her distaste for Tammy to multiply by ten.

Getting the doctors back in position, Tammy snatched her gun from a duffle bag filled with money and rushed away from the door and over to Adler. She grabbed Adler by her upper arm and jammed the handgun into her throat, orders being screamed into her face.

"You go get Hering and two others to come down here right now! Fuck waiting on them!" Tammy pointed in the direction where Bianca was being skinned by her small medical team using a dermatome. "I want organs cut out of bodies now, professionally or not!"

Adler recognized that gun. It was always pointed her way, a reminder of the mistake she'd made by accepting this job. Unhappy, overworked, and underpaid at her previous position at a private psychiatric facility in New York, Adler turned to prescription drugs. In order to cope, she'd pop pills and file her nails, day in and day out. This was her ritual, and she didn't stop, not even when fired. She just spent whatever savings she had to support her addiction, but money going out and nothing coming in forced Adler to seek another job.

After being unemployed for two months, Adler received a telephone call from Cory. A mutual friend had suggested he reach out to Adler when Cory stated he was in need of an out-of-work nurse. He offered Adler a position at Peaceful and promised she'd be in a comfortable environment with little hours and hefty pay, everything she didn't have at her last place of employment. All she had to do was keep her mouth shut and work with patients. She would be given a new identity, so she wouldn't be triggered in the system. No one wanted a nurse fired for pill-popping to help the ill. No one but Tammy.

From the outside looking in, this was Adler's only solution. It wasn't until she worked in Peaceful for five months that she learned what she had to keep her mouth closed about. It was the patients coming up missing and the screaming in the basement that drove her curiosity. She had to see what her mind had pieced together, so one day, during her late shift, Adler went down into the basement and watched familiar and unfamiliar faces being robbed of their organs. Shaken and nauseated, Adler ran to the restroom to relieve herself. It was when she turned to wipe her mouth that she came face to face with Tammy.

"Stay quiet now. It's part of your job description."

"What are you doing? You're stealing people's—" Her lunch crept up her throat and ran out her mouth. Images of blood, fingers, and legs on tables invaded her mind. She quickly turned to the toilet.

"And that is something no one will ever know. You keep my secret, and I keep yours. No one made you take this job and sign off on a false identity. That's against the law. And let's not forget the patients who went without their medicine because you couldn't control your habit." Tammy's voice was high-pitched and innocent, sounding as if what Adler had done was worse than her activities.

"It's—it's just wrong," Adler pushed out. She fought back vomiting again. Her hand was over her mouth, prepared to push in whatever tried coming out without her permission.

"It's business, and if you want your body to stay intact, you'll do your job."

Adler's dismay over Tammy's "enterprise" grew from that point on. Like everyone else on staff, she was trapped in a job due to past mistakes and the need for money. Her attitude, and her one-time complaint to Layla, was what kept her in close proximity to Tammy's handgun. There was nothing Layla wouldn't do to restore Peaceful's good name as long as money was being directed into her bank account; therefore leaving Tammy to do whatever she wanted.

"I'm tired of you pointing that thing at me," Adler hissed, her pitch low. She didn't know where the words came from; she only knew Tammy's personality was touch-and-go and always in the mood to taunt her.

"Oh, really? So, what the fuck are you going to do about it?" Tammy pushed the muzzle deeper inside her skin, the discomfort pushing Adler to swallow. "You never could get on board. So, what would it take to get you on board?"

Tammy pushed the gun farther into Adler's throat until Tammy's ears perked up. The room fell silent, and the concentration Adler once placed on Tammy was diverted. Tammy kept her position and seconds later turned around, realizing why Adler was distracted. She pushed bullets out of her gun, leaving two holes in the chest of the hostage who was slated to have his liver removed. He dropped mere steps from where she stood.

His comrades went crazy, extremely motivated to break free. Screams and vague words were now heard through taped mouths, and tears appeared under the women's eyes, distraught over the death of their colleague.

"On second thought—" Tammy pushed Adler away.

Adler's feet stumbled over one another and caused her to land in a streak of blood. In the next moment, Tammy shot everyone on the floor except for Baldwin's girlfriend. Fresh blood meshed with the old and seeped into the turquoise tiles. A slow river of blood easing toward the operating room caught Adler's eye. Adler screamed long and high, the sounds transporting from the pit of her stomach down to the tips of her toes.

"Shut up!" Tammy told her, her gun waving uncontrollably at her. "Shut the fuck up!"

Sniffling and consumed with regret, Adler dropped her head against the wall, holding future tears and screams inside.

The doctor peered from inside the operating room, realizing there had been a lot of commotion while they were working. His question was delivered in a calm manner, but one glance around the room would have inspired a wholly different emotional response. "We're done. Who's next?"

"Him." Tammy's head pointed to the man who had tried to tackle her. "Take his liver, but I need more manpower."

"Give me a second. I'll have three surgeons here within an hour."

"I want my brother. Get me my brother."

"Not a problem." The doctor fell back inside the room, instructing his team about what was to happen next. He then walked out, heading to the bathroom to make some calls.

Tammy never took her gun off Adler, who was still lying in a crying heap on the floor. Hering appeared, his throat swallowing pretend saliva.

"Take her, the one in the green shirt. Set her up in one of the rooms. I want her kidneys."

Hering nodded his head slowly without speaking and walked over to the woman Tammy had identified. He threw her over his shoulder and left the liquidly red area.

"Get back to work," Tammy told Adler, pointing upstairs.

Adler looked at her, her muscles stiff and forgetful on how to move.

"Now!" Tammy snarled.

Adler used the blood she sat on to slide away from Tammy and toward the door. Once close to her exit, she used the doorknob to help pull her up, and she ran far from the murder scene.

Tammy dropped the gun, and so things could get started, she grabbed the body that housed the liver by the hands and pulled it into the operating room.

"Prep him," she told her staff and closed the door.

Chapter 5

Cory's phone incessantly vibrated inside his coat pocket as he sat in Baldwin's office, dealing with an issue that made the series of phone calls irrelevant in that moment. Baldwin was tense, insistent on answers Cory did not want to provide.

"I don't know where they are," Cory replied.

"The last time I spoke with Cinder, she was heading out to meet with you." Baldwin stared at him, trying to gauge his body language. "She would have texted me to let me know she made it there in one piece."

"And she never showed." Cory sat straight-faced, holding in the secrecy of where Baldwin's girlfriend and workers were at that moment. There was only one place they'd be. No one just disappeared when revenge was on the radar.

"Cinder and five of my men, my best men, my most profitable men, disappear into thin air, and you can't tell me where they are?" Baldwin's hand gripped the armrest of his La-Z-Boy, the beat-up cushion forming into the print of his fingers.

"Cinder never showed at Marbles, and as for your men, I can't speak on that." Cory's phone vibrated again. With Baldwin's vision locked on the television screen, he slammed his hand in his pocket again, hoping its noise had gone unnoticed.

"Cinder would never miss a chance to eat at Marbles." Baldwin's fist slammed down on his chair. The stress was overwhelming him.

Cory was lying, and sooner or later, Baldwin would figure that out. He was better served finding a quick exit before deciding what Baldwin was going to do once he'd made up his mind that Cory was lying.

He stood up, his face cleanly shaven by a razor, his beard and sidelocks no longer a part of his face. He pointed his finger at Cory in an accusatory manner. "You're lying."

"I'm not lying, but instead of you standing here and questioning me, why aren't you out searching for her?" Cory threw this question into the conversation, his way of sidetracking Baldwin.

"My men went searching hours ago. Because of Shabbat, I cannot drive until sundown."

Cory dropped his head and smirked. It had been dark for hours, so he knew Baldwin was stretching the truth again. Baldwin had broken so many rules when it came to Jewish beliefs, but the one he held onto the most fervently was not driving. He flip-flopped and chose what he wanted to uphold. His house smelled of sausage when Cory entered, yet he always dressed in the correct attire. It was mindboggling and, in Cory's opinion, odd and disturbing.

"I hope they find them," Cory said.

Baldwin looked at Cory, his hand landing on his chin, and, out of habit, pulling on the hair that was no longer there. "If I don't find them, our deal is off."

Cory's eyes took note of the arsenal adorning the gun rack on the wall near the exit of his office. The vast selection of pistols, revolvers, and semi-automatics gave him pause. He began to see the inconsistencies in his potential business partner, and he wasn't sure if he liked what he saw.

"That is irrational, Baldwin."

"That is reality. If your sister harms my girlfriend, there will be hell to pay. Moving into organ harvesting was supposed to be easy; your plan was supposed to be easy. Possibly going into business with you is supposed to be for profit, not war."

"There is no war." Cory having to convince Baldwin was becoming aggravating. The regret over going down this path overshadowed any profit he would have made. He was supposed to be the puppeteer, pulling the strings while Baldwin got his hands dirty.

"There's a war, and you know every move that is occurring. I followed your lead. I listened to your plan on landing your sister in jail, but it didn't work, so why should I believe that she isn't behind the disappearance of my men? First, Ray comes up dead; now Cinder and my people disappear. Why should I not think you didn't turn on me like you turned on Tammy?"

Baldwin was making the situation personal, and that fact was not lost on Cory. Until that moment, he had never referred to Tammy by her first name.

Planning Tammy's demise in the organ harvesting business was no easy decision. Cory didn't want to harm his sister, but what he did want was to gain his independence. Being the talent wasn't enough for him. Cory needed to be the brains of the operation, and the only way he could realistically see that happening was if Tammy was out of the picture completely.

He engineered the setup, fed Baldwin the plan to step in on Tammy's business, take away her Delaware staff and clientele, and benefit off of the profits Cory helped produce. The money Baldwin would see come in based off the organ operation was supposed to show Cory's worth in a business. Because of Cory's clientele and contacts, Tammy's business was profitable, and that was supposed to help Baldwin decide to make Cory a part of his drug operation and sell the drug Cory had been working on. Not start a war.

"There is no war," Cory repeated.

"Which mental institution is your sister being held in?" Baldwin sat on the shortest sofa in the room.

Cory didn't answer. He looked Baldwin's way, his hands in his pockets while shaking his head, insinuating that Baldwin was losing it.

"She's in a hospital. I know jail was not accomplished," Baldwin informed him. "I hate repeating myself. Which mental institution is Tammy being held in?"

Cory turned away and laughed silently. He had underestimated Baldwin and his need for proof. Still, he needed to get him off his sister's scent before the trail began to lead back to him. "You think she's in a mental institution? Are you believing eyes and ears that aren't your own? Not everyone can be trusted."

"I see that now." Baldwin paused. He felt the need to deliver a final warning. "But if my woman does not reappear soon, business between us will not happen, and yours and Tammy's lives are on the clock."

Baldwin looked at the clock hanging on the wall. Cory understood the significance. The time reflected that Cinder and his men had now been missing for twenty-four hours.

Cory didn't flinch. "You should search for your people. The more people are searching, the faster you'll find them."

Baldwin's face tightened. Every hour that passed, he knew that the truth of what he might find could devastate him. He couldn't allow Cory to see that fear. "Bring them back, Cory. Your life depends on it."

Walking down the pathway that led to his car, Cory bypassed a gentleman heading toward the front door. Baldwin stood in the doorway to give a warm greeting. Cory's instincts went crazy, realizing that he'd recognized his face before. Things were about to get hot, and he had no other choice but to put an end to this before he ended up dead.

On the doorstep, looking out at the neighborhood, Baldwin's partner delivered the disturbing news. "Cinder was never at Marbles. There was no reservation for her. I spoke to the owner herself."

"Follow him. He'll take you to her." Baldwin's finger followed Cory's car as it drove to the destination where, Baldwin was convinced, his girlfriend was being held captive.

Chapter 6

"Where is she?" Cory looked around Tammy's room. Although he knew Cinder would be nowhere in this small area, he still chose to investigate.

Bags sat under Tammy's eyes. She had taken a mental break in order to rejuvenate her body and get some rest. A day of surgeries and murder drained whatever energy she had left, and now her brother was taking the little she tried to regain.

"Go home, Cory."

He stood over his sister. Her eyes were closed, and her body lay in a position devoted to sleep. The idea of killing her right there, where she lay, crossed his mind. Maybe if he did it now, things would fall into place so much easier. Maybe if he did it, the stress of holding together secrets and a remaining alliance amongst two enemies would fizzle away. Maybe if he did it, he'd have his own spotlight. Betraying his sister was a long, drawn-out decision made months ago when his need to grow within his own skin took him over. However, the more Tammy fought and the more she held on like a cat with nine lives, the more conniving Cory set out to be.

"He knows it's you. He knows where you are." It was a scare tactic, the next best thing Cory saw fit to use for not only running his sister off, but also possibly saving her life. Like a bipolar individual, one second Cory wanted her gone, and the next he needed her around.

"Good for him. Things should now get more interesting. It's not fun hitting someone who's not hitting back."

Cory slammed himself down on her bed, his presence rocking her foundation. Desperation peppered his words. "This isn't a game, Tammy. You need to return his people and return them now. You're in over your head. You will not win."

Tammy opened her eyes, the heaviness in her dark browns pulling her down as she pushed herself up on her elbows. "You really want out. What is he promising you? Besides selling your drug, what is in it for you?"

Cory sat silent, his thoughts saying what his mouth never could: *freedom, power*. He wished he could tell her everything he wanted and everything he had done, but he knew he couldn't. Since they were children, Tammy had always told him he could tell her anything, but that was a lie. It was only kind words people told others, empty words we all wished we could believe but knew couldn't be achieved.

Tammy could not see past herself once Cory joined her business. She set her sights on caring for herself. Helping the growth of another was not an option if it didn't benefit her. Tammy went from a nurturing, supportive, protective sister to a self-absorbed cunt with the speed of a cream-colored page of a book being flipped. If it wasn't about her business, it wasn't her business, and that's when the selfish bug bit Cory and he knew his life needed to be about him.

"A change of pace. Now stop this," Cory demanded. He meant what he said and hoped for this one moment in time Tammy would be the selfless sister he remembered from his youth.

"I'll never give you a change of pace." Harsh, solid, and without regret, she told him the truth. "This idea of yours, this . . . need goes against what I do. It goes against our grain as a family, and you're fine with that?"

She waited for Cory to respond, to speak against her accusations, but he didn't. His need to spread his wings and leave the business told her what he wanted was bigger than what she had established. She sat up to give him her undivided attention. "Tell me this: where is your conscience? I can understand you wanting to try something else, but why with someone who's done wrong against your own flesh and blood?"

It was a damn good question, and a question Cory hoped to have never had to answer. "My conscience departed the day you wouldn't let me be just the surgeon I worked hard to be; the day I realized the only reason you even put me through medical school was so that I could carry your business."

"My job is to make you better, to help you grow! I did nothing but help take you to the next level." Tammy's eyebrows sank downward.

"You did nothing but use me!" Cory's fist slammed into the bed. A knot the size of his fist sank into the mattress only to push itself upward and regain its natural form. "And you're not my mother. It's not your place to act the way you do!"

The words were sharper than a gang of knives in a knife block.

"Think what you want, say what you want, and do what you plan. But know this: if you cross over to the other side, if you betray me, there's no going back." Tammy held her arms wide apart in the air, letting Cory know that his actions dictated hers, and if that happened, there was nothing left to do except go to war.

"Then I guess there's no going back. Consider this my resignation." Cory stood as the weights of worry and betrayal fell from his frame.

Tammy hopped off the bed, her tired eyes fully alert. "You don't know what you're doing, Cory."

"I know exactly what I'm doing." He opened the door, watching his staff scatter after being caught eavesdropping.

Racing to the doorway, Tammy watched Cory walk down the hall and out of sight.

Hering appeared next to her, waiting a few seconds before speaking. "I can talk to him."

When Tammy didn't respond, he continued. "I can . . ." Hering couldn't finish. Offering to kill a man Tammy considered her world could not easily be said, but Hering knew that it had to be done. Cory knew too much, and that information could do nothing but demolish Tammy.

Without looking his way, Tammy told him, "Get away from me."

Hering left her alone, understanding the time she needed to make that decision.

Tammy walked to her room, preparing to slam the door shut, when she saw Adler looking at her. For the first time, Adler understood Tammy and could relate to family walking away. She led the world to believe she abused prescription drugs because of her job, when in reality it was because she was alone.

Adler forced herself to walk over to Tammy to speak with her, but when she took a few steps Tammy's way, Tammy slammed the door. Adler stepped back, a patient running through the halls catching her attention. She looked once more at Tammy's door, shook her head, and did what she was hired to do—her job.

Chapter 7

After being knocked out with an encyclopedia, Cinder woke up hours later to the assassination of her crew, people she considered family, and some she'd known since childhood. Seeing that, she knew her fate. Cinder's friends' body parts lay scattered around the room, thrown where she could see them after the removal of their organs. She cried, not out loud, but low, despair-filled sobs. No one was in the room, no one to take pleasure in her pain, so there she cried and got it all out, because once Tammy saw she was awake, she could not cry anymore.

Nothing went like Cinder thought it would once someone entered the room. One of Tammy's nurses discovered she was awake and left her alone to go tell Tammy. Minutes later, the nurse returned with one of the surgeons.

"You sure that's what she said?" the doctor asked his nurse of five years.

"Yup, word for word."

"Ooooookaaaaay."

Unsure of why Tammy had made such a request, he went with it and vanished into a small room filled with medications that lined the walls and cabinets filled with equipment. Minutes later, he returned with a syringe in hand. He bent down in front of Cinder, drew back his hand, and prepared to jam it inside her when she gave her last fight.

Cinder flung herself on him and dug her nails into his eyes. The fashionable nails Baldwin always complained about paying for were finally useful. Her intent was to rip his eyeballs out and throw them across the room, something for Tammy to see when she came downstairs.

The pale, porcelain-colored man screamed. He grabbed her by her shoulders and tried forcing her away, but like a cat, Cinder's claws held on firmly and didn't budge. The frantic movements of his body and wild yells shook the basement's foundation and caused her to push her nails deeper. Her fight was small compared to the blows given by Tammy, but it was an accomplishment, a headache given to the enemy.

Puncturing his skin and getting a firm hold on his eye, Cinder pulled his right eye out. Blood and tissue released from his interior and made half of his white-colored face red. The pain was violently excruciating and ran so deep it was bone-cracking. Turning his hands into fists, he punched at her sides, but Cinder blocked out the pain and constantly told herself, *Just one more*. The hold she had on his remaining eye told her she was ready; just one strong fast pull and it was over, but Cinder collapsed, the grip on his eye lost.

"I told you just jam the shit in right away. Don't give her a chance to move!" the nurse screamed.

The doctor looked at an unconscious Cinder, then at the nurse holding the empty syringe, the same one he'd dropped when Cinder caught him off guard.

"My fuckin' eye! She took my fuckin' eye!" he hollered.

The nurse ignored his screams and looked at the blood and eye on the floor.

"Just more shit to clean up," she complained.

Her limbs were missing. There was almost nothing left of Cinder. Both her legs had been removed, and one of her arms. She lay in the operating room, weak in spirit but very calm. When she woke up from her battle, she had a view of the eyeless doctor in the next room. That caused a smile to cover her face. However, the drugs pumped into her weakened her. Cinder had yet to see Tammy after she knocked her out the first time, and she wasn't dead, so she knew Tammy wanted her for one more thing.

After an hour of wondering thoughts, Tammy finally came inside the room. Cinder observed puffy eyes with a hint of red when Tammy pulled up a seat beside her.

"You live if your boyfriend leaves my brother alone. Working with Cory is not an option."

Cinder took note of the red lines planted in Tammy's eyes and laughed. "Not even if you begged. Your brother's a gold mine, and we're going to milk him for all he's worth!" Cinder laughed a wretched, demeaning howl. She had to fight to push the noise out of her, but it was worth it.

Tammy pounced from her seat and pulled Cinder from her bed, throwing her onto the shiny marble floor with the strength of a man. Pain hit every part of Cinder's body, yet her loud giggles continued to dance inside of Tammy's ears. Cinder shoved the hurt away, but not the chuckles.

Eventually, Cinder's face became serious, and her personality turned sullen and unrecognizable. "I'm pushing for this deal to go through. After this, Baldwin will no longer be rich, but wealthy. And if that means I have to die in order for it to happen, then so be it."

Pulled into reality, Tammy discovered the kidnappings and murders were not a solution, but quicksand. Tammy was drowning, and she wouldn't come up for air until she forced things back to the way they were.

Kill her. Kill her now.

Tammy kneeled down, pasted the palms of her hands against the icy floor, and pushed her face close to Cinder's. "You're not understanding me. This will not end well." Tammy's eyes batted at an alarmingly fast rate and enlarged within the snap of a finger.

Cinder smiled. "I understand completely. What you don't understand is that you will not win."

Tammy saw Cinder laugh at her, point at her, and jump up and down in pure amusement over her roadblock. She would not cross Cory out of their future business endeavors. There was too much money to be earned, and a small circle of people in hopes of receiving it.

Cinder proceeded to leave, happy and unbothered by the situation. Stepping outside the door, she turned around and told Tammy, "Good luck to you."

Kill her. Kill her now.

Tammy closed her eyes. The cool air choked the room and turned it dry and humid. Shaking her head, she opened them and found Cinder staring at her. Cinder was confused, her face scrunched up with unlimited lines, and her limbless body still on the ground.

"Where did your legs go?" Tammy asked. "You just had them."

Cinder didn't answer.

"How the fuck did you do that?" Tammy grabbed her close, saliva creating puddles on Cinder's cheeks. "Where did they go?" she growled.

"You're more fucked up than I thought." Cinder's voice was nothing but a whisper. It didn't take her long to figure out that Tammy was seeing things, a delusional mind unraveling in front of her.

From her waistband, Tammy pulled out a gun and held it under Cinder's chin. "How did you do it?"

Unraveled and at ease, Cinder's aura turned cold and withdrawn. Her response was a bitter chill. "Exactly how I'm going to destroy you—behind your back."

Tammy pushed her away. Cinder fell over, her head banging against the tiles like a stone. Two seconds hadn't passed before Tammy sprang up, wrapped Cinder's hair around her free hand, formed a fist, and yanked her head up.

"I'ma have fun killing you." Tammy's volume was low and blood-curdling, the gun pointing at Cinder's skull.

No footsteps were heard, nor did the ladies hear Adler call for Tammy several times. It was when Adler screamed like an opera singer on opening night that Tammy broke her focus.

"What!" Tammy let out.

"There's something I need to tell you. Something I've seen." Adler tried hard not to look at Cinder, but it was no use. She looked, and for a moment, she got lost in the dreadful scene.

Frustrated with being interrupted, Tammy let go of Cinder. Her body dropped, her sarcastic comebacks kicked out of her. Tammy stood and headed for the door. When she had one foot over the doorstep, Cinder used her only arm to pull her upper body up as much as she could, her neck stretched out.

"Before you kill me, do me a favor, Tammy!" she yelled. "Tell Cory his setup to take you down was genius!"

At the same time, both Tammy and Adler looked Cinder's way, not believing what they had just heard.

Chapter 8

15 minutes prior

On the outside, everything looked normal, from the colorful flowered walkway to the steel park benches and the large glass windows. The building stood tall, the face of good mental health staring out at the community. Looks could be deceiving. The truth could not always be found in the light, but sometimes the darkness could reveal all. That was why he made his way to the back door of the hospital.

Appearances had to be kept, and that was why Cory's footsteps appeared before his. The place was quiet when he entered, and that alone was reason enough for him not to want to move. The hospital was spacious, clean, and happy in appearance; no unconformable vibes pumped throughout the upper level. It was the lower level that held the depression, blood, and horror.

Unaware of where to look, he walked in the dark, in between furniture and objects capable of hiding him. Halfway into the television room, that's when he heard her. Her laughter seemed to float throughout the hospital.

He followed the cackling and imagined Cory must have taken this same route earlier. The stairs were slippery, easy for anyone in a rush to fall. He walked slowly, poking his head inside the door located in the lower level of the hospital, and held in his stomach's contents before they escaped. There was so much blood, so many body parts, and so many of his friends.

He looked up in front of him, noticing three rooms lined up back to back. In the second room sat Cinder and Tammy. He didn't notice it right away, but after staring closely, and definitely when Tammy flung Cinder from the bed, he noticed her missing body parts. A hit of shock consumed him, and the smell seeping from the dirty tools and corpse suffocated him.

Suddenly, danger crept into his mind, and the idea of departing the hospital seemed right. He left the way he had come in, slowly and alert, then slid out the back door. He never noticed Adler watching him.

Cory poured another glass of rum. It was the only thing he could do since he couldn't sleep after seeing his sister. Everything was backfiring, and his selfishness had pinned him against the wall. He didn't know what to do next, so he drank. He needed a break from the devastation he'd caused and an idea on how to repair it all, but that seemed unrealistic. Cory had forced his sister into the woods with wolves, and now she was forcing their leader to step down. That wasn't a part of the plan. She was supposed to step down from her position and Cory into a new one, but now he'd learned a side of Tammy he had never known. She was an outlaw, society's outsider forced into power from the inside.

There was never enough liquor when needed. The fifth of rum was down to its last cup without assisting Cory with the peace he needed. He poured the last of his drink, took a sip, and knocked the remaining over when trying to place the glass down. Brown liquid spread itself across the table and dripped on his bedroom rug. Cory slammed his hand down in the sugary fluid, flipped the table over, and searched around the room for an answer. Alcohol had failed him; he needed something that could take him out of the real world and place him somewhere all of his troubles didn't exist.

The bottom drawer of his dresser was where his eyes landed, hiding its true identity. Cory opened its drawer, punched in numbers, and waited for the safe to pop open. Inside sat a small bottle with a screw on top. Opening it, he sniffed it like he had countless times before, swirled it around, and observed it like fine wine ready to be consumed after years of aging. This was what it was all for, the nameless drug he created that would make him wealthy.

It was a few steps from being complete, but Cory's drunken mind needed to experience where the drug actually was in reference to its effects. Normally he'd test it on willing participants in need of cash, but tonight, he would test it on himself, a willing participant in need of an escape.

It took just a small sip. After indulging in the turquoise liquid, he waited and watched the clock. His last tester experienced results within ten minutes; he needed to beat that time. Five was the goal. Eight minutes later, an uncontrollable smile stretched its way onto Cory's face. Pushing the liquor's effects out of his system, it produced a rush of energy and positivity. From his eyes, the world was perfect, and he wanted to venture out. He had to remain focused, which was exactly why he took a small dose. If not, he would not have been able to control its results. It was something he had to remember to jot down: he could not sell a drug that deprived people of some sort of control the more they took it. He wanted a longevity drug, not a drug that would wipe out his costumers within months.

He walked inside the kitchen, dug inside his junk drawer, and pulled out a razor. With its small, sharp tip, he cut into his palm. Blood and the sight of tissue shown; yet physical pain never came. Cory screamed and laughed. What he had set out to accomplish had been obtained. Besides a few side effects, such as the itching and rash appearing on his arms, the drug was almost perfect. People would feel no physical pain. When he thought of his troubles, he felt nothing emotionally. He rushed to his room, grabbed the notebook he wrote the drug's progress in, and on a new page, wrote what he thought would rid the drug of its negative aspects.

The drug had induced Cory's muse to supply him with the ideas needed to mature his drug, so he sat at his desk and wrote it all down—the ingredients and steps needed in order to better the fluid, the last steps needed in finalizing his cash cow.

Time passed when under the influence. It was scary thing when you what you thought was a half hour was really two. The pages were filled in the notebook, a result of Cory finishing his research. Book and drug in hand, he walked to the safe, put them inside, and grabbed its door. Before he could shut it, he was grabbed from behind. A gloved hand covered his nose with a soiled rag, knocking him out within seconds.

Chapter 9

7 a.m.

"Was she there?"

He looked anywhere except in Baldwin's direction. He could see Cinder in his mind, at least what was left of her. He had taken the long way back to Baldwin's. Rushing there was not high on his priority list when the information he had to relay wasn't good.

"Yes."

"Was she alive?"

"Yes."

He was not giving Baldwin anything, not elaborating nor saying more than one-word answers. Baldwin knew what that meant, and he deliberated on whether he wanted to ask future questions.

"Was she hurt?"

Looking past him, Baldwin's partner answered, "Yes."

Baldwin looked his way, his forehead crunched, and battled to contain himself.

"What was done to her? And no one-word answers." Baldwin jammed his hands into his pockets and pinched himself, praying this was a dream he could wake himself up from.

"She was missing her . . ." He stopped talking, the imagery too much to revisit.

"Say it!" Baldwin hollered. Done with being calm, or at least pretending to be, he demanded answers faster than he could ask them.

"She was missing her legs and her right arm." He spat his observation out, but the speed of which it came did not eliminate the distress from his tone. He thought back to what he'd seen, and his stomach started to rumble.

Baldwin looked at his partner, his eyes large and holding multiple questions. He felt like digging his finger into his ear and asking him to repeat himself. Years of selling drugs never prepared him for hearing those type of words, and never had it introduced him to such ruthlessness. Tammy was in the organ harvesting business. This fight should have been easy; she should have stepped away from the game board willingly after being arrested. It was never in the deck of cards for her to rip the game from under Baldwin's feet and supply them with a new one.

"And the rest of them?"

He shook his head. He tried not to think of the rest of them. "Chopped up into pieces."

Baldwin's hand slapped against his stomach. His mind told him to race to the downstairs bathroom, but his feet wouldn't move, and his mouth opened anyway. Only in control of his torso, he turned away and threw up in the middle of the living room floor. Liquor and the drugs he sold splattered onto the wooden floorboards, the stench hitting his partner's nostrils. He could have been timed for how long it took him to finish puking. He released everything his stomach contained. When he was done, he breathed heavily and took a moment to straighten out his mental faculties.

"That's exactly how I felt when I saw it, but the weird thing about it was Cinder was laughing. That psychopath was right in her face, and still she laughed. After all of that, she still couldn't break her."

Baldwin's shoes smacked against the floor. Vomit in the corner of his mouth came into clear view as he approached his partner. "You saw her around my girl and you did nothing?" Baldwin grabbed him by the neck. Both hands firmly blocked off his breathing as he forced his friend to walk backward until the wall stopped him. "And you left her there!"

The wrath from Baldwin released from his horrid breath, leftover vomit fell from the side of his mouth. Baldwin's partner was fighting to remove his hands and gasping for air; however, Baldwin's strength only increased with the struggle.

The weakening of his friend's effort and the dimming of his eyes snapped Baldwin out of his rage. He let him go, and he dropped to the floor and grabbed his neck. Air didn't make its way back into his body easily due to the constant coughs. Embarrassed that his three-hundred-pound weight did nothing to assist him, he watched a man nearly half his size walk away.

"There was no way I could have gotten her out alive!" his partner screamed, discomfort surrounding his voice box. "They would have killed us both had we been caught. But we know where she is now, so I suggest we form a plan and go get her!"

The doorbell rang, drowning him out and sending Baldwin marching to the front of his house.

"Go get her! Go get her now!" Baldwin ordered.

Baldwin braced himself for the endless reasons why someone other than his men would have been at his home at that time of morning. Opening the door, he saw a woman dressed in a black-and-blue delivery uniform equipped with a hat. She stood with a smile plastered on her face. A delivery van sat parked behind her, and a large silver gift-wrapped box tied with a bow sat in her hands.

"What the fuck is this?" The exhaustion was evident on his face.

The white girl perked up, straightened her back, and pushed the box out in front of her.

"Delivery!" she yelled, her smile undeniably obvious.

Baldwin growled, "Put the box down."

The girl shook her head, shoving the package into his hands, ignoring the muffled sounds coming from the box.

"Enjoy!" Turning her back, she walked to a miniature delivery truck, its first and last delivery completed.

The box was anything but light. Baldwin wanted to drop the package and unwrap it out in the open, but knew it was risky. People were always watching. Making his way inside the house, he slammed the door shut and released the box from his grasp. It crashed against the wood, and with his foot, he pushed it toward his partner.

"Open it."

He looked at Baldwin. In reality, the box was pretty. Wrapping paper glistened with a big red bow and invisible tape. But in his mind, it was a disease, hot coal that shouldn't be touched. He saw how the gift was brought to Baldwin, but curiosity won him over and forced him to open the box.

He looked inside and stared at its contents. Seconds later, when he found the strength to move his legs, he walked backward, stumbling to get away. Without meaning to, he bent over and threw up, his days' worth of meals mixing with Baldwin's.

Baldwin slowly headed to the box. His friend took a second to fight back bile and scream in a breathless tone, "Don't look inside!"

Baldwin didn't listen. Bending down on one knee, he flipped open the flaps of the box and saw a heart-numbing shocker. He saw what broke him. Cinder's heart sat trapped in the confines of a Ziploc bag next to her liver, kidneys, and lungs. So that there was no mistaking that the organs belonged to Cinder, her head sat in full view. Her pretty head, exactly how Baldwin last remembered, had blood splatter on her cheeks. Baldwin took her head from the box, holding her in front of his face. Her eyes looked into his as rage stampeded from his mouth.

"Get her, then bring her here," he ordered.

Baldwin dropped his head, his forehead touching Cinder's. When his partner walked past him and out the door, Baldwin closed his eyes and allowed tears to fall from his eyes.

Chapter 10

It was quick, without thought and off adrenalin. Adler raced back over to Cinder and smashed her face into the floor. A strand of blood discolored her hand when blood and teeth erupted from Cinder's mouth. The visual of it all forced Adler to take a step back. She had never behaved in such a way. She looked at Tammy, shocked with herself; yet Tammy's only response was a jolly smile. Adler appeared to be at a loss for words. She questioned who she really was.

Adler wasn't sure if it was the results of the violence she'd been exposed to, or her understanding of Tammy being rejected by her brother. Adler understood the feeling of abandonment and neglect, and for the first time, she felt badly for Tammy. Adler was taken down memory lane when she saw how Tammy watched her brother walk from her. That's how she always looked whenever her father walked out on them for an additional time. Maybe that was it: Cinder throwing a dig at Tammy and revealing Cory's disloyalty added salt to an already sensitive wound and forced a wave of aggression to pump through Adler's veins and show her father's face on Cinder's body.

She stepped back, making her way beside Tammy. "I'm sorry," she mumbled.

Tammy's smile never withdrew. "Don't be," she told Adler. Tammy ran up on Cinder as if they were in the street and shot her in the neck. She didn't stop until the gun was empty and her feelings a little more at ease. Smoke trailed in the air, the smell adding to an already bad scent.

"Now that that's done," Tammy said, putting her gun away, "what did you have to tell me?" Tammy's disregard for life and her hand in it did not include remorse.

Adler's eyes were stuck on Cinder, but still she spoke. "Someone was here. He snuck down here then left out the back."

"Baldwin's men. Cory told me they knew where I was."

"So, what do we do now?" Adler didn't know why she used the word "we," but then again, she didn't know why she did half the things she did.

"I believe her." Tammy paused. "Cory planned it all. He's smart enough and determined enough to." She looked around, trying to accept the pain and make room for it. "Now, you go and bring him to me."

"Me? Why?"

"Because it's time you get your hands dirty. Time you really join the team. After that, we'll send Baldwin his girlfriend's organs, something I've learned from Bobbi, a close friend of mine."

The night Adler watched Cinder die, the same night she participated in Cory's kidnapping, played constantly in her head. Walking down memory lane, Adler took Cory's drug and discovered his notes were right; it erased any negative feelings and only supplied happiness. Since the events took place it had haunted her, but now that she gulped the turquoise, it all went away.

Knocking Cory out, Hering had carried him out of his apartment wrapped inside of an area rug. Before Adler left Cory's room, she had noticed the drug and spiral notebook. Looking at it all, she brought it back to Tammy. Tammy read the information and came to one conclusion: she would take over Cory's project, sell it as her own, and reap all the benefits.

That suggestion was what won Adler over to the drug. Tammy needed a tester, and she knew Adler's addiction to prescription pills made her the perfect fit. If Adler gave good feedback and the product took off, she'd have a lifetime supply, free of charge, and at the end of the day, that's all Adler wanted, a getaway from reality.

Adler stuck her finger inside the glass bottle, desperate to empty it of his contents even though nothing was left. Her shift was ending, and she needed more of the drug. She couldn't stay locked in the staff room forever. She had to remain happy while at home, so she continued to try to dig out more of the drug.

Baldwin's partner in crime was in his car. Visuals danced in front of his eyes, far too many seen within a few hours. Reaching a red light a few blocks from Baldwin's home, he saw the delivery truck used to deliver Cinder on the corner, the engine off and in close proximity. He looked over, leaned into the passenger's seat for a better look into the isolated truck. The emptiness sent an uneasy, eerie feeling inside him.

He sat back in his seat, waiting for the red light to turn green, when a blue automobile turned into the next lane. He saw a woman dressed in a delivery outfit beside the driver, a man with a matching uniform, smiling and waving at him. Suddenly, the car took off, and before he could make a U-turn, a button was pressed on a bulky remote, and his car blew up in the middle of the street. Smoke and car parts sat in a bonfire, the car alarm blaring. The team of delivery people raced down the street, homes disappearing in the windows, their laughter carried in the wind.

The explosion was heard near and far. Neighbors walked out from their homes, onto their lawns, and looked in the direction the destruction came from. No one spoke; they only looked at one another and gradually walked out into the street and closer in route of the car. Like zombies, they walked in union, scared but curious about what they'd see.

From the window, Baldwin looked outside. His conscience told him to stay inside, yet the number of people leaving their homes and venturing out tore him from out of his safety net.

As he parted from the living room window, a car zoomed by in the opposite direction from where everyone's attention was placed. This time of morning caused everyone to be on high alert, and the sound of fire trucks and police vehicles drew twice as much attention. For a few minutes, Baldwin stood there, looking toward the accident from of the sidewalk of his home. His loss of sleep and energy fogged his brain and made it so he didn't remember his partner had just left and could possibly be in the accident.

Turning away, he walked back home. When he was halfway inside, Mrs. Evans, the 55-year-old retired wife and mom, walked over from next door. She always watched Baldwin's home whenever he went away, and she was the only person he could stomach on the block.

"Baldwin, did you hear that? What's going on?" She walked to his side, concern and the need for answers written on her wrinkled brown face.

"Good morning, Mrs. Evans. I think it was an accident."

"Wow!" The arms of Mrs. Evans' fluffy robe fell below her elbows. "I hope everything's okay. Did you go over there?"

"No, I've only been out here for a few minutes and am actually heading back inside. Good—" He was on the verge of telling her bye, but Mrs. Evans cut him off and spoke.

"Before you do, can you please put my microwave on the counter? It's still in the box, and my husband won't be in town for another two days."

Baldwin really wanted to get in the house and close his eyes, but the old woman's hopeful stare made him take away a few minutes of sleep to help her.

"Okay, lead the way."

Happy he accepted, Mrs. Evans walked around her lawn on the walkway and into her house within a total of ten seconds. For an older woman, she moved fast. Her swiftness put a spotlight on Baldwin's gradual movement. Finally making it inside of Mrs. Evans' house, Baldwin bypassed the spring-colored living room and met Mrs. Evans in the kitchen. Next to her feet sat a microwave box.

"You can put it right there." Mrs. Evans pointed to the counter next to the refrigerator.

Baldwin walked over to the box, took the appliance from the confines of the cardboard, and faced the counter, his back to Mrs. Evans. Pushing seasonings and dishes aside, he placed the microwave on the countertop.

"Thank you. That's perfect!"

Baldwin turned to tell her "you're welcome" and was met with a stab in his side—a stab that turned into multiples. Baldwin's body froze, and before he could react, Mrs. Evans aimed for the human body's major arteries. Within minutes, Baldwin was on the floor, and Mrs. Evans was stepping over him.

"We won't be needing your organs!" she screamed out to him, pretending he could hear her.

Outside in her backyard, she searched for the delivery truck parked behind her flowerbed, waiting to remove Baldwin's body.

Chapter 11

It was a parallel universe, a lost world unattainable even when imagined, however created through greed and revenge. The ceiling lamps showed off the blood painting the room and highlighted the violence given to Cory. On a stool surrounded by darkness, Tammy watched Cory's punishment and the inevitable future transpire in front of her. The shadows hid the dried tears, which left behind stripes. Forcing herself into another world, Tammy mentally escaped reality. There was no staying in a world where she had ordered her brother's harm and watched. She pushed away the fact that Cory's face was a bruised puddle of blood. The punches Hering gave him melted into his flesh and cracked his bones. Tammy counted the number of hits landing on him, and when she got to ten, she spoke.

"Is it true?"

It took time for Cory to answer; conversation would not be easy.

"I don't know what you're talking about." Cory inspected every angle on how Tammy could have found out he had orchestrated it all. His encouraging Baldwin to sponsor his drug and take over the organ harvesting business was now public record, and his plans were shattered.

"Cory Ward, is it true?" Tammy wanted to know nothing except that.

Looking out of his one good eye, he thought about what telling the truth would result in and what becoming a traitor had caused. Tammy hadn't looked him in the eye the entire time he was being beaten, and that meant one thing: they were no longer family, but enemies. And that was what Cory concentrated on when deciding what he should and shouldn't admit.

"Yes," he said.

Tammy should have taken it. She should have tested the chemicals responsible for crushing her relationship with her brother, because if she had, this would have been a lot easier. And it may have even helped her mentally.

"Why?" she asked.

Cory's bloodshot eye scanned the interior design of the basement—the colors, the texture, the bloody wallpaper. "I wanted out, something I knew you would never give me of your own free will. I wanted my own identity."

The corners of Tammy's mouth flipped downward, and her head nodding indicated her belief in his statement. "Some things are not negotiable. I know what's best." She paused, her finger pointing to herself. She looked at her brother, and a puddle of tears formed in the corners of her eyes. "But know this: although it's wrong, your dream will live on." Tammy reached behind her and freed the gun with a suppressor attached from the shadows she hid in.

Cory didn't look her way. He only took in the area that surrounded him, a mental photograph he'd hold with him for eternity.

Tammy placed the firearm under his chin. “I’m sorry,” she whispered. Turning her head from him, she pulled the trigger. The insides of his head spit out and flew into the air, membranes falling into Tammy’s hair as a strong force knocked her off her feet. Tammy remembered hearing that when someone died, you should open a window; that way their soul could leave. Sitting on the floor, disheveled and shaken up, Tammy wondered if she should have listened, because had Cory’s soul entered her body, he’d haunt her forever.

Chapter 12

Three months later

"How are you today, Tammy? Have you given some thought about our last session?" Dr. Connor looked at Tammy.

She gave eye contact; however, her facial expression was molded into a hard, cold stare. Unfazed by their session's opening sentence, she blinked a few times then turned away.

Dr. Connor acknowledged her lack of participation, nodded his head, jotted a couple of words down in his notepad, and continued speaking.

"Would you like to share anything you've seen or heard lately?"

Tammy thought about that question and revisited the last few months in her mind. The hospital had become a place of death after Cory's murder. Coming to terms with the fact that she killed Cory could not be and was not accomplished. Tammy's delusional disorder fed her mind the lie that she was not responsible for the crime, and in its place formulated the tale that a patient within Peaceful was to blame. Tammy saw it with her very own eyes: Hunter, the hospital's trichotillomania patient, had beat Cory to death. He had slammed Cory's head against the basement floor until he was lifeless. Because of this, Tammy had strangled Hunter. The next day, his body was found in the TV room.

After Hunter's killing, the voices returned. They told Tammy that Hunter had accomplices and she had to avenge her brother's death. Each day that passed, she killed more patients and eventually started killing off staff. This was what finally made Layla uncomfortable; however, when she approached Tammy and Tammy offered her more money to keep her mouth shut and to cover up the murders, Layla complied, but under one condition. Tammy had to seek treatment for her disorder. A true believer in what she'd seen and heard, Tammy agreed to seek treatment, but only so Layla would clean up the mess.

Two months after the serial killings, things were close to being back to normal. Money fixed a lot of things when needed. Everyone knew who was responsible for Cory's death, and that was what made Tammy's team ten times stronger—fear. Until Tammy was capable of doing so, Adler had taken on the business dealings surrounding Cory's drug, and she finally gave it a name: Painless.

Two days earlier, it had been one month since Tammy had uttered a word. Staring out in front of her, Tammy hadn't blinked since Dr. Connor asked his last question. She appeared trapped in another world, so Dr. Connor repeated the question.

"Would you like to share anything you've seen or heard lately?"

Tammy looked his way. Sixty seconds passed before she opened her mouth and told him, "Yes."

Shocked, Dr. Connor held his composure. He didn't want to deter Tammy from opening up. So, he acted as if, for the last month, she always spoke.

"Tell me what's on your mind," he encouraged.

"The voices. The voices tell me to kill myself."

Alarmed, Dr. Connor proceeded to ask, "Why would they tell you to do such a thing?"

Tears welled in Tammy's eyes, water threatening to fall over the brim of a glass.

"Because I killed my son," she confessed. The voices in her head finally allowed her to speak.

About the Author

Born and raised in New York City where she lives with her husband, Brandie Davis-White graduated with a bachelor's degree in English from York College and is the founder of My Urban Books blog and Facebook book club. From home, she continues to pen drama-filled novels.

IG: authorbrandiedavis
Twitter: @AuthorBrandieD

One in the Chamber

by

N'TYSE

48 hours later

Master P's "Break 'Em Off Somethin'" could be heard through the thin walls of one of the upstairs apartments in the dilapidated complex. It was competing against the fifteens shaking in someone's trunk from the adjacent parking lot, where the twins had just parked their two-toned white-and-blue Cutlass. They liked to ride nice, and before they switched their part-time occupation from slanging chicken at the local chicken spot to hitting licks, they could only afford the slightly roughed-up Oldsmobile, which, for the time being, was sitting on a quarter tank of petrol. However, after the other night, they knew things were certainly about to take a drastic turn for the betterment of their pockets.

Quamin knocked on the door with a heavy hand.

"Who the fuck is it?" the voice boomed from the other side.

"Dominos, nigga!" Quamin rattled off after glancing to his left and spotting a delivery guy heading to the next unit over. He was surprised the pizza joint would even deliver in a neighborhood so rough, especially after dark, and at an hour when it seemed the entire hood was out. Hell, it didn't matter that it was a Sunday. Anybody who looked like a quick come-up was liable to get their ass jacked any day of the week in those grimy parts of Oak Cliff, including the pizza man.

"Guess he got amnesia now. He just let us in the fuckin' gate," Quamina quipped. Her perfectly arched eyebrows wrinkled in confusion. "Who else would it be knocking at the door? Publishers Clearing House with a million-dollar check?" She lowered her face to the peephole so that she could be seen more clearly. Her long, wavy black hair, which was usually braided back in two Iversons, was neatly pulled into a single twisted ponytail that hung like a rope midway down her wife beater. Unlike her brother, she was tatted all over from the stomach and arms up to both sides of her neck. And while they both had tight, athletic frames, Quamina appeared the more muscular of the two.

"Anybody else with y'all?" Kevin called out, obviously more paranoid than usual.

"Naw, man. It's just us," Quamin reassured him.

"This bucket-headed nigga be on one," Quamina half whispered. "I'm too fuckin' high for this shit tonight."

"Chill out, Mina," Quamin said, dying laughing on the inside.

After what felt like forever, Kevin finally unchained the door and slowly pulled it open. He nervously peeked out into the dark hallway and took a quick look around before inviting the twins into his girlfriend's two-bedroom apartment. He had only been dating Rasheda for three months and was already sick and tired of playing stepdaddy to the little bastard. He didn't think Rasheda even knew who the little girl's daddy was, but he definitely didn't recall signing up for that shit.

"Come on, come on!" Kevin hurriedly ushered them inside, locking both locks and the deadbolt behind them.

"Man, you actin' like the boogeyman after your ass!" Quamina said matter-of-factly.

"Awww, I see you got jokes."

Her eyes roamed around the scarcely furnished apartment the second they stepped inside.

Kevin embraced the Muhammad twins with a pound-hug. They were his latest partners in crime, and after witnessing what they were capable of forty-eight hours ago, he had gained mad respect for them. Unlike Kevin, who'd be pushing twenty-seven in a week, Quamin and Quamina were only seventeen years old, yet all of them were equally savage and thirsty for that almighty dollar.

"Y'all burn the clothes and the surveillance tape?" Kevin drilled, cutting straight to the chase.

The twins nodded in unison as they took a seat on the green suede sofa.

Kevin picked up the television remote and lowered the volume. Before they arrived, he had been eating some Top Ramen chicken noodles smothered in hot sauce and watching a rerun of the television sitcom *Martin*. He tossed his chick's two-year-old's teddy bear clean across the room before reclaiming his spot on the filthy, mismatched loveseat directly across from them.

"Shit, the law's been real hot around this motherfucker lately. But we cool. Ain't nobody seen shit or heard shit, and for *y'all's* sake, as long as you don't go yapping your gums to your friends, trying to show off and shit, everything will stay that way." Kevin looked them dead in the eyes. "Because I ain't going back to jail." He paused to make sure his point was taken. "For *nobody*!"

"Everything straight, bro. We even got an alibi," Quamin reassured him.

"Well, that shit better be air fuckin' tight."

Silence.

Quamina cleared her throat. "Man, I was just thinking. Them white folks were getting hella rich off of our black, dead bodies. No wonder they had their funeral home smack in the middle of the hood." She shook her head at the painful realization. "But aye, we some lucky motherfuckers to pull that off like that! I mean, a funeral home, cuz. Who would have thought they'd be loaded like *that*!"

"I told y'all once before, I don't believe in luck. It's all ordained by the man above, and that lick was fate, got dammit! Besides, they were gon' get their feathers plucked sooner or later. I'm sure I ain't the only one who scoped out that they made the families who didn't have life insurance pay damn near double—in cash and in full—before they would even touch them. I betcha they didn't do their own people like that. Hell, we just took back what was ours." Kevin acted as though they had merely completed some type of community service. That's how heartless he was.

Kevin reached in his pocket and pulled out a wad of money, mostly large bills.

Quamina's tight, hazel brown eyes widened in excitement. She rubbed her hands together, ready for her big payday.

"Time to cash out," Kevin said as he peeled off a few bills. He handed the twins their cut from the job the other night, a meek smirk on his face. He felt like a boss and was treating them like employees in training.

"This what I'm talking about!" Quamina acted like she had never seen that kind of green all at once in her lifetime, and she hadn't, not working at Henny's Chicken part-time. "Yo, this like nine hundred dollars, Q! I'm definitely getting those new baby blue Air

Jordans first thing in the morning, bro. I'm gon' be the flyest cat in the school. Even the straight bitches gon' be jocking me. Including your girl, bro." Quamina playfully elbowed Quamin. The twins always joked and scored on one another, but for the first time, Quamin didn't have a quick comeback.

Quamin's silence rested on his sister's bragging fest as he sat in deep thought, counting up the same nine hundred dollars in his hands. His expression quickly transformed from contentment to bafflement.

"Stay down with me and you'll see there's way more where that came from, playa!" Kevin promised. "I'ma show you how to eat off these streets. That way you ain't never gotta worry about no handouts. Ever!"

Quamina nodded her head in agreement. "I like the sound of that shit. Let's cuff this money!"

"Fire up a blunt then, sis. Let's toast to the good life and stacking paper!"

Quamina shoved her earnings deep into her right pocket, reached for the weed and cigarillos already spread out on the table, and began stuffing the Swisher Sweets like the pro that she was becoming. She fit in well with the guys, and it didn't matter that she was a hardcore stud. In fact, being a lesbian had its benefits. She was able to teach them a thing or two when it came down to the female psychology and anatomy, so the way she saw it, her contributions to the squad outweighed the fact that she was a chick. She could keep up and was harder than a lot of the guys she associated with.

"Say, bro, I don't mean to question your math, but this not really adding up," Quamin pointed out, finally breaking his silence.

Kevin busied himself with his blue pager and acted as though he hadn't heard Quamin's comment. He was too busy thinking about the pussy invitation he'd just received from a chick he'd met five days ago. She had alerted him with the code 69*911.

"Yeah, we gon' have to wrap this up early, kinfolk. I gotta go handle somethin'," Kevin said, placing the pager on the glass table.

Quamin continued. "You said your girl told you they average about twenty-five thousand a day in cash. Split that three ways, and shit, I'm like seventy-four hundred short. That's not including all the embalming fluid you took. The street value gotta be worth over a hundred K on the low end. Am I right?"

Kevin finally locked eyes with Quamin. His eyes were bloodshot, and the bags under them were evidence of his sleepless nights. "Fuck you tryna say, my nigga?"

Quamina locked eyes with her brother. "We good, Q. Chill out." Her words came out muttered, yet her slanted eyes begged Quamin to just shut up and relax. She didn't want any problems.

"Naw, fuck that! This nigga playing us like some dummies." Quamin stood up, towering beyond six feet. "We got two bodies, *white bodies*, on our hands because *this* nigga forgot to mention that both of the owners would be there. And now he wanna fuck us again by screwing with our money? Nah, I'm not letting that shit ride, Mina."

As if searching her mind, Quamina quietly calculated her brother's math.

Kevin's pager vibrated across the table. This time he ignored the alert. He let out a guttural chuckle. "Sounds like you tryna accuse me of—"

"Give us the rest of our money, Kev, and we won't have no problems," Quamin interjected.

Kevin jumped to his feet and pulled out his .45. "You catch your first body, and now you think you the king of the motherfuckin' streets, huh?" Kevin aimed the gun at Quamin. "I bet you ain't all hard now, nigga, with this gat aimed at your dome!"

Quamin didn't move a muscle. His unflinching eyes, cold and stark, zeroed in on Kevin. If he had to die today, he refused to die like a bitch. Quamin was one of Carter High School's basketball all-stars, and other than his twin, no one could outrun or out-ball him on the court. But in that very moment, Kevin had him trapped and out of moves.

"The fuck! Chill, bro. We good, we good," Quamina said, slowly rising to her feet. Her eyes were nailed to Kevin's strap, and her heart pumped just as loud as the music on the other side of that door.

With his lower lip tucked between his full rack of shiny gold teeth, Kevin began to breathe hard and aggressively. "You think I'm just gon' let you stand there and disrespect me in my crib, nigga? Nah, you gon' learn today what happens to li'l boys when they disrespect their elders."

"Bro, we don't want no problems." Quamina put her hands up respectfully, in surrender mode. She stepped in between Kevin and Quamin. She tried to defuse the situation before it got out of control. "We just gon' be out. We ain't sweating that shit."

Quamina turned to Quamin. "What the fuck, bro? This man tryna feed us, and you gon' stand here and disrespect him in his own house. Let's just bounce!"

"You better get this li'l nigga together before I have to," Kevin spat, spit flying out of his mouth.

"We cool. I got him."

"Nah, nigga, I want my money!"

"You know what, bitch-ass nigga? I got your money right—"

Before Kevin could conclude his sentence, Quamina turned around so fast, brandishing a weapon of her own. Without a second thought, she fired one relentless shot, sending that bullet right between his eyes. Kevin let off one not even a full second behind hers, but the trajectory of his release was unknown. He fell onto the glass table, shattering it before hitting the floor hard. The dual shots had echoed so loudly in the apartment but were masked by the loud music outside and rowdy neighbors.

"Mina!" Quamin screamed at the top of his lungs. He caught his sister's body before it could hit the floor completely. Tears rushed the twins' eyes. Quamina made a gurgling sound as she fought to breathe and speak. "Mina!" Q screamed again, pain etched in his voice. "Not my fuckin' sister," he said. "Come on, Mina!" Blood oozed out of Quamina's body.

It was then Quamin realized she had been hit on the right side of her neck. Panicked and desperate to save her life, he plugged the hole with his fingers, all while crying, "Mina!" It didn't do any good. Blood continued to gush like shower jets.

"Arghckkk . . . arghckkk . . ." Quamina choked on the blood filling her throat. She fought for every single breath. "Argggghckkkk!"

"Don't leave me, sis. Help! Somebody help me!" Quamin screamed at the top of his lungs as tears poured down his face. If no one heard the gunshots, surely no one heard his cries for help. He wanted to go run for help, but he couldn't bring himself to leave her side. He screamed for help once more and began to rock back and forth uncontrollably with his arms wrapped tightly around his better half. With tears blinding him, he looked back down at Quamina. Her beautiful hazel eyes stared blankly at him.

"No! Mina!" He shook her, but she had stopped breathing. Stopped fighting. Just like that, in the blink of an eye, Quamina was gone. Forever.

Gotta Do It Yourself

Quamin let out a loud screech as he held Quamina tightly. He shed more tears, all while knowing he couldn't stay and risk being caught.

"I'm so sorry," he managed through the tears, blaming himself.

He stood to his feet and was covered in Quamina's warm blood, which was indeed his own. That tiny apartment was now a crime scene. He had to get out of there before Kevin's girl got home and made the grim discovery, but before he left, he wanted what was due to him and his sister.

Quamin quickly ransacked the house and found the rest of the money, along with a pound of weed and several boxes of embalming fluid. And Kevin had thought Quamin was just some dumb kid. Quamin knew the wetheads paid good money for laced marijuana, and now he had all the money and the product at his disposal.

He made a few trips back and forth to the car, and just before the last trip, he rummaged through Kevin's pockets and took all the money he had flaunted earlier in their faces.

"Ho-ass nigga," he spat.

And just like that, Quamin was on top, only without his ace—his sister. He took the necklace off Quamina's neck to remember her by. He didn't want to leave her side, but he had to. She wouldn't have wanted him to risk getting caught.

Just before he could open the door and make his escape, the doorbell rang.

"Fuck!" Quamin panicked and began to look around for someplace to hide, certain that it was Kevin's girl. The doorbell rang again. This time, a female's voice called out, "Dominos!"

Letting his guard down, Quamin rounded the kitchen corner he had ducked off into and went to answer the door. He unlocked every lock and slowly pulled the door open, baffled.

"We didn't order any—"

POW!

Quamin's body dropped where it stood. He didn't know where the shot had come from. All he knew for certain was that he was hit, but when he saw the pizza box drop to the ground and the chubby Hispanic girl take off screaming and running in the opposite direction, he knew the shot had come from behind him. He clutched his stomach, biting down on the burning sensation ripping through his torso.

"Arrgmmmm," he groaned in pain, spitting out the blood that filled his mouth.

He managed to flip onto his backside, and that's when he faced off with the mastermind herself. Unbeknownst to them all, Rasheda had been in the apartment the entire time.

Rasheda hunkered beside Quamin. She forced the chrome 9 mm into Quamin's mouth so fast and hard it juddered against the back of his throat. His eyes begged for her not to pull the trigger, but then he thought about

Quamina. In that split second of a moment, he made peace with his fate. There was no way he could live without his twin sister. They had come into this world together, and they would die together. He quietly prayed to his Maker and closed his eyes tightly.

"When you want shit done right, you gotta do it yourself," Rasheda seethed.

POW!

Brain matter splattered everywhere. Rasheda's words were the last Quamin heard before she rocked him into a deep sleep for eternity.

And as if it were just an ordinary day in the Cliff, Rasheda casually searched Quamin's pockets for the car keys. He was insane to believe for one second he would get away with her money and her product. She looked around at the three dead bodies and realized she had to get out of there fast, but not without sending one final message. She walked over to Kevin's lifeless body and emptied the rest of her clip into him.

Dressed incognito in one of Kevin's oversized black jogging suits, his dopeman Nikes, and black shades, with her hair stuffed under a black baseball cap, Rasheda was unrecognizable that night. She didn't think she could pull it off, but their plan had worked out perfectly—just as Dino had said it would.

She made sure the coast was clear before powerwalking toward the twins' car, headed straight for her baby daddy's house.

Stick to the Script

Rasheda pulled into the alleyway and drove until she came to the back of her baby daddy's house. She then pulled into the driveway and into the garage. She practically jumped out of the car, nearly tripping over her own two feet. She hit the switch on the wall for the garage door to close, and only then was she able to breathe a little easier.

"Dino!" Rasheda called out as she entered the house through the kitchen.

She snatched off the baseball cap and revealed the tapered Halle Berry–inspired pixie cut she usually rocked.

"Dino!" she called out again, hoping she didn't wake their daughter, LaLa, who was likely upstairs with Dino's mother, tucked in bed for the night.

Rasheda could hear the video game in the back room, and she knew exactly where to find Dino. She followed the sound. When she made it to the den, she found Dino parked in front of the television, playing football. She walked right over to him, waving a huge smile. She pulled all the money out of her pockets and tossed it onto his lap.

"The embalming fluid and the rest of the money is in the garage," she confirmed.

Dino tossed the video controller to the ottoman and pulled Rasheda closer to him. She straddled his lap and looped her arms around his neck. Her long fingers caressed the side of his face. She kissed him deeply and with such aching passion. Their plan had worked beautifully, as he knew it would. In fact, it had turned out even better because he didn't have to lift a fucking finger. Kevin had fallen right into their little rabbit hole and had done all of the dirty work of robbing the funeral home, leaving Dino and Rasheda to reap the benefits. Dino felt extreme gratification in that moment. And while that little altercation with Kevin nine months ago might have left Dino scarred, paralyzed, and bound to a wheelchair, it was Dino who ultimately got street justice, thanks to his main bitch, Rasheda—the one he aptly called his One in the Chamber. She was the epitome of ride or die, and as long as she was by his side, he knew the streets would be his for the taking. It wouldn't be long. He just had to be patient. For now, Dino only wished he could see the dead man's face so that he could spit in it.

On the other hand, the only thing Rasheda was saddened by after everything was said and done was learning of the brutal reality that her best friend's adopted parents had been murdered during the heist. She had not expected that anybody would be killed, and she should have known that Kevin's hot-headed ass wasn't leaving any eyewitnesses behind. Rasheda couldn't dwell on that now. It would only interfere with her concentration, and with what Dino had envisioned for the two of them, she needed to remain focused and stick to the script. She still had to get through the interrogation that would follow.

"Well done, baby," Dino said between more intense kisses. "Now all we have to do is wait for things to calm down. And as soon as it does, we'll make our next move."

Rasheda loved the sound of that.

"Now, g'on and get cleaned up so Daddy can eat."

Rasheda's pussy grew moist at the thought. She planted another kiss on his thick, full lips before heading for the bathroom.

Dino's smile stretched across his face as he admired his lady from behind. She was beautiful, but what he loved about her most was her loyalty.

Seventeen-year-old Carmelita, better known at school as Carma, laid in her bed with the blankets pulled over her uncombed head. She hadn't been able to sleep or eat for the past two nights after witnessing three armed goons rob the funeral home that her parents owned and worked in. It had all happened so fast, but it played out slowly in her mind, over and over again. She remembered their faces, remembered their voices; however, what really sent chills up her spine was that she could almost feel the two gunshots that followed, as if the bullets had found their way to her.

Joe and Sheila had been working late, and Carma had gone to the Mannings' funeral home to borrow money from her father, Joe. She had lied and said it was for gas and a movie, when in actuality it was for gas and the nightclub. Her best friend, Rasheda, had already paged her twenty minutes before, alerting Carma in their own little code that she had made it to GG's. It was their little hangout spot whenever one or the other needed to get away. And that particular night, all Carma had to do was show up, because Rasheda had told her when they spoke earlier that day that she would pay for everything. Unlike Rasheda, who seemingly kept a man with money, Carma had to ask her parents for it. She hated going anywhere broke, and that night was no different, even if Rasheda was going to pay her way.

While Carma was only seventeen, Rasheda was nineteen and much more advanced in life. She was independent and was already living on her own. She had even offered Carma a place to stay, but Carma never took her up on the offer. They both had their fair share of past run-ins with the law and had done everything under the sun in the chase for the Benjamins. That's what they had in common—their streetwise mentality and a thirsty pocket.

Although the two had first met in the juvenile detention center when Carma was only fourteen, they officially linked up a year ago after bumping into one another at the Red Bird Mall in Oak Cliff. It was all she wrote after that reunion. They didn't miss a beat, reconnecting and catching up on life's happenings. They even talked about all the crazy shit they had witnessed in juvenile and recalled all the times they had to have each other's backs. From what Carma could tell, Rasheda hadn't changed a bit. She was still up to her conniving scams and running game on men who were weak behind beautiful women. Only difference this time around was that Rasheda had her daughter, LaLa, and was basically getting adjusted to being a mom. She was a hustler at heart. She had a job selling shoes full-time and weed part-time, getting paid by any means necessary.

Carma hated having to rely on her parents, which was why, after graduation, she had already made up her mind to ditch college. She had grown up in the Dallas, Texas foster care system and had bounced around from house to house most of her adolescent life, so college was never an aspiration of hers. Since the day she was conceived, her birth mother had been on drugs, but it wasn't until Carmelita was three years old that CPS got involved and decided it was best to remove her from the home. While Carmelita didn't remember her mother, one thing she did know for certain was that she didn't want to end up like her. And despite how much hell she'd taken her adoptive parents through, they would do anything for Carmelita. They never treated her any different from their two biological children, and had Carma not been black, no one would have known that she wasn't the Mannings' blood child. They were good to her, better than her own birth parents had ever been. They were the most loving human beings she had ever met, so why on earth would anyone want to hurt them?

Watching them be murdered in cold blood the way they had, had poor Carma both angry and scared to death for her own life, especially since she had recognized two of the three robbers. Quamina and her twin brother, Quamin, hadn't been wearing a mask like the third guy had. So, from the second they entered the funeral home, Carma had gotten a really good look at their faces from a hidden closet where they kept a second hidden surveillance camera. She had just come out of the restroom and ran inside the small closet in the nick of time when she heard her mother's frightened scream. She watched in agony as the unwanted guests demanded money and embalming fluid.

Of what Carmelita knew of the twins, they were star athletes at their high school and very popular. But the question remained: why would they want to hurt her parents?

"Knock, knock!" Bianca sang softly. She was the Mannings' oldest daughter. "Are you in here, Carmelita?"

Carma sniffed as tears skated down her cheeks. She pulled the covers down from over her head. "Yeah."

Bianca walked over and took a seat on the edge of Carma's bed. "Supper's ready."

"I'm not hungry."

"But you haven't eaten all day."

"I'm not hungry."

Bianca took a deep breath. She knew her sister was stubborn, but not this stubborn.

"Okay, if you're not going to eat, at least let me bring you something to drink."

Carma thought about it. Her throat was so dry it felt like she'd been chewing on cotton all day. "I'll take a water."

"You got it." Bianca smiled and then leaned over to give her sister a peck on the cheek. "We're going to get through this. Together," Bianca promised, before standing up to go fetch Carma some water.

Carma watched as Bianca's feet disappeared out into the hallway.

Ring! Ring!

Carma looked over on the nightstand at the ringing phone. She thought about snatching the cord out of the wall, but instead answered on the third ring.

"Hello?" she said weakly.

"What's up, chick? I think you have some explaining to do, Missy. You stood me up at the club the other night."

It was Rasheda.

Carma slowly pulled herself up in the bed. She thought about telling Rasheda everything. Thought about telling her that she knew her parents' killers and how she was afraid they would come for her next.

"I can't talk right now," Carma managed instead.

"Why? Wait! Are you okay?" Rasheda rushed her with questions.

Carma exhaled deeply as tears flooded her eyes and cascaded uncontrollably down her face.

"It's Joe and Sheila. They were killed during a robbery at the funeral home Friday night."

"What the fuck! Oh my God, sis! Are you serious? I had no idea!" Rasheda took a long pause. "Who did that shit?"

"I don't know," Carma lied. "The police haven't said much."

"That's so fucked up! But don't worry, sis. Whoever was behind that will definitely pay in due time. Karma's a sneaky little bitch, and one you'll never see coming."

Carma sniffed again. "Yeah. That she is."

20 years later

Carmelita Jenkins raced against the clock to get to her second showing of the day. Ordinarily, she wouldn't be in such a rush, but she had gotten held up in traffic. It had been raining all morning long, and that had slowed things down. The meeting was with a prospective client, so she had to impress and show the doctor and his wife why she was one of the top real estate brokers in the region, and more importantly, why she was the perfect person to secure this contract and hopefully save them a lot of money in the process.

Carmelita wasn't rich, but she was doing extremely well for herself and had made a very good living from brokering real estate. She was naturally gifted at selling things and persuading her clients to go in one direction over another, especially if it was in their best interests based on future development projections.

She loved her job and all of her accomplishments, but there was indeed a time in her life when she thought the streets would swallow her whole. She had been living life in the fast lane, but that tragic night her parents were murdered left Carma traumatized. It had also set her on a different path in life—a better path than the one she had been on. She changed her surroundings and detached herself from a lot of old friends and associates. The way she saw it, she was striving to be the best version of herself, and she couldn't be that person still stuck in the hood and doing the same thing that had gotten her locked up before. She owed it to her parents to strive for better.

Far from the old Carma who used to rob, steal, and do whatever it took to get ahead, Carmelita was walking a different path. Her hair, nails, and makeup were flawless. She was dressed in the finest of fashions. Besides her physical appearance being on fleek, she was driving a sexy black 2019 Mercedes Benz G-class with red leather seats. Only the best for a hardworking boss.

Carmelita pulled into the stunning multimillion-dollar estate and followed her car's GPS. The home she was getting ready to show was a beauty. It was priced at $2.6 million, but Carmelita knew the seller's agent and was certain she could convince him to persuade his client to be flexible with the numbers. Now, how flexible depended on the upgrades inside, which Carmelita couldn't wait to feast her eyes on.

She could tell from the exterior that the home was well kept. The video she had watched in advance didn't do the exterior of the property any justice. Before pulling onto the cobblestone driveway, Carmelita spotted, for the first time in all of her years of selling houses, a porte cochere near the entranceway. She knew right away that it was only going to be more beautiful on the inside.

As Carmelita put the truck in park and turned off the windshield wipers, an old, beat-up Honda Accord pulled up beside her. Carmelita thought perhaps the woman was lost and needed directions. They both rolled their windows down at the same time.

"Hi." Carmelita spoke first to the brown-skinned woman.

"Are you Carmelita?" the woman asked.

Carmelita was caught off guard. "Yes, I am."

The woman smiled. "I'm Tracy. My husband, Dr. Young, got called in for an emergency C-section, so it's just me today," she said. "Hope that's okay."

"Um, absolutely. Just give me about five minutes to disarm the alarm." Carmelita grabbed her phone and folder. She was still puzzled by the sight and how the woman's presentation didn't fit the description in Carmelita's head. She definitely didn't expect a doctor's wife to be driving an old, beat-up car. She sighed deeply.

Carmelita entered her access code into the pad to unlock the door. It took her exactly five minutes to disarm and make clearance. She then opened the front door and invited Mrs. Young inside.

"Oh my God!" Tracy said as if she had never seen anything like it before.

"Isn't it lovely?" Carmelita said. Remembering that she didn't have much info on the woman, she began to dig a little deeper. "So, who do I need to thank for the referral?" she asked.

Tracy had a sinister grin on her face. "Let me just cut the bullshit and get straight to it."

Carmelita's eyes bucked. "I beg your pardon?"

"Come on now. You and I both know I don't look like I can afford a damn thing you're selling." The woman looked around the immaculate eight-thousand-square-foot house again in admiration. "This motherfucker sure is nice, though, but I'd have to hit the lottery to be able to afford one of these." She laughed.

Carmelita's breathing intensified. She had already broken her number-one rule: never leave home without the pepper spray. Her first mind told her to run, but Carmelita knew she wouldn't get far in her Louboutins.

"I don't think I follow," Carmelita said. *Who is this crazy bitch?* she thought.

"Let me ease your mind because you look like you're ready to attack my ass," Tracy said. "I come in peace, but with some valuable information that you're going to want to hear."

Carmelita narrowed her eyes at the woman. What kind of game was she playing today?

"For starters, my name ain't Tracy. It's Bridgette. And your old best friend, Rasheda, well . . ."

Carmelita waited with bated breath. She hadn't seen or heard from Rasheda in twenty years. Her mind instantly thought the worst. "Is she dead?" Carmelita asked, praying to God that wasn't the case.

"Hell naw, that bitch ain't dead!"

"Then what is it, Tracy—I mean Bridgette? What's wrong with Rasheda?"

There was a long pause before Bridgette finally said anything. "She's the *real* reason your parents are dead."

Karma's A Sneaky Little Bitch

It had only been two weeks since Bridgette presented the information to Carmelita. She had told her everything she knew, in hopes of only one thing—sending Rasheda to jail for life. Come to find out, Bridgette and Rasheda shared the same baby father; however, Bridgette was the mother of Dino's firstborn son, Emanual. She couldn't stand Rasheda and felt that she had come between her and Dino when they were younger. But after Rasheda's latest stunt, she was indefinitely on Dino's hate list. Never in a million years had he imagined that Rasheda would do him that dirty. She had stolen all of his work, all ten kilos of cocaine.

Bridgette knew there was only one person who could help her find Rasheda. Even if they couldn't find her, she would have to come out of hiding sooner or later, and when she did, Bridgette was going to be right there waiting for her. With Dino by her side.

Carmelita didn't want to walk back through her painful past, but there were a lot of unresolved issues, and she wanted answers. Rasheda was the only person who could provide them to her.

She sent a text to the number that Bridgette had given her. In the text, Carmelita simply put the same code they used to use back when beepers were popular and they would alert one another that they were at their spot, GG's. Carmelita waited and waited. About an hour later, her phone rang.

"Hello?" she answered.

"Carma, is this really you?" Rasheda asked on the other end of the line.

"Yes, it's me. How have you been?" Carmelita asked, keeping the conversation light and copacetic.

"Whewww . . . that's a good question. I guess I'm peachy."

Carmelita knew that meant she was in trouble.

"Well, I've missed my old friend. It's been like twenty years," Carmelita reminded her.

"Wow. I guess it has been that long now that I think about it."

"I was hoping we could talk and catch up. Like the good old times," Carmelita said, hoping Rasheda would take the bait. She needed to confront Rasheda in person and not over the phone. It was the only way she would really know if she had anything to do with her parents' death.

"Sure. Tonight works for me, because I won't be here tomorrow."

"What do you mean? Where are you going?" Carmelita quizzed.

"I'm moving to Canada."

Carmelita pulled into the gated apartment complex in South Dallas. She parked the car, got out, and walked over to the unit directly in front of her. Carmelita had memorized the apartment number Rasheda had given her, and since she was right on time, she went ahead and knocked on the door.

When Rasheda opened the door, Carmelita hardly recognized her old friend. She looked sick. Very sick.

"And there she is. Give me a hug, girl," Carmelita said, giving her one good squeeze for old times' sake.

Rasheda embraced Carma as well. It had been a long time since she'd had visitors, let alone someone she considered family. "Come on in," Rasheda said. "Excuse the place. I haven't been feeling my best lately."

Carmelita took a seat near the door. She hadn't planned on staying too long anyway. She had one purpose in mind, and that was to get a confession out of her. She needed Rasheda to look her in the eyes and tell her the honest truth about what had happened twenty years ago.

Carmelita made friendly conversation with Rasheda for a good thirty minutes. They talked about the good and bad times in their childhood, and then Rasheda slowly opened up about when things went from sugar to shit, starting with that night she had Kevin and the twins rob the funeral home. She cried as she poured out her heart to Carmelita right there. It was as if her soul needed to purge that pain and guilt she had been carrying for so long.

"Why?" Carmelita cried along. "They didn't deserve to die."

"I didn't mean for it to go down like that. I didn't even think they would be there."

"But they were! And their blood is on *your* hands!" Carmelita continued to sob.

Rasheda shook her head. "I didn't pull the trigger."

"It doesn't matter! *You* put the shit in motion!" She paused to catch her breath and wipe the tears from her face. She came to her feet. "I have to go to the authorities."

"Wait a minute. What did you say?" Rasheda stopped sobbing.

"I said I have to go to the police. You have to tell them everything you told me. Let them know Dino put you up to it."

"They're not going to believe me. Besides, that was twenty years ago. The case has been closed."

"Not if I can help it," Carmelita said. She turned to head for the door.

Rasheda grabbed Carmelita by the elbow. "I can't let you do that, Carma. Please."

"Let my arm go," Carmelita said, snatching it back out of Rasheda's grip.

As soon as she did that, Rasheda pulled out a small handgun from her waist and pointed it at her old best friend. "Don't make me do something I'll regret—again," Rasheda said.

Carmelita stood in shock and fear, just as she had that night she saw her parents die. She was frozen in place. "So, you're going to shoot me?"

"Don't make me do it," Rasheda warned. "I'll never be able to forgive myself."

Carmelita gave Rasheda the most sorrowful look.

Rasheda looked on in mild confusion while Carmelita continued toward the front door. She knew Rasheda was ready to take her out. Rasheda pulled the trigger, and to her surprise, the gun jammed in her hand. Carmelita nearly pissed herself, and she took that as her cue to run.

She hopped in her BMW, and just as she was turning the corner of those apartments, she saw an old beat-up Honda Accord speeding in the direction she had just come from. She recognized the female driver, but not the other three passengers, who had ski masks covering their faces. Carmelita thought about picking up her phone and dialing 911, but then she remembered that karma was a sneaky little bitch, and that even the streets had a way of retaliating and coming back to collect its IOU. Because that, my dear, you could never run from, no matter which corners of the world you tried to hide. The streets were *always* watching, *always* listening, and stayed ready with one in the chamber!

About the Author

N'TYSE, a Dallas, Texas native, currently juggles her writing career as a mother of two, wife, and filmmaker. She is a self-proclaimed investigative journalist, documentarian, and national bestselling author of the Twisted domestic suspense series (*Twisted Seduction, Twisted Vows of Seduction, and Twisted Entrapment*). She has contributed to several national bestselling anthologies and magazines, in addition to collaborating with some of today's hottest talent. Her anthologies include *Outlaw Mamis*, *Gutta Mamis*, and *Cougar Cocktales.*

The literary artist made her directorial debut in the documentary film *Beneath My Skin* and has gone on to produce other documentaries under her Dallas-based production company, A Million Visions Productions. She is currently hard at work producing book-to-film projects.

@NTyse
FB: Author.NTyse
www.ntyseenterprises.com